BLOOD AND FAITH

a novel

JOHN FROHNMAYER

LUMINARE PRESS

WWW.LUMINAREPRESS.COM

Blood and Faith
Copyright © John Frohnmayer 1993, 2022

Printed in the United States of America

WWW.JOHNFROHNMAYER.COM

Interior line drawings of Madonna and Child by Leah Johnson,
www.leahjohnsonart.com

Luminare Press
442 Charnelton St.
Eugene, OR 97401
www.luminarepress.com

LCCN: 2022914861
ISBN: 978-1-64388-871-2

In memory of my brother Phil,
who loved all things beautiful

Table of Contents

Author's Note
BLOOD AND FAITH

I wrote this book thirty years ago, put it in a drawer, and didn't look at it again until, during a COVID clean-out, I almost threw it away. It is set in the early 1990s, before widespread use of personal computers, cell phones, and the ubiquitous internet. The original was typed on those machines we now see in museums. Deciding it was worth another look, I hired someone to put it on a computer so I could edit it, and the original was, much to my dismay, "recycled," that is to say, destroyed. I have reconstructed it as best I can, so this book and the characters in it, all of whom are fictional, are survivors.

That the players in this international drama are the United States, Russia, and Ukraine gives it some currency because of the tragic and unprovoked war Vladimir Putin's Russia has visited on Ukraine. As you will read, the tensions among these countries have long histories.

Writing in the early 1990s, having just spent three bone-crushing years as a federal agency head, I fully expected that the United States would soon have a female president, and that we would all be better off for it. I still feel that way and my treatment of President Betty Sorensen reflects that view. The Russian president portrayed here is a scoundrel, but not, like Vladimir Putin, a war criminal, and while my sympathies and hopes are for Ukraine, I have not altered the original text to portray its actors differently.

One last note: the spellings, for example Kiev rather than Kyiv, are those current in the early 1990s. Likewise, I have not altered airport and security procedures that before 9/11 were much more lax.

John Frohnmayer
Enterprise, Oregon
www.johnfrohnmayer.com
March 2022

Prologue

Unfocused eyes gaze down and away from her adoring child: languid, absorbed, fixed on eternity. Her head is inclined toward his cheek, and her arms gently cradle him in maternal embrace. Her mouth reveals neither sadness nor pleasure as she contemplates his destiny. She is both of this world and, despite her centuries of existence, untouched by it. The Virgin of Vladimir, Our Lady of Vladimir, The Mother of God. The most sacred icon in all Eastern Orthodox Christianity graces the main hall of a small northern Virginia museum called Akerhill.

Battles have been fought over this 12th century icon, and many revere her as the great Palladium—the shield, the savior—the one that preserved Moscow from the ravages of Tamerlane's hordes. When the great warrior was approaching Moscow in 1395 with his army ravaging the countryside and nothing to stop them but the air, The Mother of God was rushed from nearby Vladimir. She could protect the city; its soldiers couldn't. And that night Tamerlane, fearless warrior intent on conquering the world, dreamed about a vengeful purple lady. Without other explanation, he turned his troops and vanished to the east.

As with all icons, The Mother of God reflects heaven rather than earth and serves as an intercessor for reaching the mysteries of salvation. She is a sacrament through whose mystical communion the believer, in solemn contemplation, comes closer to God.

And she is a killer.

CHAPTER 1

God's Mother

The Last Decade of the 20th Century

The navy blue presidential helicopter, with white trim and the presidential seal of the United States on either side, landed in the Akerhill parking lot at 9:55 a.m., the wash of its rotors mixing with the saturated air and slathering the spectators in a gritty sauce.

The chase helicopters stirred up the adjacent pasture, silencing the cicadas and blasting the resident mosquitoes toward the waiting crowd that stood or squirmed or slapped, disheveled and sticky in the Northern Virginia countryside, where the bunch grass and bitternut and morning glory climbed over each other like autograph seekers to the sun. Even the air smelled green.

Betty Sorensen, ever aware that she was commander-in-chief, slapped the hull of the helicopter twice to thank the pilot for not crashing and proceeded up the red carpet to a striped awning under which a podium, Russian and American flags, and multiple microphones had been placed. She was short, with curly gray hair and glasses; pleasantly overweight, comfortably middle aged, conservatively dressed. Pavel Kiprensky, on the other hand, was

3

tall and slender and well groomed, with his light-colored, double-breasted suit, impeccably placed grayish-black hair, and manicured nails. He looked as much like a Russian president as Khrushchev had a steel worker.

Lara Cole waited for the chief of protocol to introduce her to the presidents. Her shoes were too tight. And because Igor had jumped up on her shoulders as she was dressing, she forgot one earring and had a nasty scratch on the back of her neck into which the sweat dripped and stung as she stood. Pavel Kiprensky grasped her hand in both of his, giving her an unapologetic and approving inventory from head to toe as he congratulated her for directing the museum that now housed "his most prized possession."

Cameron Aker then elbowed her off the platform and took the seat designated for the museum director. He was chairman of the board, family namesake, and resident tycoon of Akerhill. Moreover, he and President Kiprensky were old buddies.

Contrary to typical protocol, Kiprensky spoke first since he, on behalf of all Russians, was graciously loaning the most prized icon in all Eastern Orthodoxy to demonstrate the affection between the people of Russia and the United States. He said that the days were gone when our countries threatened to send ballistic missiles across the oceans toward each other. Instead, he presented to the people of the United States an object that, for eight hundred years, had stirred the passions and devotion of his people. It consisted not of tons of metal, gyros, and explosives, but weighed less than fifty pounds and was made merely of egg yolk, pigment, and wood.

The inspiration of The Mother of God, he said, was that she captured the spirit, the humanity, the devotion, and the hope of the entire Russian people. He omitted to say that she also had presided over centuries of carnage.

Kiprensky was a politician from the moment he arose in the morning until he tumbled into bed, and perhaps in his dreams as well. His every action was filtered through a maze of political possibilities. Like a cosmic chess match, each political ploy unlocked hundreds of other moves, the results of which not even he could fathom. But that was the thrill of the game—to be at least one move ahead and keep the chess board twirling so that only the nimblest opponent could maintain his orientation.

President Sorensen rose, and the protocol chief slid out a small box upon which she could stand so that the television cameras would see more than her gray curls above the podium. Reading from five-by-eight-inch cards on which her remarks were typed, she thanked Kiprensky and the Russian people for the generous loan (which came, incidentally, from the Tretyakov Museum in Moscow, not from Kiprensky himself as he had suggested), acknowledged the priceless and symbolic quality of the loan, and thanked Cameron Aker for his part in brokering and hosting the icon's visit.

She looked up and saw three hand-lettered signs, silently held just behind the restraining ropes. SHAME. BLASPHEMY. SACRILEGE. Her aids had briefed her of no protest, foreseen no disruption.

Seasoned politician that she was, she continued, saying that The Mother of God signifies the spirituality and peace that the world seeks and that these three months in the United States would solidify the bond of friendship and the mutual respect of the peoples of these two great nations.

Lara watched from the side of the dais as the Secret Service talked into the microphones on their lapels, and the crowd began to vibrate uncomfortably. This day should have been the most exciting of her thirty-four years, but long before now she had dreaded it.

Akerhill Museum, the toy of Cameron Aker III, was no place for a priceless artwork like the Vladimir Mother of God. She could not escape the feeling that both she and The Mother of God were merely appetizers at a grand feast—planned, attended, and to be consumed by others.

She took a step toward her head guard, Wesley Foster, and was quick-frozen by the gesture of a Secret Service man, in mirrored sunglasses, whose manner convinced her that she should not take another.

Now the crowd was turning and stirring as an increasing number began, quietly at first, to repeat: SHAME, SHAME, SHAME. Then a tall, gray-haired man with gold, wire-rimmed glasses stooped and picked up a handful of gravel, letting the dust and rock chips sift through his fingers as he said, "Ashes to ashes; dust to dust." Next to him a woman did the same, and the man next to her, and the dozen on either side of them.

Although Willy Mays in his prime could not have thrown the gravel to the podium, the Secret Service doesn't hesitate, and as President Sorensen labored on, agents wrestled the tall man to the ground, carried him, as he went limp, by hands and feet back through the crowd and handcuffed him to Akerhill's massive iron gates. As others continued to sift gravel through their fingers, they were likewise carried away until two dozen, like fleshy gargoyles, were attached with plastic strapping to the gates.

The television cameras swung around to record the drag away. Then the presidents and dignitaries, more quickly than dignity would dictate, retreated to the museum to view the icon. The fleshy gargoyled fence was the next day's front-page photo.

Cameron Aker was pissed off.

No Bible thumpers were going to ruin his celebration. He called up every swear word in his vocabulary, and he knew plenty, to exhort Lara (whose project and museum it suddenly was), the sheriff, the Secret Service, and the Virginia State Police to erase the protesters. As Aker ranted, the gray-haired man, in a clear tenor, led the plastic-bound gargoyles in a lusty rendition of "The Old Rugged Cross."

By the time the sheriff's jail bus arrived, the presidents were long departed, and the searing sun, annoyed mosquitoes, and orifice-seeking gnats made the protesters' circumstances cruel and unusual. The yellow and green bus, ungainly but slow, belched blue-gray diesel smoke as it lumbered away between the white board fences of Akerhill's driveway. The rapping engine noise at the top of each gear collided with the incessant bragging of the cicadas, each competing to be most obnoxious.

"They could have just shot the sons of bitches," said one Wilson Porter, Lara's assistant director.

"You're not much of a civil libertarian," said Lara.

"Been black for a long time," he replied, "and so I know protests are supposed to mean something. Here these people appear, and obviously surprised all the suits with their mirrored shades and curly wires down the back of their necks, but what did they accomplish? I'd shoot 'em because it was such a dorky protest."

Wesley Foster, head guard of the museum, had been standing next to them on the massive stone steps of Akerhill, observing their conversation and holding his coffee cup and his tongue. About sixty, with thinning reddish hair, and in relatively good physical condition (that is, his chest and stomach were still distinct parts of his anatomy), he was born to take orders. Foster admired and respected Lara. In her crisp business suits, short, bobbed hair, and brisk manner, she struck him as quite pretty, although he would have sooner swallowed his tongue than to say so. His was a life of service, and he asked her what he should do.

"Cameron has vanished, but I see no reason why we shouldn't open. Have you checked the security?"

Foster replied, as if he were a recording, that the perimeter alarm, the window and door alarms, the video cameras focused on the main hall and the icon itself, and the central console in the guard station were functioning fine. He added that the vertical wire from the ceiling and an infrared beam that surrounded the icon's case were tested this morning. He had done that himself.

"What if these yo-yos come back and decide to storm the place?" asked Wilson. "Can we repel boarders?"

"I would defend the icon with my life," proclaimed Foster melodramatically, eliciting a snort from Wilson and a shudder from Lara, who knew how utterly unequipped her museum was to house such an object.

That afternoon the American public got its first glimpse of The Mother of God. Like the Mona Lisa, she was smaller than life, no bigger than the front of your dishwasher. But if you stopped and looked at her, she would arrest you with eyes so intense that they commanded you to follow her gaze to the baby Jesus. The infant, in turn, adored his mother, completing the triangle between the Virgin, the viewer, and God.

The power of this image was measured in megatons.

CHAPTER 2

The Odd Trio

Cameron Aker III was in the barn collecting semen. His beloved polled Hereford bull, shamelessly named Peter the Great, had been reserve grand national champion at Denver, which meant that he was second best in the attributes bulldom most cherishes. Because of this honor, Peter's semen was in high demand, and being none too bright, he could be tricked out of copious quantities of it several times a day. This semen was promptly divided into "straws," frozen, and sold at insane prices for insemination of polled Hereford cows all over the world.

Aker wallowed in money. Granddaddy had acquired, through piracy no doubt, huge tracts of land in Northern Virginia. Daddy parlayed that land into cash as Dulles airport, scores of bedroom communities, and a miasma of urban despoilment pushed west from the nation's capital. Cameron III, (known as "Three" or "I, I, I", or, not to his face and in a Brooklyn accent "da Turd," usually accompanied by a Bronx cheer) fancied himself a trader—in stocks, commodities, land. Everything in his world was for sale. He had done brilliantly, primarily because of that business genius, inherent, not taught, by which his risks were taken with other people's money. He even made money in polled Hereford breeding, through fortuitous timing—the kind of luck that seemed to follow him around—and hiring knowledgeable help whom he treated like stable droppings.

Aker, as an undergraduate of minimal academic distinction at Stanford, became acquainted with Pavel Kiprensky at Zott's. Zott's was a drinking establishment, not a classroom, and Aker considered it his informal headquarters. He was comforted by the knowledge that, through some astute trades he was one of the few Stanford students who actually got richer, much richer, during his four years there.

Kiprensky wandered in from the brilliant California sun one day and, blinking to adjust to Zott's perpetual twilight, sat down on a beer-stained stool next to Aker and started up a conversation. That the jukebox twanged incessantly, or the ferns survived without light or the stumbling undergraduates came and went totally escaped Aker's attention. He was far more interested in what this Soviet, who was undoubtedly a Commie, had to say.

Kiprensky was a phenomenon. Few Russian students attended American universities in the fifties. But not only was his English excellent, his interest in American politics was so compelling that he had persuaded both his Soviet benefactors and the American government to allow him to pursue a PhD in American history.

His Stanford days were the subject of intense interest to both the Americans and the Soviets, and functionaries of both governments, like shy suitors on the edge of the dance floor, watched and wrote as the two friends drank and talked.

Over the years they had kept in loose touch, and in the eighties when trade with the Soviet Union was becoming a real possibility, and Kiprensky was a rising star in the Soviet political firmament, the telephone calls and faxes and visits by Aker to Moscow multiplied.

Aker wanted to be the next Armand Hammer, establishing such an intense personal relationship with Russian leaders that he would be the clearinghouse through which all commerce flowed.

Kiprensky, on the other hand, saw Aker as one of the chief sources of hard currency—American dollars—that the failing Communist economic system and the emerging but bewildered Soviet capitalist system so desperately needed.

Kiprensky was neither idealogue nor altruist. Nor was he inconveniently honest. Politics, as the Soviet Union crumbled, opened up opportunities and, with Aker's financial support, they both made tidy profits diverting and exporting Soviet minerals and chemicals and selling them in Europe and Asia. Sometimes they acted alone, other times with a network of KGB operatives, foreign financiers, weapons merchants, and other purveyors of international disruption. Profits in the new Russia were satisfying.

Lara Cole was named after Larissa Feodorovna Guishar from the Boris Pasternak novel, Dr. Zhivago. Since Lara's parents were readers rather than moviegoers, she preceded the plethora of girls of that name by about five years. Lara had directed Akerhill for a little over eighteen months. Before that, she worked at the Metropolitan Museum in New York City, utilizing her knowledge of medieval art gained in college and by working for Sotheby's in London. Before that, she was embraced to the point of suffocation by the Roman Catholic Church.

Catholicism had chosen her, as it had also consumed her parents. Protest about instructional classes, daily Mass, or the dark omnipresent shadow of sin had not crossed her mind in the early years. Every school from kindergarten on was taught by nuns and presided over by a priest, often distant, occasionally gentle, ever answering to a humorless and exacting God. When rebellion arose in her, it was accompanied with periodic payments in the currency of guilt, and like a mortgage, those payments came due eternally. But the curious part of it was that Lara always viewed her life as happening to someone else.

Her father died while she was in Catholic boarding school. She hardly knew him. She was only ten and had already logged four regimented years there. Her unassuming mother had given her soul to Jesus, and He kept it, leaving little for her to share with Lara. Although they maintained constant, if strained, communication, Lara's visits always left her with a suitcase of guilt and unspecified anger.

Her earliest memories, then, were not of her biological family, but of the family of faith: the nuns and the lay sisters and the male authority figures in cassocks. She imprinted the smell of candle wax, furniture polish, and incense as she struggled with her missal, rosaries, kneeling benches, and mental confusion.

I HAVE SINNED, FATHER.

Confess, my child. Unburden your soul.

Well, we were playing, jumping rope, taking turns. And you know, we would make up rhymes as we jumped—to help with the timing—and I...I...well, we were...

Tell me...Yes...?

Well, Patricia had been bothering me all morning, poking me in the back and asking questions during class when we were supposed to be quiet...

And?

And then she made a face at me just before her turn to jump. And I was holding the rope, so when she was jumping, I jerked it, and she tripped and fell. And I said, "Fat Pat fell on her prat." And then the other girls started to say it too, and she started to cry...and Sister said I should come over and see you.

Do you think Jesus would have done that? It was an accusation, not a question.

N-n-n-no.

All her life, intoned the disembodied voice, **she will carry the scars you have inflicted...**

The thing was, Lara still thought of her as a "Fat Pat," and it made her smile. She couldn't help it.

LARA'S SCARS WERE NOT ALL EARNED IN THE SERVICE of God. Man had inflicted a few, and one man in particular, had cut some deep and lasting ones. Derrick Cole, Wadham College, Oxford, started at Sotheby's about the same time as Lara, and, through his persistence, they became friendly, first at work, then after work, then in bed. They married.

Lara discovered, too late, that she was a spectator of human emotions. Throughout her parochial school years she had almost never dated, in part because she, and others for her, assumed that she would follow a life of singular devotion. In college she had male friends, but none of any sexual consequence, and she simply never mastered the natural give-and-take between the sexes that she might have learned from watching her parents, her peers, or even herself, by trial and error.

And so, as much as she wanted to love Derrick, and be loved, she acted like a straight-legged cat, squirming and arching to liberate herself from emotional proximity, only to return, inopportunely, to be cuddled. Neither of them could be a teacher, and so they emotionally dismembered each other, the prelude to divorce being a long and escalating battle of mutual degradation in which he convinced her, at least for a time, that a nunnery was where she belonged, so cold and dead was her soul toward man.

Since she had forsaken her faith, retreat to the church was foreclosed, and with a soul incapable of loving man, she found herself in chilly and uncharted waters. But it never occurred to her to despair. Her technique, unselfconsciously assumed, was not to think about herself and to be "on with it" in a flurry of work directed toward the beautiful and totally accepting world of art objects. Her good nature, steady disposition, and semi-detachment from the sweat and grunts of life were both virtue and vice. She succeeded brilliantly at work while issuing an unspoken invitation for others to stand clear—the kind of invitation that Cameron Aker III gleefully ignored. At abuse he was a virtuoso.

It was he who interrupted Lara's reverie with the insistent honking of the horn of his Mercedes. Lara left her office, forgetting her briefcase, purse, and other professional props. Emerging from the climate-controlled museum, the humidity and heat were so oppressive as to almost knock her back into the building. The dizzying white sky hung close to the ground, seeming to shimmer up from the superheated earth.

Cameron's Mercedes 560 SL coupe was green with a white convertible top, thankfully up. Cameron, himself, had on a blue hopsack blazer, open collar shirt, khaki pants, loafers, no socks. They were on their way to see Vincent Buckley, Cameron's Washington lawyer.

"These butt hooks aren't going to screw with my museum," he said without preliminary. "Buckley will tell us what to do, and then you'll do it."

Lara wiggled in the seat trying to unstick her blouse from her back.

"In case you didn't know it, it was embarrassing as hell when those mouth breathers disrupted the president. Kiprensky laughed about it afterwards, but it sure as hell wouldn't have happened to him. I thought you knew something about security."

Lara was not unused to accusations from Aker. She just was not very good at reply. It was he, against her strongest advice, who wanted to house the icon. It was too valuable, too fragile: the wood could split or the pigment flake or the plane crash. It just wasn't an item suitable for either travel or commerce.

Aker could have cared less. He wanted to host the icon, and he had the juice to make it happen.

Then she had pleaded with him that the icon go to the National Gallery in Washington or the Metropolitan Museum in New York. Akerhill, for all its bucolic setting in the rolling hills of Virginia, and its lovely stone building and gardens, was no place for such an international treasure.

But Aker was determined. His daddy had set up a not-for-profit corporation that had gotten much of the inheritance Aker coveted. Normally, the Aker Foundation was a pain in the ass, but in this case, it could provide some not-for-profit grease for his venal machine. So the foundation put up a $5 million honorarium for the loan. If he could bring this symbol of Russia to Akerhill, with his own house right next door, he would have, symbolically, brought Russia home for a visit. How could he more clearly demonstrate that as far as trade with Russia was concerned, he was the man to see.

"Who was that guy—the tall, gray-haired one that the Secret Service should have clubbed senseless?" asked Aker as he entered Highway 66 eastbound, cutting off a semi and darting directly into the fast lane. Lara was totally passive to his dangerous driving. She wondered, to herself, about her lack of concern for her personal safety.

"His name is Reverend Bob Sounder. His group is called the Constants of Leo."

"Those are supposed to be jokes?"

"To know who they are you need a little background in church history." She waited for a rejoinder, but for a change, he was looking at the road.

"From Pontius Pilate on, Christians were persecuted in the Roman Empire, but all that changed in the fourth century when the Emperor Constantine embraced Christianity, founded Constantinople, and granted Christians full civil rights. Eastern Christianity matured into Orthodoxy. As its name suggests, it represented a fixed and proscribed kind of religion, both in its liturgy and in its artistic depictions." Aker gave her a sidelong glance as if she were speaking an alien dialect.

"Orthodoxy did not allow for ad-libbing, and icons became the way religious concepts were portrayed—a fixed, stylized medium through which the worshipper could reach God. The problem came from some rather loose ecclesiastical writing that suggested that the icon had become more than an avenue for access to God and, in fact, was God Itself: in other words, the icon had become an idol, a graven image, a violation of the commandment against man creating God."

Cameron sighed.

"I'm almost to the point, Cameron, stay with me. In the early eighth century, Leo III became persuaded that artworks of Christ, the Holy Family, and the Apostles violated the injunction against graven images, and he took down the image of Christ on his bronze gate and replaced it with a cross. This seemingly inconsequential act precipitated the struggle between the iconoclasts and those who favored human images. Fear of idolatry gained momentum, and much irreplaceable religious art was destroyed. For about 150 years, off and on, the iconoclasts held sway until Theodora—not the one you probably associate with Justinian—"

"Not hardly," interrupted Aker.

"Theodora restored the veneration, not worship, of icons to the Orthodox Church. Orthodox believers now parade their icons on the first Sunday of Lent to commemorate the victory over iconoclasm. But apparently, iconoclasm still has some vigor as those people in front of the museum demonstrate."

"So they named themselves after Leo and Constantine," said Aker. "How clever." He braked violently to avoid climbing into the trunk of a Toyota, jerked the wheel to the right and shot across two lanes only to brake again behind a slow-moving pickup.

"A world of idiots," he said as he flashed his lights.

"I'm surprised the Secret Service didn't know about them," she said. "They were written up a couple of months ago in the Post."

"And you just let it happen?"

"You were the one who insisted on talking to the Secret Service, remember? Neither my opinion nor my counsel were regarded."

Bob Sounder grew up in rural Texas, the son of a Pentecostal minister who served churches in storefronts and tents and clapboard buildings in so many towns that they seemed to meld into a swirling memory of speaking in tongues, praying till dawn, and dunking in the river.

A story he had heard, too many times to count, was that he and his twin brother were sleeping on a pallet in a hayfield as their father, to make ends meet, worked as a field hand. Pa turned to see a rattler, coiled and rising next to the pallet. With three large bounds and a swing that separated his hayfork from its handle, he beat the snake into bloody pieces.

Somehow this incident confirmed that the Lord protects His flock, and it had been recounted from pulpit to riverbank across the country.

The same faith was able to deal with Bob Sounder's twin brother's ruptured appendix that took his life at age 15. No matter what happened, "God had his hand in it," and no matter how great the sacrifice, Sounder's father was grateful to the Lord.

Bob vowed to liberate himself at the first opportunity. He was an avid reader and had a fine singing voice. He loved the harmonies of the simple, traditional hymns. But he also knew field work, auto mechanics, and common labor. Shortly after his brother's death, he left, working from job to job, reading more broadly, and ultimately getting a scholarship to Montana State, where he graduated with honors.

He strayed from the church.

His marriage to a devout and sensible girl of a Montana ranching family, and his desire to set an example for their two small children gradually returned him to the fold.

Because he was articulate, after a while he found himself preaching. But he was hollow—disconnected, detached. He was still fighting his father's profession when God spoke by saving his child. That was his conversion on the road to Damascus.

One thing he knew for certain: affluence had it all over poverty. Preaching didn't have to be joined with material denial, and his break in that regard came during a frigid winter when a local grocery chain owner whom Sounder had been courting, both for his money and his soul, decided it was time to make an altar call, confess Christ, and be baptized. The problem was that the gentleman was 75, in failing health, and it was 22 degrees outside.

In the parlance of the church, the businessman was "hungry for the Lord," and Sounder challenged him to meet his Maker, either by worldly or heavenly salvation. They broke the ice on the river, dunked him in, and called upon the Spirit. Not only did he survive it, but he grew more vigorous and, toward Sounder, much more generous.

Sounder moved his headquarters to Northern Virginia, started a radio show, and waxed charismatic.

He saw mankind as being faced with too many obstacles and distractions on the road to faith. He was, by intellectual inclination, a simplifier. Complicators are compelled to place each piece of human information on the appropriate twig on the right branch of the tree of knowledge. To

Sounder, particularly having dealt with congregants who were, for the most part, unsophisticated people, the message should be as simple as possible.

He came to the conclusion, not unlike Emperor Leo, the iconoclast, that it was time to strip away the chaff. Take, for example, God's injunction in Exodus 20:4-5, "Thou shalt not make any graven image, or any likeness of anything that is in Heaven above…for I, the Lord Thy God, am a jealous God." That was clear.

Add to that, the first chapter and verse of the Gospel John: "In the beginning was the Word and the Word was with God, and the Word was God."

No graven images. Christianity is a religion of the Word. Sounder the simplifier became Sounder the twentieth century iconoclast. He was the brush hog that cleared away the symbols, the vestments, the trappings that blurred the eyes of believers. He embraced Deuteronomy's exhortation to burn graven images with fire.

What's more, he had the appetite of a martyr.

VINCENT BUCKLEY'S LAW FIRM, BUCKLEY AND SPENCER, on the north side of Pennsylvania Avenue, kitty-corner from the Gothic-towered Old Post Office building, occupied what was reputed to be the most expensive commercial real estate in Washington, D.C. The offices were appointed with the obligatory rich wood, sparking glass, thick carpets, and smartly dressed help.

Buckley's secretary led them back to his corner office. He rose to greet them. Lean and fit, fifty-eight years old, dark blue suit, dark blue and white striped shirt with a white collar, French cuffs, red tie, black Allen Edmunds lace-up shoes—ready to appear on television at a moment's notice.

Buckley started with the preliminary pleasantries, but Aker cut in; "We've got some God-intoxicated assholes around Akerhill, and I want you to get rid of them, Vince. What we need is some law and order—some good old ass-kicking family values."

"I need the facts, Cam. Tell me who they are and what they did," Buckley commanded, ignoring Aker and looking at Lara.

She filled him in on yesterday's events discussing her theory about what motivated the Constants of Leo. When she was done, Buckley leaned back, hands behind his head, and sucked in his breath.

"They haven't done enough yet to really threaten you. But you should be prepared." (Thus, they indeed needed his expensive wisdom.) "What you have got," he said, "is a clash between your right to run a museum, on the one hand, and their right to assemble and speak on the other. Now, if it were just your own private little plaything out there, Cam, the First Amendment might not make much difference because the government wouldn't be involved. State action is what it's called. But you are open to the public, and this display of the icon is officially sanctioned by the United States government. The First Amendment says they can assemble and protest."

"Well, what's our role?" asked Aker. "Just to sit around and wait until they push open the doors, knock over the icon, and stomp it into the floor? Why can't you throw their asses in jail until the Second Coming?"

"What evidence do you have that they will do that?"

"But they threatened us," whined Aker.

"That's your problem," lawyered Buckley. "Being annoying is one thing; endangering your property is quite another."

He smiled as if he had just delivered a papal blessing. Then he said, "Lara, you told us that Reverend Sounder—is that really his name?" Buckley stopped and shook his head. "Great name for a preacher. I once knew a lawyer named Harrang," and he laughed as if that were about as funny as the law got. "The issue that a judge would have to decide is whether there is a sufficient threat of violence to overcome the presumption that speech, and particularly political speech or religious speech such as this, has an absolute right to protection."

"Dammit, Vince..."

"It's too early, Cam. We will do the research, but my memory is that a court will balance the potential restriction of speech on the one hand against the potential for physical harm on the other. To prevail you would have to show that ultimately you will win a lawsuit and that the danger to your icon is immediate and substantial. It's called a clear and present danger of imminent lawlessness." Always research, thought Buckley, a happy combination of the lawyer's urge to be careful and his need to be rich.

"That was about as satisfying as kissing your sister," fumed Aker when they reached the street. It was even hotter here, and the wind blowing down Pennsylvania Avenue had just deposited what felt like several pounds of grit underneath Lara's contact lenses.

Aker told her that he had an appointment and Estelle, his wife, was coming in for a play at the Kennedy Center, so Lara could just drive his car back. He dropped the keys in her hand like a tip to a doorman and strolled off toward the Willard Hotel. He was around the corner before Lara remembered that she had no purse, no money, and no driver's license.

Inside a drugstore and out of the wind, she flipped out her hard contact, spit into her palm to wash it, and put it back in her eye. She considered returning to Vince Buckley's office to borrow enough for parking, but she had, for the day, reached her degradation quota. Instead, she walked to the garage, drove up three levels, and when she reached the attendant's station, waved and pointed to the nonexistent monthly sticker that wasn't hanging from her mirror. The attendant hesitated just long enough that she was out. But as she hurriedly pulled into traffic, a woman in a large sedan swerved around her, laid on the horn, and gave her the finger.

She spent the next ten miles wondering about the human race and why she so little desired to be part of it. Her mind wandered back to her parochial school, and she was wearing the regulation blue jumper with white blouse.

How can we be born in a state of sin, Father?

Adam's sin is visited upon us all, my child.

But that's not fair.

Lara, Lara, remember St. Anselm's question: Cur deus homo—why did God become man? Because only through God's grace of Christ becoming man, and taking on man's sins, can we escape eternal damnation.

But if God is love, why is there damnation at all?

Man has free will. And free will, in the hands of a sinner, leads to the very real possibility of eternal damnation.

Is this supposed to make me feel better, Father?

You are dwelling in sin and selfishness, my child. You must put aside yourself…Remember to count as lost all time not spent loving God.

And I'm still a doormat twenty years later, thought Lara as she stomped the accelerator and the 5.6-liter engine pressed her back into the glove leather seat.

CHAPTER 3

Preening in Indignation

———◆———

L ara lived in Bear Hollow, near the edge of the Shenandoah National Forest in what was something more than a cabin, something less than a house. Up a gravel driveway and flagstone steps, one entered into a single room with a high beamed ceiling and a large stone fireplace at the end. An upholstered chair faced the raised stone hearth, and a narrow refectory table with mismatched hand-joined chairs filled the space between the sitting area and the kitchen. A sleeping loft and bathroom comprised the upstairs, and the only other room, incongruously, was a well-appointed "guest room" she never used. The pond at the bottom of the lawn was a favorite watering hole for local deer.

Lara lived with Igor. Igor was a cat, a Russian blue with gray-blue fur that seemed to have a silver hue around its contours. He had yellow eyes, a handsome rounded face, and a lover's disposition. Igor craved food, sleep, and attention. For the latter, he butted her arm until he gained access to her lap and was not one to be denied. When she wanted to protect a freshly pressed light-colored skirt, he simply approached from different angles as many times as necessary to gain access, and, if thwarted enough times, he jumped to her shoulders, gripping fabric or skin with his claws, and draped himself around the back of her neck.

·—·—·

Lara never minded waking up but hated spitting fur. She pushed Igor out of her face, started the coffee, and glanced, without really caring, to see if there were any deer at the pond. Thirty-four was late for self-discovery, she thought, but even more troubling was the prospect that, ten, twenty years hence she would still be searching, having lived her life as a stranger to herself.

What she knew for sure was that her single-minded devotion to art that had led her to Akerhill was a frail foundation upon which to build a life. And even her bravest delusion could hardly allow her to pretend, after yesterday, that she was in control there.

She called the Rappahannock County Sheriff's Office and confirmed that they would send up a few deputies about opening time, then had two cups of coffee and a piece of toast, and put her stomach into spin cycle.

She was pretty good with her makeup, quick with the eyebrow pencil and a little bit of color that accentuated her cheekbones. She said "Hi!" to the mirror. The reflection said "Hi!" back—a pretty girl with fine features, square shoulders, and a muddled mind.

Outside it hadn't even pretended to cool off during the night, and the gnats, intoxicated by the CO_2 she exhaled, attacked her as she hurried to her car.

Twenty minutes later, Akerhill appeared on the crown of a small hill, facing westward toward the Blue Ridge Mountains. Approximately 100 yards behind it, partly hidden by

Akerhill's bulk, was a modern house, built by Aker II for his family after he decided to give the old family mansion to his newly created foundation. The former home would become a museum to display the substantial art collection amassed by Cameron's I and II. Number II then promptly died, leaving III as his less than thrilled cultural heir.

Lara drove around to the back of the museum and entered through the gardens. They were English with brick walls and white wooden trellises with pale pink New Dawn roses cascading down them. A series of boxwood and holly hedges, royal oak trees, and a row of multi-ported birdhouses on high poles served as inviting homes for swallows who paid their rent by inhaling copious quantities of insects. The gardens once sported imperious and obnoxious peacocks, constantly squawking and crapping, but a den of red foxes, denizens of the neighborhood, ate all but their feathers, and nobody much missed them.

She rang the bell, and a guard let her in. She needed some time alone, not just to collect the pieces from yesterday, but to figure out the strange combination of detachment and panic The Mother of God had created in her.

She dumped her purse and briefcase in her oak-paneled office, went to the Great Hall, and commanded an audience with the icon. The Mother of God was mounted inside a plexiglass case against a background of velvet, secured to its base by peculiar screws that looked like the point of a screwdriver. The case was put together with the same kind of screw, so that to open it one would need a screwdriver that looked like the head of a screw.

Although she had avoided entangling human alliances, Lara had an increasing sense that her one-dimensional life was watery gruel, and she would have to seriously seek some self-knowledge to thicken it. And while she might loosen the tightly fastened lid on her emotional self, the last thing she needed while she did so was The Mother of God as a houseguest.

But here she was. She held her child—a commentary on the family of man. Need to think about that one. And she gazed with devotion. Need to think about that, too. And she was strong and unbending, and beautiful and untouchable, and radiated silence of the heart. This is hitting a little too close to the mark, thought Lara, but, for a change, she didn't switch off her senses.

The great columns solidly supported the arched ceiling of the main hall. A guard's shoes squeaked as he walked through on his rounds, nodding, but not disturbing her. The ventilation kicked on.

The longer she looked at The Mother of God, the more her own memories pushed unbidden into her mind. How long had her confessional truancy been—four years—five? What would she say if she returned? I haven't missed you, Father? Nor have I missed the guilt you—sorry, not you personally, but you the church—spread on me layer after disabling layer?

Sixteen years of Catholic school and endless preparations to be a "bride of Christ:" she rose at three in the morning to pray, observing "the great silence," to listen for God's voice, through the day and the offices of lauds, vespers, compline, all the while trying to deny self and sin and pride and all the pieces of the world that intruded on her union with God. Everything but the tones of her heart told her God was her duty and her destiny. Her mind kept seeing foolish and ignorant people.

Faith, thought Lara, I can't even begin to define it.

LARA'S OFFICE, IN THE NORTH WING OF AKERHILL, HAD once been a library. It was clad in dark walnut with a fireplace in the north wall. The bleached white oak floor gleamed around the sides of the oriental carpet, and a single broad board table served Lara as a desk and a conference table. Six straight backed chairs surrounded the table, her "staff" filling only two of them.

Wilson Porter—Wilson, Wil, or Willy if you were his mama—studied classical painting at Cooper Union in New York City. Immensely talented, irreverent, impatient, and quixotic, he had all the tools to captivate or offend the world. He did both with vigor.

Wesley Foster, the head guard, had ensured that everyone was in position, the alarms were functioning, and the security was on full alert, just in case. Nobody knew if the Constants of Leo would return. How could they tell? They couldn't send up a scouting balloon; they had no intelligence from the front; so they just had to wait. With malice aforethought, the Constants had thoroughly disrupted Akerhill whether they protested there or not.

Foster raised his hand. Three of us here, thought Lara, and he thinks he's in a fourth-grade class. She nodded to him with a patient smile.

"Reverend Sounder is a minister of God. The wife and I heard him preach in Brownsville. He was real good—spoke the word. He caused a fuss yesterday, but he has something worth hearing to say. He's on the radio, too."

"Do you know him, Wesley?"

"I've never met him," said Foster, "but he healed a sick boy out to south county. His mother put the boy's forehead up against the radio, and he was well just like that."

"If he comes back, perhaps you and I can go out and talk to him," said Lara.

Wilson was seized with a fit of coughing, kicking Lara under the table before he scurried out.

SOUNDER GAVE LARA AN EARLY OPPORTUNITY. THE CARS that were pouring into her parking lot were substantially shabbier than Akerhill's usual, and their passengers didn't stroll purposefully toward the museum, but regarded it as an instrumentality of the devil as they gathered in small groups for the assault. She went out on the porch into the sweltering heat, and a Rappahannock County sheriff's deputy made his way toward her. She recognized him from a recent celebration in Front Royal in which he played lead guitar in an all-police band called Lawful Sound. Discounting the beer bellies and unlikely combination of law enforcement and country-rock, they weren't bad. His military-pressed shirt was already sweat stained, and he estimated 250 protesters, with more arriving. Sounder, he told Lara, had predicted that she would burn in the ninth circle of hell.

Her stomach did a gainer. She seemed unable to avoid undigested spiritual issues. How dare this man she had never met comment on the destination of her mortal soul. The sheriff, dealing with the temporal only, called for more men.

She retreated to her office and dialed the four-digit extension that would connect her with Cameron Aker's

house. No response. Lara put down the phone, and it immediately rang again, her secretary reporting that Wanda Chin
of the Washington News Gazette was camped in front of
her desk demanding to talk to Lara right now.

Lara reviewed her courses in art curation, conservation,
acquisition, history. She had studied painting, sculpture,
finance, and fundraising, but had taken no course in how
to talk to a reporter.

She took two aspirin instead.

Then she swept out of her office in her best Loretta
Young fashion, hoping to blow right by the waiting reporter.
Wanda Chin was out of her chair like a shot and wedged
herself squarely between Lara's path and the secretary's
desk. Wanda was vaguely Asian with gleaming black hair,
a straight high-bridged nose, and to Lara's quick appraisal,
biologically impossible green eyes. She was the kind of
person who stopped passers-by in their tracks. Her peculiar
combination of features, put together in a random genetic
mixing on God's day off, defied an easy decision whether
she was mutant or beautiful.

But if Wanda's looks could arrest the casual passer-by,
when she focused her potent intellect and pitbull personality, it was clear that no story would be denied her.

"I don't have time to talk now. Make an appointment
with my secretary, please." Lara shouldered her way past
Wanda, but Wanda was in her wake flinging questions
as Lara steamed out toward the crowd just beyond the
entrance doors. She motioned for Wesley Foster to join her.

The sun reflecting off the gravel of the parking lot caused
her a pinpoint headache behind her right eye. She walked
to the tall, distinguished looking man with gray, wavy hair
and gold-rim glasses. He was attended by a small blonde

man with a bushy mustache, with whom he was quietly conferring. Behind them stood a crowd that was now surely bigger than 250—absolutely silent, inclined slightly forward as if waiting for instructions.

"I am Lara Cole, the director of Akerhill Museum." Then she said, "May I help you?" and felt immediately like a fool.

The gray-haired man regarded her without speaking. He then said softly, "You have insulted the faith of these good people and thousands like them in the United States. You mock our religion with your graven image. You defile all that we hold sacred."

"Perhaps we should be introduced first?" asked Lara, shielding her eyes with her hand and wishing she had brought her dark glasses.

He swept out of the sun like a Japanese zero pilot. "I am Reverend Bob Sounder," he said, his eyes barely open. "You will remove this abomination."

"Excuse me, Mr. Sounder."

"Reverend Sounder."

"Reverend Sounder. If the icon offends you, you don't have to come in and see it. I don't think you would picket a Muslim congregation just because you knew that inside, they were praying differently from you."

"The difference," said Sounder, "is that you have maliciously set out to defile our religion by getting the United States government to present this image which pretends to be God. It must be destroyed, and you surely will be destroyed with it.

"The Constants of Leo," he said, turning and gesturing broadly to the crowd behind him, "are the vehicle of God's vengeance against those who create graven images."

From the corner of her eye, Lara could see Wesley Foster nodding gravely. By this time the deputy had wandered over.

Lara turned to him with a mixture of anger and entreaty, "Deputy, you heard what this gentleman said about vengeance and destruction. Please remind him of his obligation to obey the law and respect private property."

The deputy blanched. This was not a typical rural Virginia scenario. "Look, folks," he said to a random point halfway between Lara and Sounder, "I am just here to keep the peace, not to settle your dispute, whatever it is."

"Well, what are you going to do, Reverend Sounder?" asked Lara, hands on her hips and feet slightly spread in as menacing a pose as her blood-rushing combination of fear and anger would allow.

He regarded her as if she were dog poop and said quietly, "When your museum opens, we will do God's will, of course."

"You touch that icon, and you will learn what vengeance is," said Lara, looking Sounder in the eye from her full five-foot-five-and-a-half-inch frame just long enough to telegraph that she was terrified. Then she spun around and walked back to her office with Wesley Foster a few steps behind, leaving Reverend Sounder, the deputy, and a bemused Wanda Chin standing in a semicircle.

"Mr. Aker returned your call," said her secretary.

Flushed and trembling, Lara took the pink while-you-were-out slip, went into her office, and shut the door. She sat in her chair, both elbows on the desk/table, hands on her forehead. Her headache had spread to the other eye, and her stomach was doing barrel rolls as she contemplated whether she could have been more ineffectual with rehearsal. She massaged her forehead, searched her mental supply house for sources of courage and, after a few more deep breaths, found enough to punch in Cameron Aker's extension.

Aker told her to call Buckley, hanging up without awaiting either her reply or opinion.

Buckley was out.

She dialed Aker again. "Do we open or not? I need some guidance. And it's your museum."

"But I hire you to run it, Sweetie. Get some balls, Lara."

"It's my museum if there is trouble, and yours if there's praise," she blurted, thinking that getting fired might not be so bad.

"You got it, babe. But I'll tell you what. It's going to be a bank holiday. You just go out and tell them that the museum is not open today, and if they want to sit out in the hot sun all day and fry their faithful asses off, I'm sure the Lord will appreciate it."

With that, Aker treated Lara to another dial tone.

CHAPTER 4

A Blow from the Chin

W hen Lara arrived at the museum at eight the next morning, the meadows were tranquil, the parking lot empty, and the protesters absent. She hoped without conviction that they had, like the proverbial plague of locusts, departed to ravage some other field.

When she reached her desk, Wilson Porter was there with the Washington News-Gazette, shaking his head as he scanned the front-page story under the byline of Wanda Chin.

The picture showed Lara face-to-face with Sounder, and the headline screamed, "Museum Chief Threatens Protesters." Lara threw the jacket of her khaki-colored summer suit on a chair, slouched behind her desk, and just sat there staring forward, searching for the energy to let the day proceed.

"Do you want me to read it to you?"

"No, just put the paper down, and after I take in some extra oxygen, I'll read it myself."

"You look awful," said Wilson helpfully. "I will get you some therapeutic coffee."

Lara reached for the paper and began to read:

"Our lawyers will be all over you like a bad smell," vowed Museum Director Lara Cole to the Reverend Bob Sounder yesterday. The confrontation, on Akerhill Museum's well-manicured grounds west of Washington, was precipitated by the presence of the icon called The Mother of God.

Reverend Sounder, the leader of the Constants of Leo, was on hand with approximately 250 other protesters alleging that the icon offends their beliefs and is present in this country through the sponsorship of the federal government.

Sounder said, "Christ threw the money changers from the temple. Martin Luther nailed his 95 theses on the church door at Wittenberg. I am witnessing against this sacrilegious intrusion of our government into religion."

Akerhill Museum, with its whitewashed fences and gracious appointments, bespeaks the wealth and privilege of its founding family, of whom Cameron Aker III is the presiding scion. White House sources confirm that Aker's friendship with Pavel Kiprensky, president of Russia, was instrumental in making the loan of the icon possible.

The White House press office indicated that it would have no statement regarding either the icon or the protest. Cole, the museum director, refused to be interviewed by the News-Gazette."

Lara sat back and shook her head as Porter reentered her office, a coffee cup in each hand. "Precious little pissant, ain't she?" he said.

"Where'd she get that quote? I didn't say anything like that," wailed Lara. "The reporters juice you by writing a 100 percent negative story and then try to goad you into giving them more ammunition by hinting that you are hiding from the press."

"I've seen this before in my short but action-packed life," said Wilson. "You watch—within the next couple of hours, the conservative papers from Richmond and New York City will be calling up and asking you to comment on this story Wanda Chin has written. They will get the issue spinning among themselves in the hope that somebody in the mainstream press will pick it up and write about it. When they do, you going to talk to them?"

"This isn't even my party. It's Cameron's, so he should be the spokesman for the museum, but I don't know where he is today."

Wilson was sitting across from her at her table/desk, doodling on a yellow pad as they talked. "If you don't talk to 'em, they are gonna write about you. And if you do talk to 'em, they are gonna write about you. At least, if you talk, you can say why the icon is here and describe its significance as a work of art."

"I haven't been quoted very often in the press, but each time I have, they have gotten it wrong," said Lara. "This is the first time I thought it was intentional, though."

"What have you got to lose? If this morning's story is any indication, you're already a target. You have a gallery talk at ten. Why don't you call Wanda Chin and tell her to come hear why the icon is important?"

Lara sighed, wondering if her lack of breakfast was the reason she was starting to shake. "Call her and ask her to come, Wil. And get out of here so I can get my thoughts together.

"Close the door," she yelled as he walked out.

In fact, Lara's thoughts for the lecture were already

together. What was in disarray was her confidence because, while she prided herself on bulling through tough times, both her self-control and the situation were beginning to swirl. Tears formed and rolled and then gushed. She was utterly alone, unequipped, and afraid.

She went to the bathroom, locked the door, and sat on the toilet and cried some more. Then she stopped crying, fixed her makeup, and without either feeling better or resolving a single unmanageable issue, reviewed her notes for the lecture.

CAMERON AND ESTELLE AKER LOVED THE WILLARD Hotel, where they had stayed after the play at the Kennedy Center. He liked it because Abe Lincoln, the night before his inauguration, had stayed there and walked to the White House the next day to become an American hero. Abe couldn't afford to stay there now. In fact, he would have choked on its pretentious elegance. Which is precisely why Estelle Aker liked it, and why Mrs. Lincoln, with her penchant for redecorating and overspending her budget, probably liked it, too.

Cameron sat at breakfast in the dining room just off the block-long hallway. With him was the Buyer. Aker and the Buyer had been associated in dozens of deals over the years, and the effect of the Buyer on Aker was the same as always: luscious foreboding. The Buyer exuded a scent of menace like a marigold repels a mosquito. He was a violent man.

Violence, in fact, had been his profession. While most colonels in the Soviet Army in Afghanistan sought what relative safety they could find in Kabul, the Buyer craved just the opposite. He jumped out of so many Mi-8 helicopters that they nicknamed him the YoYo. His pursuit of the Afghanistan rebels—called *Dukhi*, or ghosts, because they struck and disappeared—bordered on the pathological, as if he were a duly ordained angel of destruction. Which is exactly how he viewed himself.

Aker did not doubt for an instant the report, now passed into lore, that when the Buyer's accompanying attack helicopter took heavy fire and crashed into a steep, rocky canyon, bouncing down and spewing out dead soldiers as it went, he flew into an uncontrollable rage, sprinted under fire across the narrow valley, scrambled up the other side, and took out the antiaircraft gun and every living thing around it with only his combat knife and his bare hands.

His fame as a fighter and his KGB connections propelled him into a lucrative career as a dealer in weapons, contraband, and minerals after he left the army. He and Aker had sat like this before, discussing the details of a sale, but always by indirection lest the conversation be accidentally or intentionally overheard.

This transaction, however, was different from others in that Aker, himself, was the seller, not the financier. The commodity also was curious: a polled Hereford bull named Peter the Great. Prize polled Hereford bulls are valuable for the sale of their semen for insemination of cows whose offspring must have noble bloodlines. Often prize animals have multiple investors, in a limited partnership, who reap handsome returns from semen sales. In that respect, this transaction was also different.

The Buyer looked at him intensely and said, "You realize that I am interested not in fractional shares, not in the right to sell semen, but in the bull himself."

"I realize that," said Aker. "But I don't claim to understand it."

"It's not difficult," replied the Buyer. "When Chernobyl exploded, it laid waste to the fields and pastures to the immediate north and east and irradiated, perhaps irreparably, everything in its path. The cattle industry in Ukraine, and especially the undamaged part, has been adversely affected. We must start over.

"If we are to start over, we will start with the best. That is why your bull, Peter the Great, should be the father of this new line. That is also why our people should see him in all of his magnificence."

"I thought it was more than just the name that interested you. My price is $2 million, and I'll give you the quick commercial, although the price is not negotiable. He was Reserve Grand National Champion at Denver last year. He has the right color balls to withstand cold weather. He is an indefatigable humper and docile enough, even when excited, to allow easy semen gathering. He could be productive for a decade. I could syndicate him for more than $2 million, but I would have to screw around with the securities laws, and I'd rather not answer to ignorant partners."

The Buyer disliked Aker. The man was crude and arrogant. But the Buyer was a professional, so he simply asked, "Assuming we conclude an agreement, how soon could you ship him?"

Aker paused, mentally calculating. Then he said, "I figure a week. But it's up to you to get all the export papers. He will have to be quarantined for a while to ensure he doesn't have a transportable disease. I can give you inoculation certifications, bloodlines, and a bill of sale. I will build you a crate to ship him in, so you won't have to risk the cargo planes."

"Yes," said the Buyer. "We will want a special pen to ship him in."

"Your wife?" asked the Buyer. "Will she not object to your selling the bull?"

"Estelle doesn't pay any attention to these things," said Aker. "She is so out of it, it takes her an hour and a half to watch *Sixty Minutes*."

"I will look at this bull, and then we will decide," said the Buyer.

Of course, the price was grossly inflated, but since it would be paid with US aid dollars granted to Ukraine for agriculture, and since the Buyer and numerous other functionaries would receive generous kickbacks, who was going to complain? And the Buyer would receive additional compensation when he completed the second part of the transaction that was not discussed at all.

CRUNCHING TIRES ON GRAVEL AND SLAMMING CAR doors alerted Lara that people were arriving for the museum's ten o'clock opening. They were not, she feared, all art aficionados hungry for her wisdom on iconography and church history. She wished, for once, that she had a written script for her talk rather than speaking from slides and notes. While she had prepared this lecture weeks ago, the emotional squall that had overtaken her in the last hours left her concentration shot and her whole body vibrating with tension.

The thought of praying, as she had when a child, crossed her mind and surprised her. Too late for that, she thought, and picked up her three-by-five note cards. As she was putting them in order, she glanced across the table to where Wilson had left his yellow pad. She stood, reached over, and retrieved it. In less than five minutes, while he and she were talking, he had sketched The Mother of God from memory. She held her slide of the icon up to the light. He captured both the detail and the feel of the piece with astounding accuracy.

He is wasting his talent here, she thought, and walked out to meet the enemy.

Head guard Wesley Foster—that is, the head of five other guards who were adequately trained but unarmed and physically underwhelming—had placed the podium four feet to the right of the icon and a portable projection screen four feet to the left. A velvet rope surrounded the icon's plexiglass case, and in front of the podium, approximately 150 folding metal chairs were filled. Scores more people stood around the edges and tried to push in through the main doors of the museum.

I've never been so popular, thought Lara, scanning the crowd to see if any of them were familiar museumgoers. Maybe a third my allies and two-thirds theirs.

Reverend Sounder was seated prominently in the second row, wearing a beatific smile.

Lara looked for Wanda Chin. No Wanda.

"Icon is the Greek word for image," she began. "Emperor Constantine, as the first Christian emperor, established Constantinople on the site of the historic Byzantium, an act rich with both symbolism and foresight: symbolism because, as the hymn goes, 'In Christ there is no east or west,' and foresight because in 410 AD, Alaric the Goth ruined an otherwise pleasant summer in Rome by overrunning and sacking the place.

"So the center of Christianity shifted to Constantinople, which endured for another thousand years until it fell to the Muslims in 1453."

Projecting a map of ancient Russia on the screen, Lara described trade routes from what is now St. Petersburg, through Moscow, Vladimir, and Kiev, down to Odessa on the Black Sea, and thence to Constantinople on the Bosporus.

"Keep in mind," she said, "that Russia at this time was a thinly civilized group of principalities loosely allied by trade and mutual fear of the marauding raiders that followed the slow-moving rivers from Scandinavia to Constantinople, the most majestic city in the then-known world.

"We pick up our story with Vladimir I, prince of Kiev, from 980 to 1015. Vladimir was a searcher. In his early days he worshipped a pantheon of pagan idols, but he was unfulfilled. He investigated German Christianity, the Muslim faith, and Eastern Orthodoxy, shopping for the best trade advantages, diplomatic and political alliances, and, of course, aesthetic and spiritual rewards. He was tempted by the Muslim's proposal of unlimited fornication, but that lost some of its allure in light of their ban on alcohol. 'Drinking,' quoth Vladimir, 'is the joy of the Rus. We cannot live without it.'"

She glanced at Sounder. Apparently, the reference to sex and alcohol didn't inflame him. He sat, eyes almost closed, slouched and motionless in the most tightly wound passive position she had ever seen.

"In the year 988, Vladimir's envoys returned from Constantinople so overwhelmed with the majesty of the great church St. Sophia that Vladimir accepted Orthodox Christianity and married the sister of the Byzantine emperor.

"As an absolute ruler, he ordered a mass dunking in the Dnieper River and made Orthodox Christianity the religion of all his subjects, as well as himself. He, and his son who followed him, established Kiev as the center of Russia, where fine churches and Byzantine Christianity flourished.

"Which brings us to our icon, the Vladimir Mother of God. It came to Kiev from Constantinople in 1131 and personified the union of God and man in Russia. When power shifted to the town of Vladimir, near Moscow, the icon was taken there in 1155, and subsequently to Moscow itself, where it has remained for every minute of its life until it came so gloriously to visit us here in Northern Virginia."

She paused and thought she heard some faint hisses from the crowd.

Wanda Chin had arrived and was standing in the back, notepad in hand, next to Sounder's assistant, Gary Simms. Simms was giving her his full attention.

Flashing an image of The Mother of God on the screen, Lara said, "In Eastern Orthodoxy, devotional art, such as this, is used both publicly and privately as a way of uniting heaven and earth beyond space and time. The image of the Blessed Virgin holding the Christ Child on her lap is known as Theotokos in Byzantine iconography."

"It's a graven image," said Sounder softly.

Lara swallowed hard and went on. "According to the Scriptures, Christ's image was the Word made flesh. In the Epistle to the Colossians, St. Paul asserts that Christ Himself is the image (we might say the icon) of the Invisible God."

"Man will not worship an idol nor defile Christ," said Sounder, louder this time.

Maybe I'll shift from theology to art, thought Lara, taking her pointer in hand and walking to the screen.

"The gold background behind the Virgin is the symbol of light. In an icon such as this, it signifies the unapproachable light that existed before Creation and in which St. Paul tells us God dwells.

"Over her head and around her shoulders, the Mother of God wears a cloak called a maphorion that has a gold, eight-pointed star above her forehead and on her shoulder. These are the symbols of perpetual virginity. The star on the forehead is equivalent to a halo, and the one on the shoulder is a sign of power. (In the east, a servant kisses his master on the shoulder). As you can see, her features, hands, and body position are all stylized in the prescribed Orthodox manner." Lara's voice cracked, and she was beginning to sweat. The whole room seemed to throb with the pounding of blood in her head.

"As you can see from this photograph and will be able to see better when you get closer to the icon itself, the wood is dotted with nail holes. These were caused by a metal covering, called an oklad, that both adorned the icon and protected it from damage since it is still the practice for the Orthodox faithful to kiss the icon."

Sounder leaped from his seat. "She preaches the work of the Devil. Moses, come down from the mountain."

By prearranged choreography, his followers came to their feet with such abruptness that Lara stepped back, bumping the velvet rope around the icon, interrupting the infrared beam, and triggering the high beeping alarm.

It is not clear exactly what happened next, but in some order, Sounder pressed forward, pushed aside the velvet rope, and laid his hand on the plexiglass case surrounding the icon. Wesley Foster sprang from his position in back of the icon, cocked his right hand, and popped Sounder squarely in the jaw. Members of the audience pressed against the windows, setting off the perimeter alarms, and the museum guards surrounded the icon like Secret Service agents around an endangered president.

All of this played out as if in slow motion, but in reality, it took place within a span of fifteen seconds. Then the action seemed to freeze. Wesley Foster was standing over a surprised Reverend Sounder, who had abruptly sat down upon acquaintance with Foster's fist. Foster stared dumbly at his hand, clenching and unclenching it as if it were an unknown appliance.

The rest of the crowd just stood, like accident victims still too dazed to know if they are hurt.

"Mr. Sounder, I think you had better leave," said Lara in a voice that modulated a whole octave in a single sentence.

Gary Simms was at Sounder's side, taking his arm and helping him to his feet. They walked at a moderate pace through the front door, their followers falling in step.

Next, museumgoers filed out, and Lara found herself standing next to Wanda Chin, who had enjoyed every minute of it.

"Exciting talk you gave, Madam Director."

Lara made no reply.

"What is the policy of the museum about using physical force against visitors?" Wanda asked.

"Our guards are here to protect the art and the public."

"Does that mean that they are authorized to hit them? Would you describe that as protection?"

"He was going to harm the icon," Lara said in a voice that sounded like a whimpering child.

"But you set off the alarm, didn't you?" asked Wanda. "Are you sure he touched the icon?"

"Yes, I am sure. But you just make it up any way you want." And Lara turned and fled to her office.

I've blown it again, thought Lara. "It was not so much her questions: it was that smirky smile on her face.

"Things just get worse."

CHAPTER 5

Strategies

S ounder's offices, near the Metro stop in Rosslyn just across the Potomac from Washington, D.C., were neither lavish nor shabby—just functional in an earth tones way. Behind the reception desk sat a well-scrubbed, unimposingly voluptuous young woman with the smallest possible diamond in her wedding band. To her right, down a corridor, were the offices of Sounder, Simms, and the comptroller of the Constants of Leo, along with various secretarial and accounting functionaries. Three older women, two of them volunteers, opened the stacks of mail that arrived daily with checks for ten, fifteen, and twenty-five dollars precipitated by the constant appeals, via mail and airwaves, for contributions.

Down a short hall behind the receptionist's desk a glass door simply said, "The Word." The radio studio consisted of a moderator's desk with the electronic console; a computer monitor from which the host could see the name, location, and subject of a call-in listener; a microphone on an articulated arm; and a red "scrub" button in case the caller got out of line. Radio equipment, for all its communicative power, is inexpensive and simple. For his television work, Sounder depended on the studios of the religious networks.

Gary Simms knocked and entered Reverend Bob Sounder's office. Sounder was seated at his desk, the Bible open in front of him. The left side of his jaw was swollen and beginning to discolor from the blow he had received earlier that day.

"How are you feeling, sir?"

"Many have endured far worse for their faith. Come in and pray with me."

They sat in silence, heads bowed, for forty-five seconds—Simms was looking at the dial of his watch—and then Sounder intoned a prayer for guidance. Simms joined the "Amen."

"It is often not possible to know God's plan—He works in strange and mysterious ways—but I have to think, Gary, that he has especially chosen us to witness. All my life since I was called to God's service, I have felt destined for a special mission that would bring the Kingdom closer to earth.

"I have never told you," Sounder continued, obviously anxious to talk although it must have hurt his swollen jaw, "why I became a minister."

In fact, he had—multiple times—but Simms wagged his head and encouraged Sounder to continue.

"My wife and I were driving in Minnesota one afternoon, and our two young sons were in the back seat. That was before car seats, seat belts, or even much appreciation for auto safety. Locking the door was about all we did. You are probably too young to remember, but on some cars, the back doors were hinged in the rear and latched in the front so that the front and rear handles were next to each other with only the door post between them.

"The kids were bouncing around in the back, and Matthew, in particular, was banging against the door. As I looked back, I could see it was not fully latched, and I said so to my wife. She said she'd get it and leaned back and pulled the handle. Well, I was going about forty miles an hour, and the wind caught that door and snapped it open, breaking the hinge. Matthew rolled right out after it.

"I watched him in the rearview mirror as his little body tumbled along the shoulder and down into the ditch, and I said to God at that moment, 'If you spare my child, I will serve you for the rest of my life.'

"God did spare my child, but He exacted a price. Matthew is a loving and generous son, but he will never be more than a child. And every day when I see him smile with the half of his face that isn't frozen, it's like Noah seeing the rainbow as the sign of God's promise.

"God and I made a bargain. He kept his part, and it's up to me to keep mine." Sounder wiped a small tear from the corner of his eye.

"Do you feel the Spirit, Gary?"

"I do, sir," said Simms, anxious to get down to business. "I've been reviewing all that happened the last couple of days, and it is clear that God has had His hand in it."

"Let's get to work, then. What have you brought?"

With that, Simms slid a small stack of eight-and-a-half-by-eleven-inch glossy pictures across the desk to Sounder. "The photographer from the News-Gazette let me see his contact sheets and then made these for me from the photos he took yesterday. This one shows the whole room in which the icon is displayed. This one is of the blasphemous piece itself. The other two are of the outside of the museum, one showing the front door and the other, the porch to the south."

Sounder studied the pictures intently, moving them about on his desk with the eraser of a pencil so as not to smudge them with his fingers.

Finally, he said, "Our choice is not whether to do God's will, but how to do it most effectively. Review our plan."

Like a field general placing his troops, Simms explained how many protesters would be placed at the entrance, the windows of the main hall, and in the seating area, and what they would do when they got there.

"They have threatened legal action, and we should make it clear to all of those who participate that they must be willing to endure jail for their faith."

"It is not a problem," said Simms.

"I am going to devote tomorrow morning's broadcast to this issue, and each one thereafter until the image is removed or destroyed. I will also call friends at the Round Table of Solemn Prayer and see if they will give us some assistance on their TV show. Our God is a jealous God," intoned Sounder, never questioning for a moment his authority to pronounce God's will.

LARA PULLED HER TAURUS OUT OF ITS PARKING SPOT and headed west on Highway 66 toward her house. She was exhausted and badly needed to shower away the pungent odor of a workday she would just as soon have missed.

While June was supposed to be one of Virginia's "good months," it was unseasonably humid, like the inside of a puppy's mouth. When she drove up to her house, the pregnant doe was at the salt lick, her bulging sides announcing an imminent birth. The deer looked up, determined that Lara was no threat, and resumed her licking. The acorn crop had been a good one, and the deer had kept Lara company both winter and spring.

She opened the front door to be greeted by a hungry, and not particularly cordial, Igor the cat. She fed him and, as she fixed her own dinner, listened to the television news. The sky to the northwest darkened. A thunderstorm was on its way, but in these foothills of the Blue Ridge, one valley could have an inch of rain, and the next, nothing. The weather patterns were, as an old Virginia farmer had told her, both "express and local."

She took her dinner, leftover linguine and carrot sticks, and sat on the step of the front porch. Two minutes later, she retreated inside to her dining table, not wanting to share either her meal or her body with aggressive insects. Halfway through the linguine, the wind began to rattle the tops of the broad-leafed trees so that it sounded as if a train were coming through—the old-timer's "express."

The first boom of thunder came immediately after its lightning flash, and the lights went out. Then came the rain, not on tiny feet, but in combat boots on her rolled tin roof. Within a minute, she could no longer see the pond. She got up from the table and ate her carrot sticks as she stood at the window, wondering at the violence of her day.

She didn't think she was a coward. She had tested her courage—rock climbed, even blindfolded once—and had bicycle raced when willpower was all she had left in the final five hundred meters. But what could she say for herself today? Fighting with the Constants of Leo, even if it was not a physical fight, was not why she was a museum director. Tolerance and understanding were what art could teach.

Maybe she was naïve. Or maybe she just wasn't very good at choosing.

LARA'S MIND, WITH NEITHER INVITATION NOR APOLOGY, began its self-directed reminiscence of her life. Sister Marie-Therese was washing dishes, the sleeves of her habit pushed back above her elbows. Lara, sixteen, in her uniform blue jumper and white blouse, was sitting on a stool in the kitchen.

We wash the dishes for Christ, Lara, just as we cook and clean and fast. Ours is a life of worship.

But, Sister, in class you are so funny, and you teach music with such passion and play the viola—are none of these things human?

Of course, they're human, Lara. Just because our life is dedicated to Christ doesn't mean we ignore the world.

But that's my problem—I just can't figure out how your life of worship and dedication to the spirit of Christ fits with the world and all its problems.

Service and caring and nurturing are part of Christ's message, but our lives are not self-directed; we are kneeling and waiting for the direction of Christ through prayer and tradition, and His holy church.

But what about yourself, Sister? Do you not have a life that you can direct? Can only our priests and the Holy Father tell us Christ's will?

You are strongheaded, my dear. Pray for the courage to submit your will to that of the church. Many before you have done so and have unwrapped the mystery of God's love.

I'll try to submit, Sister. I want to believe.

⸻ ◆ ⸻

WHEN THE RAIN STOPPED, SHE WENT BACK TO HER porch. Most of the insects had been discouraged, except for the fireflies, who were flashing about the lawn. She walked down the steps, waited for one to illuminate, and went toward it. It sat there dumbly, clearly not a Rhodes scholar of the insect world, while she cupped her hand around it. It had two sets of wings and a longish tail that looked as if it had been dipped in white fluorescent paint. She couldn't tell how it was wired, but she admired its singular mission: illuminate the night no matter how short the duration, no matter who the audience.

Three hours later, after she had gone to bed, the electricity returned. She got up, turned off the lights and the television, and went back to bed.

⸻ ◆ ⸻

THE HEADLINE ABOVE WANDA CHIN'S STORY THE NEXT morning screamed, "Museum Officer Slugs Minister." The picture showed Wesley Foster standing over a clearly surprised and abruptly seated Bob Sounder.

The lede was:

> An unprecedented assault of a museum visitor occurred yesterday at Akerhill Museum on the lavish estate of Cameron Aker III, west of Washington. Wesley Foster, chief of museum security, struck the Reverend Bob Sounder on the jaw in a

disturbance during a museum lecture. Sounder was treated and released at Northern Virginia Community Hospital.

The story then recounted how the icon had come to Washington, rehashed the protests of the Constants of Leo, and repeated self-righteous statements from Gary Simms on behalf of his fallen leader.

While the story was front-page news in the Washington-News Gazette, neither the Washington Post nor the New York Times acknowledged it. The White House continued to have no comment.

At nine thirty, about twenty patrons, not obviously associated with the Constants of Leo, were lined up at the front door, awaiting the ten o'clock opening. At nine forty-five, a cavalcade of cars, church vans, and pickup trucks arrived. Each disgorged its passengers who, without hesitation or conversation, walked to the front door and enveloped the queue already waiting there.

The density of the crowd, or their conscious touching of the glass doors, flexed them enough to activate the perimeter alarm, which rang out like a school bell.

After posting a guard inside the doors, Wesley Foster walked to Lara's office and asked if she wanted to open at ten o'clock.

"Can you handle it?"

"Since the alarms are tied directly to the sheriff's office, they are going to be here in a couple of minutes. If they can help with the crowd outside, we can handle security inside unless," he paused, "they decide just to charge the icon and try to smash it."

Then he said, sheepishly, "I haven't been in a fight since grade school, Miss Cole, and I'm sure ashamed of hitting

Reverend Sounder yesterday. The wife and I pray for him— listen to his program. I just feel terrible."

Lara got up from her chair and walked around the desk/ table until she was standing directly in front of Foster. She gripped him by both forearms and spoke more directly than she had with another human in months, "You did what your job required; you have no cause to be ashamed. In case you don't know it, everybody here is scared to death—at least I am—and you, you just did what was required. This is a tall order, Wesley, but you must separate your faith—and whatever feeling you have for Reverend Sounder—from your duties here. Can you do that?"

"Can I do what?"

"Can you do your job—protect the museum—the icon?"

He nodded vigorously.

"Well, then," she said, releasing his arms, "I will try to do as well as you.

"Now," she said, "I already called Vincent Buckley, Cameron's lawyer in Washington. They can't be here until four o'clock this afternoon, but Buckley told me that there is no way we can deny them access to the museum on the basis of their religious beliefs. Buckley said that would be a bad way to run a museum and a good way to get sued."

"So, we have to let them swarm in?" Foster asked.

"I asked him that, too," Lara said. "We can limit the numbers or let them in in small groups for security reasons, but we have to let them in."

"OK," said Foster. "I'll try not to hit anybody today, Miss Cole."

"Wesley, you are a comfort in times of trouble."

AT 9:50 A.M., TWO RAPPAHANNOCK COUNTY SHERIFF'S cars arrived, lights flashing. The four deputies conferred with Wesley Foster, who then turned and walked back into the museum. Lara watched the senior-most deputy mount the steps and turn to the crowd. He cleared his throat, cupped his hands around his mouth, and asked for their attention.

"I'm assumin' that all you folks here either came to see the museum or to make some point. Either way, you have got a right to do that. What you haven't got a right to do is harm anything or prevent anybody from using the museum. So, here's the deal. Twenty go in at a time. We'll see how that works and try to accommodate everybody. Keep your hands off the windows or you'll set off the alarms again. Anybody who disturbs the peace gets arrested."

He walked back down the steps. It wasn't the Gettysburg Address, but he made his point.

Wesley Foster opened the doors at 10:00, and the first twenty visitors filed in. They were, indeed, there to see the icon and spent their time doing just that. They then drifted off into other parts of the museum, and the next twenty were admitted. As the crowd around the icon thinned, twenty more came in and then another twenty.

At 11:45, by prearranged plan, eighty adherents of the Constants of Leo made their way from the wings back into the central hall, snugged up close to the velvet rope surrounding the icon, and sat down.

Wanda Chin and the photographer from the Washington News-Gazette materialized. The photographer began shooting. Wanda Chin simply stood there and smirked as Lara and Wesley Foster conferred.

"Go get the sheriff," said Lara.

"He's already on his way in."

"This is out of my league," said the deputy as he joined them. "I don't know what I am supposed to do. What do you want me to do?"

"Well, they aren't hurting anything except museum attendance yet" said Lara. "I can imagine what great photos the News-Gazette will have if we start hauling them out of here by their hands and feet. As long as they don't harm anything, I would just as soon let them sit there until after we have talked with our lawyers."

"That stone floor is going to get pretty hard on the fanny," said the sheriff.

"What do you think about me putting some guards right up next to the rope to discourage them from grabbing the icon?" said Foster.

"It's a good idea, Wesley. Do it."

FOR PERHAPS TWENTY MINUTES, THE BUYER STOOD motionless in front of an icon of the Apostles in an Orthodox church off New Hampshire Avenue in Washington. Icons only reveal themselves through prayer, and he was deep in contemplation.

"Let all mortal flesh keep silent

"And with fear and trembling stand.

"Ponder nothing earthly minded..."

In a sense he was a mystic—all Orthodox believers are. The mystery is not that God inhabits the icon, but that the icon is a window through which the wholly other shines forth. It sanctifies time and space, but only if one loses oneself in prayer.

Often, he would stand for over an hour, lost in an icon's timeless essence. Life for him consisted of simple truths. God was accessible through the icons and shielded him from an otherwise indifferent universe. He was a believer and a servant and would never be otherwise. Blood and hardship defined life. His grandfather perished in the Ukrainian famine of 1933, when Stalin ordered the peasants' grain confiscated and exported. Grandfather had a weak stomach and couldn't eat grass. His mother's right foot was sheared off by a falling sheet of steel in an aircraft plant in 1942. His brothers and sisters were dead—four of them—some by Stalin's ruthless whim, others by random fate. All died violently. So, most probably, would he.

His solace was in the imagery and liturgy of Orthodoxy, whose Mass had changed little since Saint John Chrysostom wrote it in the fifth century. It renewed him. It grounded him. Blood and faith. Death and rebirth. He emerged from the church refreshed, as if he had slept for eight hours. Now he had a little breaking and entering to attend to.

* * *

AT FOUR O'CLOCK, THE ENTOURAGE OF LAWYERS ARRIVED, Vincent Buckley in the lead and litigator Gerry Martin next, followed, like the flock of a mother duck, by two associate litigators lugging huge black rectangular briefcases called litigation satchels.

The rows around Lara's desk/table were now two-deep—a veritable Cabinet meeting. Lara and Buckley and Martin were at the table along with Cameron Aker, Wesley Foster, and Wilson Porter, the assistant museum director.

Behind Buckley and Martin were the litigation associates, briefing papers and yellow legal pads poised.

Behind Aker was his wife, Estelle, who was giving her fingernails a critical inspection with the back of her hand up and the fingers fully extended, the way men don't.

After introductions, during which Aker acknowledged that lawyers seldom leave their offices and, when they do, the client ought to feel particularly blessed, he said: "I just wish it were winter so we could turn off the heat and freeze their self-righteous butts on that marble floor."

"You were right not to toss them out," said Buckley. "Right now, they are setting the agenda and playing us like a three-dollar fiddle."

"Well, that is why you are here, counselor. Tell us some truth," said Aker.

Buckley, in his most patrician voice, turned to his anointed litigator and commanded, "Gerry, that is your department. The floor is yours."

Gerry Martin was hardly a flunky. Short and square, dark wavy hair, forty-five years old, he had been a boxer in college. Boxing, unlike football, brought little female adoration. He worked his way through law school at Yale and was smart, tough, and wordy.

He launched into a lengthy explanation of the parallel system of federal and Virginia state courts. That bored Aker after the second sentence.

"Let's cut to the chase, counselor, what are you suggesting we do?"

Martin sighed, as if he mentally were going back to his corner and loading up for another round. "No matter what strategy we choose, there are no guarantees that it will be successful because when speech, religion, or assembly are involved, the court will give them great leeway."

"The only guarantee here," said Aker, "is that you are going to get paid. So, tell."

The evidence upon which Martin would reply was the blocking of access today, the harassment of the museum by triggering the alarms, and Sounder's implied threat to destroy the icon. His reference to Moses coming down from the mountain had to mean Sounder would destroy The Mother of God as Moses had destroyed the golden calf (the associates had read Exodus 32:20).

"The relief that we will ask for is a restraining order preventing them from harming the icon or from interfering with the viewing or use of the museum by the public."

"When?" asked Aker.

"When what?" said Martin.

"When can we throw those small-brained nose-pickers out of here?"

"I'm not sure you can." Martin was accustomed to clients with selective hearing. "The museum is open to the public, and they have a right to protest—that is speech—and to follow their religious beliefs. Protesting here is assembly, and if you listen to what they are saying, they are, in fact, petitioning the government for a redress of grievances. They think that the federal government's involvement here is demeaning their beliefs."

"We are a private museum," injected Lara.

"Of course, that is what we will argue. I am just telling you that your case is not a slam dunk. You invite the public to attend and when you do that, you may be treated like a public facility."

"You didn't answer when," said Aker.

"We can seek TRO—temporary restraining order—tomorrow morning before a Rappahannock County judge."

"Why can't we go to the judge right now and tell him to order them out of here?" asked Aker.

"Couple of reasons. We don't have the necessary affidavits and legal briefs to support such an order yet. We can draw those up tonight and present them to the judge first thing in the morning. The second, and more practical reason, is that it is after five o'clock, and the judge has gone home. In fact, he is probably into his second gin and tonic by now, and I am not particularly inclined to call there."

"Suppose we get this order, and they block access and set off alarms anyway—what happens then?" asked Lara.

"Then they could be held in contempt of court and potentially jailed. But let me not mislead you—every step of the process will require them to come before the court and show cause why they should not be held in contempt, which means another hearing and a lengthier process."

"What the hell is the law for, anyway?" Aker fumed.

"I know it's frustrating," replied Martin, who was fantasizing a right, left combination to Aker's head, "but everybody is entitled to due process, and remember that the folks who are sitting on your marble floor out there are also the ones that elected the judge."

"Can I say something?" injected Wesley Foster.

Everyone looked at him and, although no one granted him audience, he went on. "We are already past closing time. When I go back out there and tell them to leave, and they don't, what am I supposed to do?"

Martin said, "Tell them they are trespassing. Don't forcibly remove them but lock the bathrooms. If they leave, don't let them back in."

"What about security for the museum?" asked Lara.

"If they don't do any more than they are doing now, we can handle it," said Foster. "We are just not going to get much sleep tonight."

"I would suggest that you get out your camera and take pictures of the protesters. Keep careful notes of exactly what you told them, about closing time and all that, and we will put that in the affidavits we submit to the judge tomorrow morning. Who knows," said Martin, "you may go out there and ask them to leave, and they will quietly get up and march out."

But they didn't.

Wesley Foster announced to the seated protesters that the museum was closing in five minutes and all visitors must leave. No one moved, no one spoke, no one left.

Five minutes later, Foster repeated the same announcement, adding that anyone who did not leave could be prosecuted for trespassing. No response, no movement.

Lara divided the staff into shifts. Wilson Porter and half the guards would go home now and return at midnight to relieve the others. Lara and Wesley Foster would stay. She asked the sheriff to post a deputy outside the museum all night.

But Wilson didn't want to go home. He remarked about how exciting museum administration was and bounced off to the conservation laboratory in the basement.

Thus, began a long and boring night. The guards stood by the velvet rope surrounding the icon. The protesters sat, or slept, using each other for pillows. Occasionally all or some of the protesters would pray aloud. Wesley Foster always bowed his head when they did.

At midnight, the guards changed, and Porter came up from the conservation lab to find Lara asleep on the couch in her office.

"I'm not worth a damn without my eight," she said. But she would not go home. She was the captain of the imperiled ship. She went back to sleep on the couch, and Porter returned to the lab.

<hr />

AT SIX THE NEXT MORNING, THE PROTESTERS STOOD AND filed out.

<hr />

LARA ASKED, "WHAT DID THEY SAY?"

"The man said they had fulfilled their promise to the Lord to not let the day pass without witness. They prayed for you during the night, Miss Cole, that you might find the Lord and renounce Satan." Lara looked into Foster's broad, open face, wondering what he really thought of her and the icon, but she said nothing.

The main hall stunk like a gymnasium. Small yellow pools dotted the floor, and the unmistakable odor of excrement described both the strength of the protesters' resolve and the frailty of their plumbing.

"Let's get the place cleaned up. Wesley, you call the cleaning crew and make sure they are here by eight o'clock, then you go home. That's where I'm going. If you and I are back here by nine thirty, we shouldn't miss any of the festivities."

"I'll leave a couple of guards here to keep an eye on things, and let the rest of them go until nine thirty," said Foster.

Lara went to find Wilson, who was singing and scrambling eggs on a hot plate in the lab downstairs. "They left, Wil," she said.

"So I saw. Want some eggs?"

"They smell revolting. Why don't you go home?"

"I'll stick around, but you go ahead," he said. "I think this is kind of fun."

"You are a warped person, and so young."

CHAPTER 6

Cause and Alarm

A fter Foster and all but two of the guards had left, Wilson Porter stood looking at the main hall. Looks like a stadium after the ball game; needs a good hosing down.

He walked up to the icon. She neither slept nor averted her gaze. The gold background lifted her face off the surface so that she floated both inert and alive. If I looked at that long enough, I could become religious man, he thought. He stared at her for a long time, as if looking for flaws in her construction. Then he nodded, mumbled something to himself, and walked down the south hall to the guard station.

One guard was dozing at the consoles; the other leaned his chairback against the wall as he read *Field and Stream*.

"You going to test the alarms?" asked Wilson.

"In a few minutes," he replied without looking up.

"Want me to crank up the emergency diesel for a test?"

"Whatever turns you on," said the guard.

Porter walked back down the hall, turned right, and descended the stairs to the basement. The alarm on the interior door at the head of the stairs was off. The diesel generator, a relic salvaged from a World War II light cruiser was five feet high, eight feet long, and looked as if it could power a city. He hit the switch, and the whoosh of the compressed air starter made him jump back. The huge diesel rattled to life. It had an ineffectual muffler mounted on top and a pipe that took the exhaust out of the building. Premature explosions as the cylinders compressed the air and fuel not only created a huge racket but vibrated the entire building and triggered both the infrared alarm around the icon and the wire alarm attached to its plexiglass case. The guard turned them off.

Porter left the diesel and walked quickly into the conservation laboratory. He worked feverishly for the next five minutes while the diesel clattered.

Then, perspiring profusely, he shut it off, and returned to the guard station.

"Diesel works," he said to the guard.

"Worked so well I could hardly read my magazine while the son of a bitch was on," the guard replied.

THE BUYER ARRIVED AT CAMERON AKER'S HOUSE AT 8:00 a.m. sharp. Cameron was sitting in the kitchen, reading the Washington Post. Estelle would not greet the new day for several more hours.

Aker offered him coffee. The Buyer declined and dropped a manila envelope on the table.

In his cowboy hat and boots (Aker always wore them when mucking about with cattle), he drove the Buyer from the house down a long lane bordered by rock walls.

Polled Hereford cows and heifers grazed in the pastures on either side of the road, but no bulls were in sight.

"We don't just let them screw indiscriminately," Aker said. "You put a bull in a pasture, and he will get right with the program, but you won't know when the insemination took place. And we don't want him breaking his back while in sexual ecstasy. We do all of ours artificially. Science has helped out nature a bit, here."

The Buyer nodded. He liked Aker less with each meeting. Aker parked the pickup in front of a large barn. As they entered, the Buyer reluctantly removed his dark glasses to see in the low light. They walked the length of the barn, passing two bulls of substantial size, and reached the end stall where a bull of truly gothic proportion stood, regarding them suspiciously, snot dripping from his nose and lower lip.

"Meet Peter the Great," said Aker.

The bull was large enough to blot out the sun—1,845 pounds of muscle and meat. Red-rimmed, beady eyes gazed from his mammoth white face as he regarded Aker and the Buyer as if he knew they were up to no good.

His coat was brown with a snow-white front brisket and underbelly. As he stood, his back was raked slightly forward so that when he lowered his head, he looked like he was charging even when standing still. His poll, on the top of his head, was the only vestige of the horns that had been bred out of his ancestors generations before. He sported a brass nose ring.

"An impressive animal," the Buyer said.

"I have all of the blood typing by both laboratory and veterinarian. He has bloodlines from both sire and dam that would impress the queen. The vet certifies that he has no blue tongue disease, no hoof disease, and no hesitation. He is fit and rarin' to go, provided you give me a cashier's check for $2 million."

"You know I am concerned about how he is transported," said the Buyer.

Aker led the way out of the barn to a reinforced wooden pen sitting on the tines of a forklift. The two spent an inordinate amount of time discussing the pen, finally nodded in agreement, and shook hands. They drove back to the house and the Buyer departed. Animals, like much else in life, annoyed him.

AT EIGHT-THIRTY, LARA RETURNED TO THE MUSEUM, HER hair still wet, her raspberry-colored summer suit bespeaking a good deal more gaiety than she felt.

Five minutes later Gerry Martin arrived with two litigation satchel-toting associates in tow and handed Lara and Aker each an affidavit for their signature. Lara read hers, which started "I, Lara Cole, having first been duly sworn, depose and say…" and then continued with sixteen numbered paragraphs in which she declared that she was the director of the museum and that Sounder and his followers had caused all manner of inconvenience and danger to the museum, its personnel and contents, and were likely to keep it up.

"This isn't the way I would say all of these things."

"The judge knows that we lawyers write the affidavits," said Martin. "You just have to be able to testify that everything in there is true. It doesn't matter if you would say it in different words. In fact, it's better if you have to testify—makes you sound for real."

"Fine with me," said Lara, and she signed it, whereupon one of the associates stamped it with a notary seal, scribbled in the date and acknowledgement, and tucked it away in the litigation satchel. Aker signed his without reading a word.

The lawyers set off to see the judge at the county courthouse ten miles away.

Fifty minutes later, the Reverend Bob Sounder arrived with 250 of his closest followers and the rest of the cast of this medieval morality play soon followed, including four Rappahannock County sheriff's cars and the ever-present Wanda Chin with her faithful photographer. At 9:52, Gerry Martin returned and walked purposefully to Lara's office, where Lara sat stone-faced in her chair and Aker lounged back with his cowboy boots on her table, twirling his hat on his finger like Bronco Billy.

"I've got the temporary restraining order," said Martin. "The judge was none too happy about it. He had read the stories in the News-Gazette and was reluctant to grant an order without the Constants having an opportunity to contest it."

"But because of your superior persuasive powers, you brought home the bacon," said Aker. "This should be a hoot." Then he swung his feet off the table and followed Martin out of Lara's office.

Sounder refused to take his hands out of his pockets when the deputy explained that he was serving him with legal papers. Accustomed to folks who were less than thrilled to see him, the deputy said, "I'm gonna put these on the ground right here in front of you. They are considered served, and I will tell the judge that. Maybe you should see a lawyer." The white papers almost glowed in the searing sunlight of another extraordinarily shitty day.

Sounder regarded the papers lying at his feet, looked as if he might grind them into the pavement, and then simply turned his back, hands still in his pockets. "I will answer to God, he said, and walked toward the museum entrance, a round imprint of sweat showing through the back of his jacket.

Martin stepped forward. "Reverend Sounder, I am Gerry Martin, attorney for Akerhill Museum."

Sounder waited for him to turn into a pillar of salt.

"The papers that you left lying there are from a judge who has ordered that you not harm the icon or anything in this museum, or interrupt its functioning, or bother its patrons. If you violate that judge's order, you may end up in jail. Do you understand me?"

Sounder spoke, but not directly to Martin. "I am here to bear witness. Those here who labor for man and ignore the injunctions of God will receive His wrath. All who attempt to portray Him by earthly means obstruct His way. Their work is vanity. The Word, God's Word, is my Truth."

"I don't doubt your faith or your sincerity, Reverend," said Martin, "but you violate the judge's order, and you subject yourself to the state of Virginia."

"The vain idols of man shall be cast down," responded Sounder.

Sounder's assistant Gary Simms had picked up the papers from the parking lot while Gerry Martin and Reverend Sounder were debating the relative merits of heaven and earth and was now talking quietly with Wanda Chin. She scribbled notes as he spoke. He nodded in response to her question and walked toward Sounder. The two conferred, and then, the Constants of Leo got back in their cars and vans and pickups and drove away.

Wanda Chin, smirk preceding the rest of her body, approached Lara, who nodded and said, "The ever-present Wanda Chin."

"Gary Simms said you have opened a can of worms. They are going to lay a counterclaim on you, in his words, that will 'fund their operations for the next ten years.' Any comment?"

"I am trying to run a museum here. I'll leave the legal saber-rattling to the lawyers. But I'll tell you this; you are making this into a circus when all we are trying to do is to show the American public one of the greatest pieces of art in the whole world."

"You don't believe these people when they say it offends their religion?" she asked.

"I don't think religion has much to do with it at this point. It has become…" She stopped. I am giving her tomorrow's story, Lara thought. "That is all I have to say," and she walked back inside, out of the oppressive day.

The afternoon was like trench warfare. Lara and her staff speculated about whether the Constants of Leo would return, whether they would step up their attack on this museum or countersue, and whether having loosed the litigation, they had created a bigger monster than the one they already had.

Few people came to the museum. Not more than a dozen looked at the icon they had spent so much effort bringing here. After the tension and stress of the day and night preceding, Lara sat at her table/desk, staring blankly at the paperwork she was not doing. At five o'clock the museum closed, and soon after, she went home.

THE PREGNANT GREY SKY SETTLED IN BY NINE O'CLOCK, and the frogs and crickets awaited the arrival of the promised storm. The day had been hot, but the night seemed worse, as if an engagement for relief had been breached.

At 9:25, the wind began to freshen and then, with nature suddenly in a hurry, picked up dramatically. The thunder boomed, and the lightning flashed and like a celestial valve opening, a river of rain deluged the Northern Virginia countryside. The lights flickered, came back on, flickered again, and went out.

At Akerhill, the compressed air starter buzzed, whooshed, and the diesel kicked to life, powering the emergency lighting and climate control, computer screens, alarms, and other necessary security equipment for the museum. The diesel generator's vibrations also set off the alarms on the icon, which the guard deactivated.

Just after midnight, a black-clad figure, wearing a balaclava, opened the garden door, and proceeded up the passageway into the basement of the museum. Shifting a large waist pack around to the front for easy access to the tools inside it, the apparition stopped and listened.

The diesel generator was cranking happily in the corner, giving the whole museum basement the smell and clatter of a ship's engine room. The figure slowly opened the door at the head of the stairs until the alarm sounded, then closed it quietly, retreated back down the stairs, and ducked into concealment that was pretty sure to be foolproof.

Within seconds, the door opened and a guard descended the stairs. The guard searched the basement. Finding nothing, he climbed the stairs, closed the door, and made sure the alarm was reset. The apparition waited five minutes— dogs and apparitions can wait timelessly—and repeated the process, opening the door, triggering the alarm, and retreating. This was the trick Peter O'Toole and Audrey Hepburn used in a classic movie, but they were just out to steal a million. This time the guard did not come down to the basement. He just opened the door at the top, looked down the stairs, and closed it again.

The third time the apparition triggered the alarm and eased through the door, closing it softly and walking swiftly to the right, then turning down the hall to the north wing. The guard came as far as the Great Hall, saw that all the doors were shut and the icon was still in place, muttered an expletive, and returned to the guard station.

The black-clad figure, with a three-foot aluminum stepladder in hand, returned to the Great Hall and stopped immediately under the camera that surveyed the entire room. From the waist pack the figure removed an eight-and-a-half-by-eleven-inch photograph of the Great Room with the icon in the center. It was mounted on foam board.

Next, like a magician pulling props from a hat, came three devices that looked like telescopic teacher's pointers, except that at the base end each had a suction cup and, at the pointer end, a small spring clip. Clipping the photograph at the bottom and on each side so that it faced inward, and then, climbing the aluminum ladder, the apparition deftly positioned the photograph in front of the camera lens, attaching the bottom suction cup to the wall and the two side ones to the sides of the camera body.

Floating noiselessly around the perimeter of the Great Hall to the camera that focused on the icon alone, the magician produced a second picture, this one of the icon in its case, and repeated the process.

Time elapsed was two minutes, fifteen seconds. Don't touch the velvet rope surrounding the icon's case, the apparition thought.

The wire from the ceiling to the case was vibrating with the emergency diesel. If the guards hadn't turned it off when the diesel started, the moment the case was touched, the guards would swarm in like flies on manure. By the same token, if a guard walked through on his roving rounds, it was all over. No time now to assess risks.

The screwdriver used to open the case had the head of a screw rather than a blade. Obviously, the screws were not burglarproof; the theory simply was that, by reversing the normal configuration of screwhead and screwdriver, your average thief would be delayed. Magician/apparitions were never average.

The four screws around a plate that secured the icon to its earthquake-proof, spring-mounted base came out surprisingly easily. It was heavy, more so than expected. The figure had planned to carry it under one arm, leaving the other arm free to carry the ladder. Almost tripped over the velvet rope. Should have practiced. Five minutes and thirty-two seconds. Too long.

The door alarm sounded as the apparition scurried down to the basement. Stumbling and missing the final step entirely, caroming off a structural support but staying upright. Fucking balaclava. What about footprints? Residual soot? Too late.

With flashlight in mouth and a quick sprint down the passageway, the apparition was out the garden door. No alarm sounded. Home free. Sure, there were a few glitches, but nasty consequences were for others. It was a great heist; an enjoyable romp. There would be great benefits.

Lara was in bed, trying to decide whether she should kick out Igor. First, he wanted to snuggle underneath her nose; then, when she slept on her back, he climbed up on her chest like a lilliputian lover. If she turned on her side, he would mount her hip. She knew he was not comfortable there, but perhaps being on top was a universal male hang-up. If she thought she could sleep, she would have minded more, but as it was, her mind was churning through the day's events, kaleidoscopically mixing the political and social and religious forces that had brought her into this maelstrom.

When she had picked up The Mother of God at the Tretyakov Museum in Moscow, Madam Doctor Kopulskaya told her that she would die to protect the icon. Lara thought of herself as a Secret Service agent, taking a bullet for the president. I don't know if I would do that for a work of art. But she admired Dr. Kopulskaya's passion as demonstrated by her tears and her incantations as Lara left with the icon. No doubt about its centrality to the Russians' image of themselves.

What was more remarkable was that the Russians would let the icon out of their control and that it would have such galvanizing effect on the Constants of Leo. And what about them? Was their passion as great, or did they simulate offense so they could feel persecuted, so they could whip themselves into a frenzy, so they could demand redress? She coveted the certainty of absolutes, erasing the blurry grey of her life. The church had promised her that certainty, that shelter. Could she have submitted? Should she have?

The phone rang; Igor leapt from the bed. Lara reached over to the nightstand and picked up the receiver. She listened to the guard for not more than a minute, stumbled to her bathroom, and threw up.

CHAPTER 7

Recriminations

P resident Sorensen's advisers did not generally meet in the Roosevelt Room. Granted, it was right across the hall from the Oval Office, had the requisite long wooden table, and even boasted pictures of both Theodore and Franklin Roosevelt lest anyone's partisan inclinations be wounded. But this was no usual meeting. Not just the early hour distinguished it. It was the first international policy meeting in her administration, or any other, caused by a work of art.

The implications of the theft for relations with Russia were legion. Sensitive trade, disarmament, and aid negotiations were underway, but more than that, President Sorensen needed to keep Kiprensky in power. He wasn't a saint, perhaps not even a good man, but he represented stability, and stability was the key to America's policy. Relations among the republics of the former Soviet Union could degenerate into an all-out civil war—anarchy enhanced by the presence of nuclear weapons. Ukraine was the world's third-largest nuclear-armed country. Equally unpalatable would be the resurgence of the military, promising order and security to a people quick to renounce their freedom.

And so the big room was filled with her economic, political, sociological, and military advisers—almost everyone who held an opinion about Russia and the countries of the former Soviet Union was there.

President Sorensen was not a feminist. She was an elitist. All things being equal, she preferred people who were smart. Some smart people were female, some male.

Her chief of staff got the meeting underway, cut short the recriminations about the icon's shoddy security, and told them that Cameron Aker was on his way to the White House so that he could be on the line when President Sorensen called Pavel Kiprensky. Each person around the table was relieved that he or she didn't have to make that call. But Sorensen took no comfort in Cameron Aker. She had not been close to him before her election, and she didn't trust anybody who hadn't done something substantial for her.

The Russian expert explained that, although faith was discouraged during the communist domination, all churches were not destroyed, and the art of the past was carefully preserved and venerated. It was that fierce pride in their heritage, the love of the land, the identification with the past, that had fueled the iron will that withstood nine hundred days of siege at Leningrad during World War II. Enduring inhuman hardships forged and annealed the Russian identity.

Unlike the United States, where we define ourselves individually, by our own freedom and personal rights, the Russian expert explained, The Mother of God is a symbol of collective identity with which all Russians and, indeed, all Ukrainians, and many others within the former Soviet Union identify even more than we might with our flag. It is a unique object of veneration, of description, and of transportation between this life and another, for which we have no equivalent.

Not only would Pavel Kiprensky's political opponents deride him, calling him reckless and incompetent, but the other republics, Ukraine in particular, would use this as yet another instance of why Russia cannot be trusted. If it can't keep control of cultural patrimony, how can it be trusted with nuclear weapons, warships in the Black Sea, or economic coordination? The list of potential headaches was beyond the reach of the strongest pain reliever.

President Sorensen listened and then said, "Continue your economic negotiations, your aid talks, and your weapons talks. If we can help Kiprensky with his internal and border country problems, do so, but discreetly. Keep the chief informed on a daily basis so he can coordinate.

"General," she said, addressing her attorney general, "put your people on this investigation like you have nothing else to do.

"Just one caution," she paused, "there will be lots of yelling and pounding of fists. My guess, however, is that after they get over the initial shock, the Russians will try to use this little mishap to steal our knickers. We have a delicate game to play—to help Kiprensky stay in power and not give him the farm. You would not be sitting at this table if you didn't play that game like pros."

She got up, swept a glance around the table, meeting the eyes of each person there, and as she left the room, she lightly laid her hand on the shoulder of the adviser nearest to the door. Sorensen was a combination of your mom, your teacher, your priest, and your coach. Charisma was more sparkly. She was just solid.

When Cameron Aker returned from the White House, Lara called her staff together. She had spent a good part of the night trying to dissuade Wesley Foster from falling on his sword in expiation for the breach of security.

The museum was swarming with police and FBI. Wilson Porter, uncharacteristically subdued, was just sitting with an unfocused gaze as if he were trying to get his mind around a problem that was several sizes too large.

Without preliminaries, Aker said, "Kiprensky climbed through the line and all over us in a way I never hope to hear again. The president gave him all that soothing, grandmotherly shit. He didn't buy a bit of it. After about ten minutes he was still screaming when she finally hung up. I suspect he will throttle two or three aides, just to relieve some stress."

Aker hardly sat down before he sprung up to leave—distracted and hurried. He asked Lara about the evidence and hardly listened as she described how the perimeter security was not breached at all, the gate was not opened, and no door or window showed any sign of entry.

The guard checked the first three times the basement door alarm sounded and concluded that the emergency generator was jiggling the door. He called the sheriff's office and told them to ignore the alarm, even though a sign right above the phone says, "Alarms shall not be ignored nor assumptions made about their origin." So much for procedures. The fourth time he strolled out and found the icon gone.

"It's my fault," said Lara. "I'm in charge, and you have my resignation if you want it."

"I don't want your goddamn resignation," growled Aker. "We haven't got time to air the laundry. We need to figure out who could have done it so we can get it back."

Wilson, returning from his mental walkabout, said, "If it was Reverend Sounder or his group, they have probably smashed it to bits or driven a stake through its heart, or whatever they do to destroy idols."

"If it wasn't Sounder," said Lara, "who could it be? No art thief could fence The Mother of God anywhere in the world. It's too well known."

"It's not up to you all to solve the crime, but you may be able to give information, so be cooperative. I'm gonna go eat and see about replacing that damn diesel generator so I can say we closed the barn door after we lost the world's most valuable horse." Aker got up and left.

As the others were leaving Wilson hesitated, half-turned toward Lara, shook his head slightly as if changing his mind, and walked out.

———————

GEORGE GRAHAM GREW UP IN GARDNER, NORTH CAROlina, a few miles from Durham. His mama raised beans and corn, a few cattle, and saw to it that her five children got the best education available to black children in the forties. She wrote poetry on scraps of fertilizer bags, envelopes, and anything else she could find. George was third of the five children, enveloped by a kind of family cocoon that gave him a sense of security and worth but did not erase the edge necessary to drive him to succeed in the world outside.

He went to college at Howard University in Washington, DC, and law school, on scholarship, at George Washington.

He wasn't recruited by the FBI, nor did J. Edgar Hoover, then in his third decade of tyranny over the agency, particularly like Black agents, but he got a job and, over the years, filed three discrimination complaints when promotion boards ignored him.

For those who tried to know him, and for the many agents both above and below him who admired him, he could best be described as self-contained. His job was simply to solve the case, no matter what it was, how long it took, or who it implicated. He was now a top agent. He was the first one the director called after the White House meeting.

Graham had three agents with him at Akerhill that morning, one of whom was spreading black fingerprint powder on doorknobs, the icon case, and any other surface the thief might have touched. The scene was thoroughly photographed. The evidence that was left, the stepladder, the suction cups and expandable clamps, the pictures in front of the surveillance cameras, and the pieces of the case that had enclosed the icon were tagged, bagged, and prepared for scrutiny.

As soon as the FBI Laboratory had finished its analysis, a crime bulletin would be issued, and an international report distributed so that the law enforcement agencies around the world would be aware of the theft.

International trade in stolen art was big business, especially art smuggled out of the former Soviet republics. This piece, however, was universally known. If the word "unique" were subject to superlatives, it was the "uniquest" of Eastern icons. There was, therefore, no market for it. Maybe the thief did not care about a market. He either wanted it for his own private collection—the Dr. No of Orthodox religious art—or he wanted the icon out of circulation, to be destroyed or hidden.

After talking to investigating authorities, Lara had

granted fourteen press interviews: no, she didn't have any idea who took it; yes, every effort was being made to get it back; no, she didn't know of any reason it would be taken; yes, the museum had been harassed by the Constants of Leo; no, she didn't think that the museum's security was incompetent (that last question from Wanda Chin); and so forth.

Now she was sitting in her office contemplating what life as an actuary might have been like when Special Agent George Graham knocked and asked if he could have a few more minutes of her time.

She nodded and said, "Come in. I don't seem to have much control over my museum, my schedule, or my emotions today."

He sat down, not directly across from her at her table/desk, but at a slight angle. He had on a green and white striped seersucker suit, a white shirt, crisp and pressed ten hours ago, and a yellow tie with blue amoebas on it. His shoes were black wingtips, but the soles were rubber. The top of his brown, bald head glistened, and he wiped it with a handkerchief as he said, "I've been around the outside of this building. I've been around the inside. I sat and looked at that room where the icon was for forty-five minutes. Nothing I see so far tells me very much. You probably know this building better than anybody. How would you steal it?"

"That wasn't how did I steal it, was it?"

"Everybody is a suspect," said Graham. "I'll make up a statistic for you: 73 percent of all museum thefts are inside jobs."

"I suppose I should take the Fifth Amendment, be discrete, but it's my museum and my professional reputation, and I don't have any desire to be careful with you, Agent Graham. I'll tell you everything I possibly can. So, your question is, how would I steal it? One way to avoid the perimeter alarms would be to stay in the museum—to hide in a lavatory or a cleaning closet, or simply to be a member of the staff—a guard or an administrator.

"Whoever did it would have to know the kinds of screwheads that held the case together and the icon to its base," she said. "That person either would have had to know where our tool was kept or have made one himself. The thief knew where the security cameras were, how the alarm around the icon was triggered, and where the guards were likely to be.

"Knowing that the alarm would be off while the diesel was on? That's either pure luck or real inside knowledge that only the staff would have," she mused, "and what thief can time an electrical storm, know the power will go off, and do the deed within that window? If I had had a better idea of how to steal it, I would have done a better job of making sure no one could."

He then asked Lara about each member of her staff. She showed him, over the next hours, each of their personnel files, although she wondered if she were breaching some confidence that she shouldn't be. When he asked if any of the staff had a reason to steal the icon, she could think of no one—she couldn't even fathom the possibility.

In the ensuing days she walked the museum, its grounds, its basement with George Graham. They looked at the outside doors, the door to the basement where the alarm had sounded the night of the theft. They looked at the emergency diesel. They looked at the huge octopus-arm furnace, flush up against the basement wall with pipes snaking out to every area of the museum. They looked at the storage room, the electronic tape on the windows, the guard station console, the main electronic gate on the driveway.

They talked.

They talked about Eastern art. They talked about running a museum. Lara learned that Graham, much to the disappointment of himself and his grade school princi-pal wife, had no children. "Lord knows," he said, without embarrassment, "we tried." And he coaxed more informa-tion out of Lara about herself than she had told any other human being, including her erstwhile husband.

She liked him, and he her, although both knew that if he decided she were the one who had stolen the icon, he would spare no effort to convict her.

THREE DAYS AFTER THE THEFT, A BRIGHT GREEN INTER-national truck with small high windows in the enclosed cargo box lumbered up the drive toward the museum. Oh, good, thought Lara, they are coming to steal the rest of our collection. But the truck labored on by the museum, around Cameron Aker's house, and on down the lane toward the barns.

Lara was curious, and since nothing was happening at the museum anyway (it had been closed since the theft), she got into her car and followed the truck. It had come to fetch Peter the Great.

Aker greeted her with a cheery wave and said, "Delighted you are here to witness the start of Peter the Great's journey back to his homeland," and, with an elaborate Elizabethan bow, he doffed his Stetson and pointed toward the large wooden pen that was sitting on the tines of a forklift in the barnyard.

"Constructed the pen with my own two hands. Just goes to show you that education has not deprived me of my manual skills."

The pen sported a new plywood floor, strong braces around the edges, and a newly hinged and clasped gate at the end.

"Look at this prodigious animal," said Aker, shoving

away the farm attendants. "And yet, with this ring in his nose, I can lead him anywhere. I will demonstrate."

"Not with me standing here, you won't," said Lara, and she retreated toward the barn door where, if necessary, she could sprint to the safety of the truck cab.

But Aker was right. With his hand on the nose ring, he opened the stall door and led Peter the Great into the waiting pen. The only tricky part was that after Aker had led Peter into the pen, he was against the end wall with a ton of animal between himself and the gate. It was a mistake no knowledgeable animal handler would have made. Gripping the nose ring with one hand, he climbed the first rung of the pen, swung his leg over and, dropping the ring, bolted off the other side.

Peter let out a huge bellow as the pen was raised by the forklift and moved toward the waiting truck.

As the truck departed down the gravel road, Aker pulled a paper from his shirt pocket. "Have you ever seen $2 million in cash?" he asked Lara. The cashier's check was payable to Cameron Aker and drawn on the Barons Bank of Washington, DC.

"Who pays $2 million for a bull?"

"A consortium of Ukrainian businessmen. Give me a ride back to the house, and we'll have a celebratory drink."

"I'm not much for drinks at ten o'clock in the morning, but I'll give you a ride back."

On the short drive from the barn, Aker's arm lay casually across the seat near the back of her neck. All of her "on-guard" bells sounded. By the time she stopped, Aker was caressing her neck and said, "We don't have to have a drink. There are other ways to celebrate. Estelle has been in New York for the last week. Come on in with me."

Lara had nothing against sex. In fact, she wished she

were better at it. But she also knew that going to bed with her boss was terminally dumb, and, anyway, he was a jerk. She said, "A celebration is certainly in order, Cameron, but I'm not going to bed with you."

"Coffee, then?" said Aker, removing his arm from the back of the seat and holding up both palms as he leaned against his door. "But it's a standing offer."

Yeah, I should feel honored among women, thought Lara.

DURING THE DAY PRESIDENT SORENSEN RECEIVED ONE aide after another for short conversations on a rainbow of problems, went to meetings, performed ceremonial functions, and gave speeches. The real work came early in the morning or on the weekends, when she thought about her policies and tried to keep from being overwhelmed by the world's most demanding job.

Right now, she and her chief of staff were reviewing the latest call—the seventh in as many days—from President Kiprensky.

It was like a litany: he would scream at her about how could she be so stupid, how she didn't have enough soldiers or police to keep an eye on a little piece of wood, how she would cause his government to fall…

After about three minutes, he would settle down and start working the angles, probing for concessions.

Sorensen's problem was that she didn't have anything new to tell him except that the Constants of Leo were the prime suspect, that Gary Simms's fingerprints were on the photographs that the thief put in front of the surveillance cameras, and that the Justice Department was preparing a case against them as rapidly as possible.

Kiprensky demanded that they be jailed, knowing from his Stanford studies that holding them would be impossible. Due process, bail, a fair trial—he scoffed at such window dressing. What he demanded was justice. In this case, perfect justice could only be the return of The Mother of God—with some reparations for the insult, of course.

The indictment on a number of crimes including criminal RICO charges against Gary Simms, the Constants of Leo and Reverend Bob Sounder, would be filed that afternoon.

RICO—the Racketeer Influenced and Corrupt Organizations Act—was a bludgeon that, in addition to criminal penalties, carried treble monetary forfeitures and attorney's fees. Originally designed to halt organized crime, its scope and reach had evolved to spread a wide and terrifying net. The government's case was sketchy, but President Sorensen needed some action.

The separation of powers is only a theory. The courts could be useful in the political process.

CHAPTER 8

June into July

O ver the next month, June into July, time moved in languid half steps. For Lara, it was too much attention, by half, and not enough to do.

She spent much of her time grieving. Having forsaken religion and believing love had forsaken her, she had built a life of singular devotion to beauty. While having The Mother of God terrified her—because she didn't at first want it, and then because of its awesome power—she had come to regard it as her charge, her entrustment, her Holy Grail. Its loss, as surely as the loss of a blood relation, rent her heart.

Could she have reached out to another human, she would have. Wilson—Wil—was the only local candidate, and he was, for reasons she didn't know or question, avoiding her. The chairman of the National Endowment for the Arts had called her the day after the heist to assure that the NEA was not—that is, NOT—insuring the icon. Her museum had not previously hosted an international exhibition and therefore did not qualify, and she had not applied, but if there were anything he could do…He then went on to bitch that he had not been invited to the president's high level strategy meetings, and perhaps Lara could put in a good word for him…What a butthook.

Could she have flown into furious activity to overwhelm her angst, she would have, but there was simply nothing to do.

The Akerhill Heist, or Icongate, or Sorensen's Folly, or a dozen other journalistic inventions kept the story alive in the United States and Russia. Reporters in groups of half a dozen squawked and honked, like geese dropping guano as they flew by, each day with a new angle to old news.

Lara was amazed. Each story sounded new but was simply a rehash of what had been in the paper the day before, and the day before that. The lede would say something about a new clue, or new speculation, or heightening political tensions between the United States and Russia, or new defenses raised by the Constants of Leo (like their claim that the photographs used in the robbery had disappeared from their offices the night before the icon theft). The next paragraphs would be from prior stories, and, if it were Wanda Chin, the final paragraph would be a shot at Lara and the shoddy security of a second-rate museum that shouldn't have presumed to play in the big leagues in the first place. The last criticism particularly hurt because Lara knew it was true, and her resentment toward Aker, whose arrogance precipitated this disaster, blossomed into a noxious weed.

Most of all, she blamed herself, and this hair shirt of guilt was one reason the days passed so slowly.

The Justice Department's specially picked team that reported directly to "the general"—the attorney general of the United States—got its grand jury indictment against Gary Simms, the Constants of Leo, and Reverend Bob Sounder.

Getting a grand jury indictment is no great victory. The proceedings are secret, and the defendant isn't there unless he voluntarily appears, nor is his attorney to contradict, question, or comment on the evidence the prosecutor presents. Thus, getting a grand jury indictment is about as meaningful a legal victory as winning a tennis match by default.

The Constants of Leo, Gary Simms, and Bob Sounder had counsel—did they ever have counsel—a lawyer from the Christ's Witness Defense Fund. Lest one hastily conclude that such a lawyer would be the equivalent of an empty tennis court, this was not your archetypal shiny-suit, curl-up collar, high-waisted dipshit lawyer from God who needed a ChapStick to lip-read a brief.

Elvin Massey had been a partner with Brubaker and Solomon in New York City before he got religion. While he renounced his $450,000 annual salary, his wife, and his Upper East Side apartment to join the ranks of Christ's Witness Defense Fund, he didn't renounce his twenty-two years of trial experience as a prosecutor and then as a white-collar criminal defense lawyer. In spite of his newfound religion, he was still 100 percent mean.

For the FBI, June into July was substantially less languid than for Lara. They reinterviewed the guards, the museum personnel, the patrons. They reanalyzed the physical evidence left at the scene of the crime—the photographs, the suction cup expandable clips, the small ladder, the disassembled plexiglass case.

They pursued every lead on the vanished icon, but wherever it had gone, it did not reappear. Every third day or so, George Graham would call Lara with another question, another suggestion, another mind teaser that might pry something from her memory to help him find the edges of this jigsaw puzzle.

Graham was clearly troubled by the paucity of evidence upon which the government's case was built. A lot of swill had washed over him during his years in the FBI, but he could hardly imagine the magnitude of the putrid smell he would wear were this case to be lost. He entertained not a moment's doubt that if the time for recriminations arrived, the president would blame the attorney general, and the attorney general would blame the FBI, and the FBI would blame one George Graham, an agent whose incompetence allowed justice to be thwarted (and oh, by the way, you know, he's Black.) He also knew that the White House was pushing, pushing, pushing for results. Investigations seldom produce on demand. They watch no clock.

June half-stepped into July. The Japanese beetle arrived at Akerhill, and the most aggressive of them, disregarding the yellow bags that trapped and collected thousands of their brethren, devoured the roses with a religious appetite.

Peter the Great, in his specially built pen, traveled first to quarantine and then, by 747 cargo plane, to the city of Kiev in Ukraine, where he was met by the Buyer. A new and profitable beef business in the new and (for those who knew how) profitable capitalist society was only a short gestation period away.

But the Buyer was not pleased by Peter's arrival. A major part of the transaction had gone awry.

History confirmed that displeasing the Buyer was hazardous to one's health.

***

George Graham's snap brim straw summer hat sat on his desk—he hadn't mastered the James Bond three-point shot to the hat rack. His tie was undone, but his white shirt looked as if it had just been unfolded from the cleaner's box. He pressed the intercom, waited, and said, "Come talk to me."

Within forty-five seconds, his assistant appeared—a young woman in her late twenties, of infinite good sense and, in Graham's opinion, not enough physical strength to do anything that would, in the dime novels, be considered FBI rough stuff. She knew well that these sessions were not conversations, but an opportunity for Graham to talk through a problem. Her role, if properly played, was to listen and perhaps ask an intelligent question at an appropriate place in the monologue.

"One of the things we are trained to do is smell the phony," he mused. "Nobody's nose is perfect, but I have always trusted mine. I've gotten that aroma from lots of televangelists, but never from Sounder. He has the technique—the lowered voice and electric intensity, the burning eyes and the passion—but with him, it seems real.

"Simms, on the other hand, is a devious little suck-up who would perpetrate any crime that he thought he could get away with to improve his place in life. But I don't see him pulling this kind of a theft without Sounder's permission, and I don't see Sounder doing it at all. Suppose for a minute he did. Why would the icon simply disappear? If Sounder were behind this deal, wouldn't he bring the icon out in some dramatic fashion, stomp all over it, and take both the credit and the penalty for its destruction?"

"He could still do that," she said. "Maybe even at the time of trial for maximum dramatic effect."

"I suppose that's right, but I still don't see it. Those boys at Justice are likely to get their butts kicked by his lawyer, and I don't see Massey allowing Sounder to bring the icon to court and publicly smash it. He would lose his license and end up in jail, too. It could happen, but it doesn't feel right."

"So…" she said.

"So…Sooooo…."

"So, who else wants it?"

"It's priceless, they tell us, and therefore, on the open market, worthless. Who you gonna sell it to? The IFAR boys—the ones that work for insurance companies to recover stolen art—say that the market for smuggling icons out of Russia is a hot one, but it's not the real ones, it's the fakes they sell to the rubes in the rest of the world. Those are $10,000 deals, not megabucks."

"What about insurance?" she asked.

"You mean, somebody at the museum, maybe even Mr. Cameron Aker eye, eye, eye, sets up the heist to collect the insurance? Who does the money go to? Aker doesn't get it because it is not his icon. Russia gets it, I guess, because it came from their gallery. OK, suppose they get $25 million from the United States, so what? Russia is trolling for billions of dollars in aid, not a few million. If you believe the papers, Kiprensky is in serious political trouble over this. Why would he orchestrate a theft so he could put himself in a swamp full of alligators? It doesn't figure."

"What if it is somebody else?"

"What do you mean?"

"Suppose you don't like Kiprensky, and there are plenty who don't, both inside Russia and out. You want to embarrass him, so you steal the icon, and the believers and patriots all get their shorts in a bunch."

"Is that a legal term of art?"

She blanched just a bit, but she knew him pretty well, and he didn't mind a little levity.

"OK, then what?" he asked.

"Don't know. You would think that those who are needling him the most about the loss of the icon might be behind it."

Graham pushed back from his desk. "Why don't you spend a little time at that computer of yours and make a list of who is making political attacks on Kiprensky. Then we'll talk some more."

REVEREND BOB SOUNDER AND GARY SIMMS WERE arrested and taken from their homes in handcuffs. A federal magistrate set bail at $100,000. Under the Federal Rules of Criminal Procedure, the US attorney could have issued a summons that simply commanded the defendants to appear before a magistrate. The handcuffs and frog-march from their homes signaled the start of a legal and political war in which no quarter would be given.

The indictment alleged numerous crimes; it took forty-seven pages of legal pleading paper to detail them. While court rules provide that an indictment shall be "plain and concise," this one was neither. It alleged that the defendants, through at least two predicate acts of racketeering, established a pattern of criminal enterprise that should require them to forfeit all of their personal and corporate assets and be fined thrice the amount that the Constants of Leo had collected in the past two years.

In addition to racketeering, the defendants were charged with interfering with interstate commerce by robbery; transporting and selling goods; assault with the intent to steal the property of the United States government; advocacy of forcible resistance to the laws of the United States;

receiving stolen goods; obtaining money by false pretenses by use of the airwaves; and interfering with federally protected activities. Lots of jail time was requested.

The case was assigned to Judge Herbert R. Goldman of the United States District Court for the Eastern District of Virginia at Alexandria and was put on the "Rocket Docket."

While many federal courts are content to allow cases to languish for years, the Eastern District of Virginia at Alexandra in general and Judge Goldman in particular were committed to swift justice. The Speedy Trial Act says cases can be tried 30 days after indictment. Judge Goldman was ready and impatient. He ordered motions to be filed within ten days, briefs shortly to follow, and trial to commence sixty days from the indictment. That pace might, to the casual observer, seem leisurely; in jurisprudential circles, it was supersonic.

Elvin Massey, with God on his side, was undaunted by an ethical conflict of representing Simms, Sounder, and the Constants of Leo at the same time. In his Rule 26 Motion for Judgment of Acquittal, he attacked every count of the indictment, arguing First Amendment protection of religion and speech for those accusations based upon the radio broadcasts or mailings of the Constants of Leo, and legal insufficiency of the predicate acts necessary for claims of racketeering. His brief was soundly reasoned, beautifully written.

Judge Goldman mounted the bench in courtroom 5 of the federal courthouse in Alexandria. Old and stooped, with rimless glasses, he said, without preliminaries, "I am inclined to grant defendants motions one through three, five, seven, and nine through thirteen. Mr. US Attorney, do you have anything to say?"

The US attorney was out of his seat like a shot, bracing the lectern with both hands. "As Your Honor knows, this is a case of great significance to the United States government and, indeed, to the government of Russia."

He might as well have impugned the judge's ancestry. Outside the courtroom door, the bailiff noted that it had taken only two minutes for Judge Goldman to break the sound barrier.

"No politics in my courtroom," he screamed. "You argue the law, mister, and let politics be damned."

The US attorney reflexively replied, "Thank you, Your Honor"—which is the trial lawyer's response when he or she has just taken one between the eyes. Then he labored on manfully, citing precedents and urging the court to interpret the indictment liberally at this early stage of the proceedings. The judicial outbursts, in rough order of declaration, were:

"Young man (the US attorney was forty-four years old), you only have to prove one substantial charge against a defendant. Why waste the court's time on dozens of super-fluous claims in this forty-seven-page indictment?

"And when you cite a case to me, just cite one that makes your point. You think I'm impressed by the number of cases? One case that matches on law and fact. Do I make myself clear?" Finally, he added with a withering stare, "You would not want to mislead the court, would you, Mr. United States Attorney?"

After thirty minutes of argument Judge Goldman slammed down his gavel, directed that his ruling would be as he had initially stated and that the clerk would enter a Minute Order on the docket. Jury selection would begin promptly, as scheduled, and trial would, as was always the case with Judge Goldman, be swift and, for the attorneys, horrible.

RECENTLY LARA'S WEDNESDAY BROWN-BAG STAFF MEET-ings had had all the camaraderie of a locker room after a loss. The museum remained closed, partly because it was still "evidence" but mostly because Aker had decreed it. He assured Lara that the foundation would pick up any operating losses and that she should use this hiatus for "planning."

Planning what? If they didn't recover the icon, Lara didn't see the museum as having much of a future at all.

Wesley Foster had been so self-deprecating that Lara finally took off her reading glasses and screamed at him to knock it off. Now, he sulked and said nothing.

One day Wil Porter would bounce around the room as if on a bungee cord, and other days he would sit and inspect his belt buckle with silent detachment. Several times, as was true at the end of this Wednesday lunch, he started to approach Lara as if he had something to tell her and then, either because other staffers were there, or by a failure of resolve, he simply walked out.

Graham wouldn't tell her anything about the results of his investigation. Every time the FBI agent called, he asked questions, but he never answered hers. Lara was a bundle of undifferentiated anxiety.

THE BUYER HAD NOT INTENDED TO RETURN TO AMERICA so soon, but as he cleared customs at Dulles airport, his displeasure at the deal gone sour had only increased. He was being played for a fool. Not just him. His faith, and the faith of all Orthodox believers, was being trifled with. The first such disrespect, alone, would have been a fatal indiscretion.

He rented a car. He made a telephone call. He contacted his associates and instructed them of the search they must undertake. He went to the Orthodox church off New Hampshire Avenue and communed with his God.

CHAPTER 9

Passages

Lara's dinner consisted of fresh carrots, zucchini, mushrooms, potatoes, and tomatoes stir-fried with garlic, olive oil, lemon, and onions. Dessert was half of a fresh cantaloupe. Disgustingly healthy.

She was watching the pond, hoping that the doe would reappear with her newborn fawns, but the only animal activity was the family of woodchucks grazing on the lawn, occasionally standing on their back feet, listening for danger. Lara had never known how much wood a woodchuck could chuck, if any.

The telephone interrupted her dinner (and gave Igor the cat an unobstructed opportunity to determine whether anything on her plate interested him). Lara picked up the receiver and, without preliminaries, heard:

"Lara, this is Estelle Aker. Have you seen my husband?" The question was laden with accusation and left Lara without a ready reply.

Finally, she stammered, "No, I haven't seen him. I have called him all day with no response."

"He's not with you?"

"No, Estelle, he has never been 'with me.' Check your message machine if you don't believe I have been trying to get him."

"Well, I haven't seen him since yesterday. He went off on his horse about four o'clock. A groom said the horse was back in the morning with the reins under the saddle. But I haven't seen Cameron."

"Doesn't that suggest something might have happened to him, Estelle?"

"I don't know," she said, her voice shedding some of the accusatory tone and adopting, instead, indiscriminate panic. "He has wandered off so many times to…whatever. He thinks I don't know anything…But this time he didn't say…" Her voice trailed off. "What should I do?"

"Have you called his friends, his clubs, wherever he usually goes?"

"Yes," said Estelle, now in a small and plaintive voice, "but I just don't much know where he goes. No one does, I guess."

"But, when he goes, is it for this long?"

"Not without some excuse."

"Have you called the sheriff, Estelle?

"No," this time in a little girl's voice.

"Is anyone there with you, Estelle?

"No, just the maid." The little girl again.

"Estelle, call the sheriff now, and I'll come over. I should be there in twenty minutes."

AFTER THE RUDE SURGERY ON HIS INDICTMENT, THE US attorney told the attorney general who, in turn, reported to the president that three-quarters of the government's case against Simms, Sounder, and the Constants of Leo had been tossed out by the Honorable Herbert R. Goldman, judge. No appeal is available from rulings on preliminary motions.

Kiprensky was on the phone. Again.

The president listened, occasionally uttering a sympathetic response as she heard the usual litany of horrors over his political embarrassment.

But today, Kiprensky was different—more agitated and more insistent. "It is as if we had sent thugs to your country and abducted Wayne Gretzky, Ella Fitzgerald, Cardinal O'Connor, and your entire National Gallery. Centuries of Russians have spilled their blood for this icon you have wantonly lost.

"Now I have new problems," he went on, barely pausing to breathe. "Not only are Ukrainians and my Russian enemies screaming, but Patriarch Alexei IV wants all property confiscated by the Communists returned to the Orthodox Church. He demands an icon I don't even have. How can I answer?"

President Sorensen reminded Kiprensky that the Orthodox Church's demands were not new and then told him that certain motions had been granted against the indictment.

"What do I care for your judicial proceedings? You can send someone to jail, but it does me no good. No more promises. No more soothing talk. Here is my nonnegotiable demand."

He paused, and President Sorensen leaned forward in her chair, reaching for a pencil.

"I had hoped that this sharing of Russia's artistic and religious wealth would bring us closer together, but it has had the opposite effect. Now I am desperate, and I need a sign of your absolute good faith."

He paused again. President Sorensen, pencil poised, did not really want to hear what was coming.

"You will, within three days, bring the original Declaration of Independence and the original Emancipation

Proclamation, personally accompanied by your secretary of state to the Kremlin. Both the courier and the documents will remain in Russia until The Mother of God is returned in the same condition in which it was loaned."

"Can't do, Mr. President," she said.

"I am demanding a show of good faith from the United States. I will relate these demands to the press immediately upon hanging up. You must appreciate the seriousness of the predicament you have put me in."

President Sorensen held the phone to her ear for several seconds after Kiprensky abruptly rang off. Then she replaced it in its cradle and looked up at the attorney general, who had been listening on the call.

"He will NEVER get hostages," she said.

CAMERON AKER III WAS NOWHERE TO BE FOUND. LARA had comforted Estelle as best she could, but the conversation was one to which Lara was incidental. Estelle, in a soliloquy, to which she apparently expected no response, kept asking, "How should I feel? If he is out shacking up, he can go straight to hell. But if he doesn't come back, what happens to me?"

At this point, she would assume the little girl voice and call upon herself all manner of self-pity as only one worth $16 million in her own right can do.

Lara fixed tea and made herself available, stolidly but approachably, until 1 a.m., at which point she tucked Estelle into bed, told the maid to call her if necessary, and went home.

The next morning George Graham arrived at the Akers' house. After ascertaining that Aker had been last seen on his horse but that the horse had returned without him, and then conferring with the sheriff's office, which in his opinion was best suited for directing traffic, he set about getting more FBI agents to Akerhill.

Graham left Estelle sitting at the counter in her kitchen, drinking coffee, and walked the one hundred yards to Akerhill Museum. A guard let him in. Lara looked up from her table/desk, saw Graham's slightly sweating bald head, and said, "Your presence here, High Inspector Graham, no doubt symbolizes a major breakthrough in our case?"

"'Fraid not," said Graham. "You know what happened to Mr. Aker III?"

"I sat with Estelle until one o'clock last night; I am not even sure she knew I was there. I could have been anyone from Mother Teresa to Bette Midler."

"Well, I'm back to check the place out again," said Graham. "I've got a bunch of agents coming to organize a search in case Aker is missing involuntarily. I have to wonder, though, whether there is some connection between his disappearance and the theft of the icon. So, if you don't mind, I'll just take another look around here and embarrass myself with how much I missed."

"Want some company?" said Lara. "I've been sitting here at my desk getting nothing done for the last two months."

"If you are thinking about taking up police work, I advise you to stay with the sculptures," said Graham. "But if you are looking for company, I'd be glad to have you along."

Graham started with the Great Room in which the icon had been displayed, working his way in from the door, trying to look without preconception at every detail. He continued downstairs to the basement, examining the rock wall foundation, the octopus furnace, the hulking form of the emergency diesel generator, and then he stopped.

"That's a furnace?"

"Of course, it's a furnace," said Lara.

"But that other thing, with all of the arms and pipes and boiler, that's a furnace, too?"

"It was," said Lara, "but it hasn't been used for years."

"So why is it still there?"

"I don't know. It was there when I came, and I assumed that it was more trouble to take it out than just to leave it. We don't need the space for storage, and I have always thought it was sort of…I don't know, attractive in an ungainly way."

Graham was feeling around the furnace door and, after opening it and sticking his head in the hole originally used for shoveling in coal, he turned to Lara and asked for a flashlight.

When Lara returned, Graham had his coat off, his tie tucked into his shirt. He took the flashlight from Lara and shed the beam around the interior floor.

"Son of a bitch," he muttered.

THE BROWN-GRAY PANELS ON THE WALLS OF JUDGE HERbert Goldman's courtroom, and the blue-green rug seemed chosen to cover but not decorate. They were purposefully neutral, unobtrusive, unremarkable.

Looking straight at the elevated judge's bench from the back of the room, the jury box was on the left, separated from the well of the court by a low wall faced in walnut. It held twelve seats with more for the alternates. In the back of the room, behind the rail (the bar from which the lawyers' fraternity takes its name), were three long church-like pews into which the US marshal ushered the prospective jurors.

One by one, names were drawn from a circular bin with a crank handle, and as each juror was called, he or she walked from the back of the courtroom to take a seat in the jury box.

Over this proceeding, Herbert R. Goldman watched impassively. Never in the imagination of anyone who ventured into his courtroom was there any doubt about who was in charge. When the last juror had been seated, the judge swiveled slightly in his red leather chair and addressed the jury in a nasal tenor: "Jury service is your duty as a citizen of the United States. It is both a high calling and a privilege. While my decisions as a judge are reviewable by a higher court, your decision about the facts of this case cannot be reviewed by any court.

"Because you must be impartial, it is my duty to inquire of you about your suitability to serve. Some of you may be annoyed that you have been summoned from your jobs or other daily endeavors, but I assure you, if you were seated in the position of any of the parties in this courtroom, you would want jurors who had put aside their own problems and were prepared, as fairly as humanly possible, to find the truth.

"I am the sole authority in this courtroom about the law that governs this case. You will administer the law as I explain it to you, even if it strikes you as arbitrary or even wrong.

"Is that clear?" He had them thoroughly cowed in less than a minute. Judge Goldman then proceeded to question the jury. Finally, he turned to the US attorney and said, in a manner that sounded more like a dare, "Do you wish to inquire further, counselor?"

Counsel for both the government and the defense did.

Two hours later, Judge Goldman called for the first peremptory challenge. Peremptory challenges require no explanation. The government had six, and the defendants had ten among them. The game here—at which Sounder's lawyer, Elvin Massey, was a master—was to lay traps during questioning so that the US attorney would use his challenges to remove jurors Massey wanted off. Of the six government challenges, two were spent on jurors Massey would have removed himself.

Massey's theory was that you look at the jurors' socks. You watch them as they walk to the jury box. You observe how they dress, if they carry a book, whether they wear a gadget-laden watch. You try to gather every bit of information about them you can. Then you stare them in the eye and if you don't like them, chances are they are not going to like you either. His profile of the perfect juror, that is, one who would acquit his clients, was someone who was religious and tolerant and compassionate and young and poor and unemployed. Perhaps no single juror would have all of these traits, but he knew what he was looking for, and most of all, he trusted not the handwriting specialists, social psychologists, or other high-priced purveyors of sociological theories in choosing a jury. He trusted his gut.

The US attorney's opening statement was a study in caution. The government's case would be based on circumstantial evidence: the motive of the Constants of Leo to steal the icon; their opportunity to do so; their passion that allowed them to see themselves as above the law. He pointed to the physical evidence: Gary Simms's fingerprints on the photos that had been placed in front of the surveillance cameras. He said that reporter Wanda Chin would testify, and he concluded, with confidence, that once the jurors heard all the evidence, they would convict.

To Elvin Massey, the opening statement was much more than a sterile recitation of expected evidence, even though that's what the rules specify. As far as he was concerned, there were two arguments in a case: the one that was traditionally called the "Opening Statement," and the usual one delivered before the jury retires to deliberate. He had caused more than one mistrial by this aggressive approach, and he was dealing with an explosive judge, but if that bothered him, he certainly did not show it.

"One of our most profound rights is to be protected from the government." Judge Goldman's head snapped up like a rubber paddle ball. "The First Amendment protects our right to practice religion. The government may not approve of the particular brand of religion that we practice, but that doesn't matter because it cannot impose any kind of restrictions on our faith. That is a right our ancestors fought and died for.

"Likewise," he said, "we can assemble and protest. If only mainstream thought were protected, it wouldn't mean much. And criticism of the government is specifically protected by the First Amendment.

"The government cannot—at least it is not supposed to—retaliate against us for our speech."

Now the judge was staring intently at Massey, color building in his forehead. Massey smoothly shifted gears to talk about the poverty of Sounder's youth and the roots of his faith and ministry, then about the elements of the various crimes and how the government's "proof" would be found merely to be speculation.

"No jury has ever found a criminal defendant innocent. The test here is that the government has to prove that the defendants are guilty, and that proof must be so compelling that you are sure beyond a reasonable doubt. You must be sure that this is not a witch hunt. And it must never be said that you, this jury, aided the government in maliciously punishing its citizens for their beliefs."

Judge Goldman slammed forward in his chair just as Massey thanked the jury, turned his back on the judge, and retreated to counsel table.

THE FOOTPRINTS IN THE OCTOPUS FURNACE WERE NOT those of the FBI investigators. They reluctantly admitted they had opened the furnace door, peeked in, and not given it a second thought.

So where had they come from?

Who made them?

When?

Why?

LARA WAS BACK IN HER OFFICE WATCHING AS GEORGE Graham put down the phone.

"If you are the thief, and you want to trigger the basement door alarm, you've got to have some place to hide when they come looking, right?"

Lara nodded.

"Get the guard who made the search in here."

She did and he didn't—didn't look in the furnace—who would do that?

Dumb question.

"OK," said Graham, "suppose the thief is hiding in the furnace while they search the basement. How does he get in the basement in the first place?"

Lara said, "He, or I suppose she, couldn't have hidden there when the museum was open because the door from the public area to the basement is always alarmed."

"Foolproof?" asked Graham.

"No, but with the intensity of the day's activity, it's going off would have been a big deal—and it didn't—go off, I mean."

"Let's go look at the door to the garden." Graham was up and moving before he finished the sentence, pulling Lara along in his wake.

"The outside door is alarmed like the rest of the perimeter," she said.

He opened it and the alarm sounded, bringing two guards on the run.

Graham said, "When the power is off, does the emergency generator power this alarm?"

"Absolutely."

"No way to beat it?"

"Not without a key."

"A key?"

"The key disables the circuit—a lousy system," said the guard, "but I didn't design it, and we don't just give keys away."

"Who has them?" asked Graham.

"Not me," said Lara. "I have to ring to get in."

"Who then?"

"Well, there is a key in the guard booth and as far as I know, Mr. Aker has the only other. The key, by the way, is one of those that you can't duplicate—or at least, you're not supposed to."

"So how does this work—the key closes the circuit?"

"No, it interrupts it, but if the door is opened with the key and then is closed and locked with the key on the other side, the alarm doesn't go off."

"Bingo" said Graham.

ESTELLE AKER KNEW LITTLE ABOUT HER HUSBAND'S activities, financial or social. It was Lara who told Graham that the Buyer had given Aker a $2 million check.

"You saw the check?" asked Graham.

"I saw it, although I could not tell you whose signature it was over. It was drawn on Baron's Bank; I remember that."

"And this was for a bull?"

"That's what he said, and I saw the bull being loaded into the crate that he built."

"He built?"

"He bragged to me that he built it. 'Simple skills' was his term."

Graham grunted.

He then asked Estelle if he might look around her house, to which she assented in an absentminded way. From the bottom of Aker's closet, Graham retrieved a black balaclava and surgeon's gloves.

He grunted again, went to his car for two plastic ziplock bags, and lifting them with the eraser end of a pencil, placed the balaclava in one, the rubber gloves in the other. They weren't, in themselves incriminating—just unusual.

He called his assistant and confirmed that Cameron Aker had not left the country, at least not legally, since the time of his disappearance.

He then turned to Estelle, who was standing with her hands at her side looking as if she were on stage, about to sing an aria.

"You last saw him yesterday afternoon, right?"

She nodded.

"Riding off on his horse, and then the horse came back, and he didn't, right?"

She nodded again.

"Best to get the dogs," he said, almost to himself.

CHAPTER 10

Multiple Images

President Sorensen and her advisers were again in the Roosevelt Room. So far, she had deflected the intensity of Kiprensky's extraordinary demand by laughing and saying that no serious government in this day and age would ask such a thing.

Kiprensky did more. He called another press conference and raged, stopping just short of pounding the table with his shoe, that if Sorensen didn't give hostages, he would take them.

The attorney general wondered if there was a correlation between the disappearance of Cameron Aker and the theft of the icon. In his scenario, Kiprensky, in political trouble and trying to hold together a volatile Russian Republic and fend off the wolves from outside, needs a bold stroke. So, he gets together with his college drinking friend, Aker, and they cook up a scheme to send a fake icon to the United States that Aker can steal from himself. Aker and Kiprensky then divvy up the $5 million honorarium from Aker's foundation, and Kiprensky can beat up the United States over the loss of Russia's cultural treasure, create an outside enemy, and deflect attention from his domestic problems.

"What proof, General?" asked the president.

"None, but it's not impossible, and Aker's disappearance could mean that he and Kiprensky are sitting in the Kremlin waiting to see if we are willing to play chicken."

"But why the hostage demand?"

"Kiprensky knows that no United States president has ever agreed that any American citizen should be a hostage, let alone a Cabinet officer, so he is just upping the ante to get you, Madam President, as a reasonable negotiator, to offer some other concessions."

"And your recommendation?"

"I think you already know," said the attorney general. "You go out there and make your Thomas Jefferson and the Tripoli pirates and no US hostages, ever, speech."

AT 6:00 P.M. THE SEARCH TEAM WAS WAITING AT THE Aker residence. The sheriff was there with three of his deputies. Rappahannock County Search and Rescue brought ten volunteers. Two adults led an earnest group of Explorer Scouts ranging from ages fourteen to seventeen. George Graham had commandeered four FBI agents, dressed in waffle-soled boots, khaki pants, and the much-admired blue baseball cap with FBI in block letters above the bill.

The dogs were holding up the parade. Graham was adamant that no one go out in a search pattern until the dogs had had an opportunity to smell what, hopefully, was an uncontaminated trail.

Just after 6:30, a battered red Ford pickup rattled up the drive. Rust had consumed much of its rear fenders, a loss of no apparent concern to its scruffy driver. In the cab along with the driver were two other men, and in the bed of the pickup, three dogs: a black Lab, a yellow Lab, and one of multiple ancestry.

The dog handlers got out of the pickup, nodded to the group, and set about preparing their dogs. One put an international orange jacket on the dog, saying to no one in particular, "I spent a lot of time training her, and I'll be damned if somebody is going to shoot her thinking she's a deer."

A second simply slipped on a two-strand collar and leash, while a third outfitted his dog with a contraption composed of a saddlebag-looking vest with a nine-volt battery on either side powering a foot-long green neon tube. "Came out of a copy machine," he said. "Battery will run all night so I can find the dog after it gets dark."

Graham gave a pair of Aker's dirty socks to the handlers and asked if they wanted to explain to the Scouts how the dogs searched.

"Every human has a smell and, to these dogs, it is distinctive. We let 'em sniff socks so they know what they're lookin' for," said the head scruff. "Dogs can smell something like four hundred times better than you and me.

"Some dogs are trained to find any human, but these here two dogs, the yellow and the black, they will find a particular scent. That's why the socks. Now, these two guys work their dogs different. One keeps his on a leash and follows right along with him, and the other lets the dog roam free. If the dog smells something, it will bark or run back and forth and act real excited.

"This third dog, he be mine, and he's what we call a cadaver dog. I trained him from smell of the dirt underneath a body the sheriff found a couple of years ago out to Sperryville. Now, if the body is in a bag so the smell can't drift up, the dog may not find it. But a body that's been in the ground for a while that isn't more than six feet down, this here dog, he can smell it. And as hot as it's been, well, a human body that's dead gets smelly pretty quick. So, I just let him go, and he follows his nose and, hopefully, he don't find nothin' cause if he does, it's somebody dead."

One of the younger boys sat down.

Graham sent them off, and at nine thirty, the cadaver dog, with his eerie green sidelights glowing, began barking wildly. That frantic message made the hairs on the back of George Graham's neck prickle up. In a grove of trees by the side of a small stream a mile and a quarter from the Aker's house, they found Cameron Aker III.

He was lying in a shallow grave with a crushed windpipe and a bruised, purple face. He had been strangled, brutally and professionally.

He was totally dead.

THE US ATTORNEY WAS NOT ENJOYING THIS CASE AT ALL. It had been brought prematurely because the White House demanded it (not necessarily the president, but the "White House" as if the building itself had made the demand).

The jury would return in one half-hour, but now, at 8:30 a.m., he sat with defense attorney Elwin Massey, the court reporter, and the judge in his Honor's chambers arguing Massey's latest motions. And he was getting reamed. Massey challenged count after count, whittling the indictment to scraps. The best he could hope for was to get at least one count to the jury and hope to hell they didn't like Pentecostal preachers.

Meanwhile, all he could do was delay the inevitable rulings for twenty-four more hours while he submitted a brief full of half-assed arguments. Judge Goldman did not like half-assed arguments or the lawyers who made them.

At 9:00 a.m. sharp—Judge Goldman was a stickler for punctuality—he pushed the button that notified the US marshal he was prepared to ascend the bench. The lawyers picked up their papers and, with the court reporter, entered the courtroom through the judge's door. Thirty seconds later, not having received the responding buzz from the US marshal, Judge Goldman leaned on the button again. Still no response.

The marshal tapped on the door, opened it, and said, "We are missing one juror, Your Honor."

"You warned them?" asked Judge Goldman.

"I did, Your Honor."

"I'll take the bench," and he swept by, robe flapping as he climbed the three steps to the elevated dais. He pushed his glasses up on his nose and glared at the eleven jurors and four alternates who managed to get there on time.

Four minutes later an older woman juror, flustered and sweating, bustled into her seat. Judge Goldman pointed at the offending juror and said, "If you are late again, I will hold you in contempt."

Everybody in the courtroom felt like a criminal. Goldman spun his chair and said to the US attorney, "Recall your witness."

The US marshal sat between the witness box and counsel tables. The courtroom was originally designed with the witness box next to the judge's bench but in these days of highly charged drug trials, the US District Court administrators thought it better that the witness be next to the marshal, who was armed, rather than the judge, who presumably was not.

The US attorney recalled his fingerprint expert and led him through descriptions of whorls and lines and similarities on a fingerprint-matching scale. The fingerprint expert, using blown up and mounted exhibits, compared the fingerprints taken from the photos recovered at the museum and those taken from Gary Simms when he was arrested. The match, he testified, was exact.

"Cross-examination," said Judge Goldman.

"May the witness be shown defense exhibit three?" asked Massey.

The marshal rose from his chair, retrieved the exhibit from the clerk's table, and handed it to the witness. If the lawyer himself directly approaches a witness in federal court, the ceiling will fall.

"Do you recognize this document?" asked Massey.

"Yes, sir."

"What is it?"

"It is a notice of alibi, sir."

"And it says that the photographs upon which you have based your testimony were stolen from the headquarters of the Constants of Leo the night before the alleged theft of the icon, doesn't it?"

"Yes, sir, it says that."

"And you don't know whether they were or not, do you?"

"No, sir."

"No further questions," said Massey.

"Excused," said the judge. "Call your next."

"The United States calls Wanda Chin."

The US marshal rose, left the courtroom through the door on the right of the judge's bench, and returned followed by Wanda Chin, smirk in place. He directed her to the Bible. "You do solemnly swear that the testimony you are about to give is the truth, the whole truth, and nothing but the truth, so help you God?"

She did.

The US attorney's first question was, "You are here under subpoena, are you not?

"Objection," said Massey.

"Sustained." Goldman glared at the US attorney.

"May we approach the bench?" Judge Goldman sighed, as if a dumber attorney had never so tried his patience, but he flipped on the static machine so the jury could not overhear the sidebar conversation.

"She is a reluctant witness, Your Honor. She has treated the Constants of Leo sympathetically in her stories, and you just heard that her photographer gave them the photos found at the scene. I need to establish that adversity so I can ask her leading questions."

Elvin Massey and the judge started talking at the same time. "Shut up, Mr. Massey. I'll tell you when you can talk. Right now I'm talking." Then Goldman turned back to the US attorney and said, "You don't need to lead the witness, young man. Just ask her questions, and if she doesn't answer, then I'll ask her questions."

He flipped off the static machine and, with an impatient wave of his hand, directed counsel back to their places.

Returning to his lectern, the US attorney asked of Wanda Chin, "Your profession, please."

"Reporter."

"What paper?"

"The Washington News-Gazette," her hooded eyes stared straight at her interrogator, seldom blinking.

"And you covered the demonstrations that the Constants of Leo and the two defendants seated at counsel table participated in?"

"I covered some protests of which they were a part," she replied.

The US attorney had her identify the previously marked newspaper stories which were admitted into evidence.

"And prior to working for the Washington News-Gazette, you were a scandal reporter for The Scoop, a supermarket tabloid, weren't you?"

"Objection," yelled Massey.

"Sustained," yelled back Goldman.

The US attorney shuffled notes to find his next question. His yellow pad bumped against the stem of the microphone on the lectern filling the courtroom with static.

Elvin Massey looked at the jury and smiled.

"I refer you to the exhibit before you, United States Ten. Do you have it?"

She held it up.

"In that story you wrote, 'The icon must be destroyed. It is the manifestation of all that is evil in our society. It has no place in this country, and I will not allow it to stay.'"

"Yes, I wrote that," she said.

"Is it a direct quote from Reverend Sounder?"

"Perhaps."

"When you talked to Reverend Sounder, did you take notes?"

"I did."

"Did you bring those notes with you today?"

"No."

"Why not?"

"Because they are privileged."

"They are not privileged if they relate to what you wrote in the story," said Judge Goldman. "You were instructed to bring them, were you not, young lady?"

Wanda Chin just looked at Judge Goldman, saying nothing. She was, apparently, the only one in the courtroom he did not intimidate. The US attorney pressed on.

"Do you remember that conversation?"

"I do."

"Tell the jury what Reverend Sounder told you."

"Don't ask her that question," yelled Judge Goldman.

She looked at the judge and then at the US attorney. No one said anything. The US attorney expected, particularly after the judge's outburst, that Massey would object. But he didn't. So finally, the US attorney thought, Well, hell, I can't let the judge intimidate me, and he nodded to Wanda Chin.

She said, "Reverend Sounder said the icon was like a blasphemer. It profaned their religion, and all who were responsible for its presence in the United States would die."

The five seconds that followed that answer hung in the courtroom like the silence after the tearing metal of a car crash.

The court reporter slumped down in her chair to get out of the line of fire.

Elvin Massey rose slowly and said, "I have a matter for the court."

Judge Goldman said very softly, his lips compressed into thin parallel lines, "I told you not to ask that question. Chambers."

When the door was closed and the court reporter seated at her stenotype machine, Massey said, "Your Honor, news of Cameron Aker's murder is in the papers and on TV and radio. Reverend Sounder is not accused of murder, but now the jury will wonder if he should be, and nothing any of us can do will overcome that prejudice. I move for judgment of acquittal."

"Denied," said Goldman, "but I agree to the prejudice, and I am dismissing the indictment."

Back in the courtroom, Goldman said to the jury, "Sometimes things happen in a trial that require the court to stop the proceedings. You need not trouble yourselves about the reasons. The marshal will lead you back to the jury assembly room. You are dismissed, and I thank you for your service."

Elvin Massey smiled and nodded to Wanda Chin.

ALONG WITH A STORY ABOUT THE MYSTERIOUS DEATH of Cameron Aker III, the next day's paper carried a headline saying, "Mistrial in Cult Case." The irony was, of course, that the very reason for the mistrial—that the jury might improperly consider that one or more of the defendants was implicated in murder—was now the speculation of every newspaper. The US attorney promised a speedy retrial, and those close to him appreciated his relief at the dumping of this bogus claim in favor of an investigation that might turn up a defendant worthy of his talents as a prosecutor.

Wilson Porter burst into Lara's office at Akerhill while Lara was reading the Post. He slid a copy of the Washington News-Gazette across the table to her. Its banner headline read, "Government's Case Against Religious Group Thrown Out." Of course, that is not exactly what happened, but newsgathering had always been secondary to the editorial persuasion of the News-Gazette.

Lara pushed the paper back toward Porter. "I don't read that fish-wrapper. Many other daily sources of annoyance take precedence over that self-serving, obnoxious, inaccurate rag."

"Long as you don't have an opinion," he said, "but I'll tell you this, the next time you hire an assistant director, you won't be able to say you are just an unknown museum."

Then, as if he had clicked an entirely new slide into the projector, his expression, manner, and intensity changed completely. "Lara, we have to talk."

"Over the last two months, we certainly have had plenty of opportunity."

"No, this is serious, I have something to show you, but I don't want to do it here."

"You are afraid my office is bugged?"

"It's not that, although with all of the weirdness around here, I guess it wouldn't surprise me. No, it's…well, yes, I guess it is that I don't trust your office and I want to show you, not tell you. Come on down to the conservation lab."

She shrugged, got up, and told her secretary where she would be.

Porter locked the lab door after them, turned on the working lights over his bench, and put on his lab apron. "Sit down, Lara, and I will show you what I have done and when it is over, if you want to fire me, I'm out of here. Things are too strange and I'm getting scared."

She sat on a packing crate, and he began. "Beautiful things inspire—they excite the impulse to copy. It is like the music calling me to dance. We know the techniques they used in the early Middle Ages for hand grinding pigments and mixing paints. I learned them in school so when the icon arrived, I thought to myself, I'll make a copy. I went out to Mr. Aker's well house. A couple of suitable boards, probably 150 years old, had fallen off, and I only had to help one other fall off. Then I fastened them together the same way as The Mother of God, I roughed up the edges and made sure I got all the dimensions exactly right. The wood already had plenty of wormholes from its long life in the meadow.

"I made a gesso mixture from flake white pigment, water, and Elmer's glue. The flake white is made out of lead and is just as poisonous as a politician's breath, so I used rubber gloves and a mask when I cooked it in the double boiler because, up to this point, I was just having fun and wasn't the least bit interested in killing myself.

"When it was gooey enough, I spread it on the wood panels, sanded to get the dirt and other live bugs off, and after about five coats, I was ready to make an icon."

Lara sat transfixed. The longer Wilson talked the more excited he became, and he began to demonstrate.

"I took an egg like this," and he retrieved one from the refrigerator, "cracked the shell and let the white run out between my fingers. I then washed the yolk in the palm of my hand to get off the rest of the stuff that clings to the sac surrounding the yolk, broke the sac, and let the yolk run into a dish of pigment. I mixed it all up, added some distilled water to get the paint to the right consistency, and that's egg tempera. The old Italian masters said to always use white eggs, not brown. Who am I to argue?

"The neat thing about egg yolk is that it's an oily and a watery substance that naturally hangs together—it's an emulsifier that keeps the protein and the water from joining their own kind and reforming into separate masses. It's sort of a natural form of what we need in race relations.

"Next thing I did was to stand in front of the icon for about twenty minutes. When I was growing up, I used to do this in front of store windows. I would look at something I knew I wanted but we did not have the money to buy, and I would memorize every detail of it: its shape, its color, its texture, its dimensions. Then I would own it. I could have it in my mind's eye whenever I wanted it, or I could go back to my room and draw it. The only thing I couldn't do was touch it.

"I sketched the major features of the Madonna and the baby Jesus in India ink so I would have a permanent outline to paint over. Then I gradually brushed color onto the surface. The lab here has some unbelievable stuff, even lapis lazuli, which is crushed up semiprecious stone, for the deep-blue color in her robes.

"That is about as far as I had gotten when the Constants of Leo showed up and threatened The Mother of God. I was feeling pretty proprietary toward her and thought I could do something to help.

"During their sit-in I stayed down here most of the night and was working like hell to try to finish my icon. I got on the burnt sienna and yellow ocher and pressed on some gold leaf with a gilders brush and a glass bolè and by midnight, I had a beautiful Madonna and Child, pretty much the way it looked when it came from Byzantium to Kiev in the twelfth century. I cooked it a bit to get it dry.

"Then I had to ruin it. Practically broke my heart. I pounded small nails into the wood to make holes where the metal covering—the oklad—had been nailed on and then removed from the icon. With an electric heating lamp, I caused the alligator cracking—craquelure—on the paint's surface and then I flexed the boards to get the vertical cracks, and I kept gouging on it with a carver's tool and a bicycle chain until I was satisfied that it looked as much like the real one as I could get it. But it was still too shiny and new, so I rubbed it with 0000 steel wool and—"

He stopped and looked at Lara, and said, "And this is the really strange part. I grew up a Baptist—everybody in my family did, and we went to church and we sang and we prayed and I guess I believed, but not like my Mama did. For her, religion was a way to get through a life that had been pretty terrible. For me, religion was one of the things I didn't think I was going to need when I left my Mama's door.

"But painting that icon, even in a hurry after the protesters showed up, was a religious experience for me. It became a language my heart could read. I don't know, it is just that face and her eyes…

"Well, I am not going to go all runny on you. It was just a very emotional experience."

"Where is it, Wil?" Lara whispered.

"That's the part I came down here to tell you. Remember that after the protesters sat around the icon all night, they got up and left around six o'clock? And then you and Wesley Foster and most everybody else went home to take a shower and regroup? After you were gone, I told the guards I would test the diesel generator so they could relax, and as soon as I lit it off, I unscrewed the case and substituted my icon for the real one. The alarms were off because the diesel was running and neither guard left the guard office the whole time."

"Jesus, Wil," said Lara. "I'm not sure I want to know what happened next."

"Nothing. I didn't do anything at all. I didn't have a chance to change the icon back, and then it was stolen, so I couldn't change it back."

"Wil," said Lara softly. "Where is the real icon?"

"You are sitting on it. It's in its packing case."

"I can't believe the FBI would never have looked in the crate for all the times they searched this place."

"They didn't," he said. "I would have confessed if they found it. I was going to tell you and almost did, a dozen times. Then I thought to myself, 'Maybe I'd better not.'"

"Why would you not tell me, Wil?"

"I guess I was kind of afraid and kind of proud, too. I wanted to see how long the thief could go before he turned the icon over and found I had signed it on the back."

"You what?"

"I signed the back 'Wilson Porter.'"

"You are unbelievable," and she leaped off the packing crate and threw her arms around him. Then they opened it and she looked, for a very long time, at The Mother of God. And tears streamed down her face.

"After Mr. Aker was killed and Sounder's trial exploded, I got scared because whoever stole the icon is playing a pretty heavy game," said Porter.

"Whoever has the icon knows that they have been had by one Wilson Porter who signed his name on the fake, so it is logical, isn't it, Wil, that they are going to be coming after you?"

"That is what I was thinking."

"Your Mama still live in Montgomery?"

"Mama is dead."

"You got any place where you can't be found?"

"There is an old guy. Paints birds on Masonite with house paint. He lives in Montgomery. He or some of his neighbors could put me up, I suspect, and their intelligence system for landlords and cops is better than the CIA."

"Go quickly," said Lara. "Do you have any money?" Of course, he didn't. She wrote him a check from her personal account and said, "Call me when you get there, Wil, and let me know how I can reach you."

Pavel Kiprensky was confused. The idea behind Aker stealing the icon was to gain leverage against the United States in his negotiations. Aker would get it to the Buyer, who would return it to Kiprensky, who could then "find" it, liberate it, bring it home, be a hero, and keep whatever he had been able to extort from the US in negotiations.

Now Aker was dead, the Buyer was out of contact, and he, Kiprensky, was in trouble. Certainly, a double cross was possible. But he had no choice other than to up the ante. Confusion or not, he was enjoying this. He deserved an Oscar for the snow job he had done on President Sorensen and, perhaps, even with all the uncertainty, the best was yet to unfold.

He would miss Aker. And he should have known better than to trust the Buyer, a goddamned Ukranian.

George Graham fiddled with his snap-brim summer hat as he cradled the phone on his left shoulder. His feet were on the desk; the jacket of his seersucker suit was draped across the chair in front of his desk. "You have been more than helpful, Ma'am, and I sure appreciate it." He listened briefly to the reply and hung up the phone.

Immediately, he punched the intercom, and, within the

minute, his assistant appeared. He motioned for her to put his coat somewhere else and sit down.

"I just got off the phone with a very nice lady at the International Polled Hereford Association in Kansas City. They keep statistics on everything you can imagine about their breed. Polled, in case you didn't know, means that they don't have horns.

"Just before he got himself killed, Cameron Aker three sold a bull named Peter the Great to a Ukrainian corporation. They supposedly are going to raise a master race of cattle and reclaim the beef market that was lost after Chernobyl fried the countryside.

"The thing is, when I told the lady what Ukrainians paid for this bull, I thought the line had gone dead. She told me that was four times as much as any recent sale, and even before the tax law changed in 1986, when bulls could be syndicated with fat tax write-offs, they didn't bring such prices.

"Then she said that Peter the Great was way too big for modern tastes. The breeders follow one trend or another, and Peter was bred for size, but after they bred a few of these giants, they found they got huge amounts of meat, all of it too tough to eat. So now they are breeding for other qualities, like meat you can cut without a chain saw, and the short of it is that Peter the Great's genes are out of style. Now I grant you that Ukrainians may not follow the fad, but it seems odd. Add to that the fact that he's old, and his semen sales have dropped off progressively in the last three years. She said that to pay that kind of money for him was flat stupid."

"Maybe they are just buying his reputation?" she asked. "After all, they would need every advantage to overcome the stigma of radioactive beef."

"That's just what confuses me," Graham answered. "They should want a bull that could produce over a long period of time, and here they pay a huge sum for a senior citizen. Of course, it's possible that Aker just conned them. That could get him killed."

"Have we talked to whoever it was that represented the Ukrainian buyer?" she asked.

"Can't find him. We know that a man visited Aker's farm and a waiter at the Willard Hotel remembered Aker breakfasting with a blonde man, wiry, about five-foot-eight who spoke with an accent. But nobody seems to know him other than as 'The Buyer.' The check comes from a corporation."

"Not much to go on," she said.

"This morning I looked up Ukraine on the map. I wouldn't have passed a geography test, but I will tell you more about it when I get back."

CHAPTER 11

Righteous Fury

S ounder's press conference, the day after Judge Goldman dismissed the charges, was part revival, part game
show, and part civics lesson. His gospel choir warmed
up the audience, which in this case, was a cynical group of
Washington press flacks who were more impressed by the
donuts than the music.

But if Sounder was anything, he was a showman who
knew how to work a crowd and talk to a camera. Behind
him, flanking the lectern, was an American flag and another
unidentified flag, perhaps his, perhaps God's. Likewise,
flanking the lectern in calligraphed script on large sheets of
poster board, were the first verse of the Gospel of John, "In
the beginning was the Word…," and the First Amendment:
"Congress shall make no law regarding an establishment of
religion, or prohibiting the free exercise thereof…"

Sounder's scripture lesson was from the Gospel of the
First Amendment, namely, that the government could
establish no religion in the United States. From there, he
launched into a tirade about The Mother of God that the
United States government had not only invited to the
United States, but had installed as a part of this country's
political vocabulary.

Worse yet, the government was expending untold resources trying to recover this piece of trash, this insult, this impeachable sacrilege. When he shouted, with eyes blazing, "The president should be on her knees," the most cynical of reporters felt a little tingle.

Where else would Wanda Chin be, but in the front row, taking it all in with little squiggles in her notebook. From time to time, she caught the eye of Elvin Massey. The two of them seemed to have some unspoken communication that acknowledged, in effect, "This may be bullshit, but it is quality bullshit."

Sounder's second lesson was the second clause of the First Amendment, and he scolded that when the United States government criminally prosecutes those who are practicing their religion, it is the president and all of her flunkies who ought to be put in jail.

The irony, not lost on the reporters, was that Sounder was articulating a case that had equal appeal to televangelists and the ACLU. The measured doses of outrage and intimidation he was serving up constituted one of those stretch issues that unites conservatives (the pure ones who want the government out of their face) and liberals (the honest ones who favor proactive government but hate abuse).

For Sounder, it was gold-plated. Being publicly persecuted was a small price to pay for the kind of platform the president had handed him. That he, Sounder, should be the vessel for God's Word—the new Jeremiah to unclothe the depravity of the government—was an opportunity for which he had been born.

While he was a showman and a manipulator and a calculator, he was also a true believer, and for him there was no falsehood where he was speaking God's will. If he joined

Saint Sebastian and the other martyrs, that was fine with him; his body could absorb the arrows; he had the appetite and now, the opportunity.

Wanda Chin was not one to miss opportunity, either. She pretended no piety. Hers was a religion of power. Thousands would read what she wrote, and most of them would believe it:

> The Reverend Bob Sounder blasted back at the Sorensen administration yesterday, charging freedom of speech violations and moral depravity. Citing the bungled prosecution of himself, Gary Simms, and the Constants of Leo, he accused the administration of a politically inspired vendetta comparing it to the Salem witch trials. Sounder called for the resignation of the president and the attorney general.
>
> Sounder's lawyer urged the ACLU and unspecified religious leaders to express their outrage at the actions of the government.
>
> The Sorensen administration declined to comment, citing ongoing criminal investigations.

WHAT CHIN DID NOT MENTION, BUT SOUNDER CERTAINLY did, was that his hearers could assist this righteous crusade with their dollars, and an 800 number and Post Office box address were prominently displayed next to the Gospels of John and the First Amendment.

Sounder's greatest fury, both during and after the press conference, was directed at those who had again broken into his office looking, he said, for the evidence that the government did not have in its first maladroit prosecution. For the government to have so little respect for the law that it would break into citizens' private places—twice now—and violate the Fourth Amendment (he knew his Bill of Rights) was beyond contempt.

Here, the government didn't hesitate to deny that it had any part in this intrusion or the first one and affirmed that it would, along with the Virginia authorities, take all steps to bring the persons involved to justice. Nothing apparently had been taken, nor was there any suggestion why Sounder's offices should have been ransacked—other than the conspiracy theory that Sounder addressed.

But the break-in at Sounder's office was chilling news to Lara. Whoever had taken the icon from Akerhill was bound to come looking for one Wilson Porter who had advertised on its back side. The potential return of these malefactors to her museum, particularly if Cameron Aker had ended up dead because of the theft, turned her feet cold.

Granted, Porter was a genius. But if he could so easily copy the icon, how many other copies might there be? Had she been the No. 1 international shill when she flew to Moscow, and with that curious mixture of reluctance and self-importance, personally examined The Mother of God, declared it to be the world's priceless image, packed it up, and carried it off to the United States?

If she had borrowed a fake, her future in the art world was no more than as the butt of a joke. She needed help, which is why she called the director of the Metropolitan Museum in New York, under whom she had previously worked. "Freddy, I am in more trouble than you could possibly realize. I can't tell you a thing about it, other than what you have undoubtedly read in the newspapers, but I need your help."

"Lara, darling, I told you that you would be sorry about leaving the Met. You were a rising star, but I had no idea how fast you would become famous."

"Listen, Freddy, I really don't even have time to be friendly. What I need from you is a recommendation, or better yet, one of your best curators in early Eastern Orthodox art."

"What for?" asked Freddy.

"I told you I can't reveal that, particularly not on the phone. Just tell me who on your staff is the best."

"I'm not sure I should do that. If this somehow involves the government or if it is any number of other possibilities that are running through my careful and conservative mind, giving you somebody from the Met staff to do whatever you want done sounds like a colossally bad idea."

"Damn it, Freddy…"

He interrupted, saying, "I am not cutting you off, Lara, I am just thinking that there may be somebody who is really competent, but not directly associated with the Met, who would be better for both of us."

"Who?"

"Let me make a couple of calls and get back to you."

"Quick!" said Lara. "But call me at home." She gave him her number.

SINCE GEORGE GRAHAM'S FBI BADGE CUT HIM NO ICE outside the United States, he worked through Interpol, a network of 169 cooperating countries, each with a national central bureau to aid international law enforcement. Interpol, headquartered in Lyon, France, did not do the investigating; it just put an agent from one country together with his or her counterpart in another. (The FBI had an office for sharing information on organized crime in Moscow, but that wouldn't help him in Ukraine.)

Since Ukraine's independence in 1991, its National Central Bureau was under the minister of the Interior. The language of Interpol, especially in the former Eastern Bloc countries, was English.

Graham had sent a message requesting assistance and was told that he would be met at the Kiev airport, and "all courtesies would be extended." He wondered how good their English was. Did courtesies mean they would be polite, or did it mean substantive help in his investigation?

Some people can sleep in airplanes. Not Graham. Moreover, squashed against the window, shoulder to shoulder in tourist class, he inhaled the obnoxious reminder that this was an overseas flight (Washington/Dulles to Frankfurt), as the cloud of cigarette smoke rendered meaningless the designation "nonsmoking seats."

He took off his shoes (with some difficulty since his briefcase was jammed between his feet) and extracted the memorandum his assistant had prepared for him. Assuming an "I will overcome" attitude, he settled back and read:

Ukraine has some mountains, but you won't see them because they are west and south. Calgary and Winnipeg are about the same latitude as Kiev, which may give you some idea of what to expect climate-wise.

You are going to see a lot of flat land with black, rich soil, good for raising wheat (if the summer is long enough) and grazing cattle. Ukraine also has heavy industry—chemicals, iron, steel, rail cars, bombers, and missiles.

Historically, the flatness of the land has meant few natural barriers to keep marauding armies away, and Kiev was overrun by nearly every army that happened by. From the seventh century on, the Scandinavian Normans slashed through on their way to Byzantium. The Normans had no interest in settling, and the Slavic people that occupied the steppe were gradually able to save their lives by accepting domination and managing trade for these scoundrels (who were brothers to the Vikings that ravaged England, France, and Sicily).

With Prince Vladimir's conversion to Orthodox Christianity came Byzantine craftsmen who, in the Eleventh Century, built the St. Sophia Cathedral (it's still there and you really should see it). They also built monasteries and trained priests and adopted the elaborate liturgy that helped unify the Russian state and gave them an escape from the harshness of the climate and even greater harshness of their marauding oppressors.

Today there are sixty million Orthodox believers in what was the Soviet Union, so you get some sense that this icon is not just a work of art; it is the manifestation of history and religion and culture and politics all wrapped up in one. It is the image of a people's soul.

Remember, Russia did not have a dark ages and renaissance like Europe. Alaric sacked Rome in 410, but Constantinople lasted until 1453 and, during those thousand years, it was the pinnacle of Christian civilization to which Kiev, and later Moscow looked for inspiration.

After Constantinople fell to the Muslims, the Russians bumbled along for 250 years until Peter the Great jerked them into the Western world. The cultural split personality that this caused is held together by the Orthodox religion and, although churches were outlawed under the Soviet regime, even Stalin could not kill them. (Give him credit for trying. He did away with about twenty-five thousand churches and probably ten million believers.)

One final point. The present political interaction between Russia and Ukraine is an uncomfortable one. While many Russians live in Ukraine and many Ukrainians look to Moscow for leadership, fierce Ukrainian nationalism and long-standing suspicion of Russia make the relationship volatile.

Also, Orthodoxy has come roaring back since the disappearance of the Soviet Union, and the Orthodox Church is a political force to be reckoned with.

Fax me if you need more. And bring me back one of those nesting dolls, please. Remember, it is Ukraine, NOT The Ukraine!

As he came off the plane at the airport in Kiev, Graham was met by a Ukrainian police inspector who presented him with a single red rose wrapped in cellophane and escorted him to the VIP customs lounge. As Graham fumbled with the rose, his host explained that a car and driver had been arranged and that he was at Graham's service for as long as he was needed. They would meet with his superiors tomorrow at 10:00 a.m. to plan Graham's itinerary. Now, perhaps, he would like to go to his hotel for a nap (he pronounced it snap)?

THE CHAIKA LIMOUSINE THEY PROVIDED WAS BLACK AND looked like a cross between a 1954 DeSoto and a Pullman car, with a rectangular body and a grille designed by a committee. The upholstery had been gold or perhaps brown corduroy when the car was new (which, for all he knew, was 1954). It had black curtains that could be released from their elastic holdbacks if one wanted to feel as if he were in a funeral hearse, and enough leg room for limbo dancing.

The driver discarded his cigarette and started the car. It went whir, whir, whir, whir, clunk! and began to move. His host told him that he would stay in their newest tourist hotel built by a Finnish construction company just off the Kreschatik—the main shopping boulevard.

When Graham got to his room, it was apparent that the Finns, like their Scandinavian ancestors thirteen hundred years before, had left little of value. The bed was hard and lumpy, built on a light-colored wood frame. The paneling was the same light wood with occasional nondescript light fixtures of a design that combined the worst features of Danish modern and Soviet worker architecture. The bathroom was functional but smelled, and Graham, after his smoke-filled flights and long layover in Frankfurt, was tired and grumpy.

After deciding he could not sleep until it got dark (if it ever did at this latitude and time of year), he put his suit coat back on and strolled along Kreschatik, which was crowded with shoppers and sightseers. Linden and chestnut trees separated the sidewalk from the traffic on the wide street, and numerous flower beds made the sweltering afternoon almost pleasant.

As he always did, both because of his FBI training and his experience living in a society that never forgets skin color, he mentally took roll of the ethnic origin of those surrounding him. They were almond-eyed Central Asians, dark-skinned Uzbeks, Turks, and Bulgarians. There were Poles, and even some Roma playing music and shaking down the passers-by. He felt right at home, so he joined the line for a drink of Kvass that looked like dark beer.

He watched as the vendor, dressed in a white coat and high white hat, served the patrons in front of him. At that point, he realized that she was using the same glass for everybody. He stepped out of the line.

The Orthodox church was packed with worshippers spilling out onto the sidewalk. Inside, low light, candles, incense, and rich, polyphonic singing invited him to linger and examine the heavily decorated screen of icons, starting with the Old Testament patriarchs at the top, Christ and Mary in the middle, and the local saints along the bottom. Everyone stood, the women with scarves over their heads. Worshippers wandered in and out at will during the service. They kissed the icon held by the bearded, white-robed priests.

He meandered back to his hotel, dined on meat dumplings, pickled beets, mushrooms, and black bread, downed a few shots of an unbelievably potent pepper vodka called something like Gorilla, and drifted off to sleep thinking that, were he to be granted a second life, he would come to Ukraine as a dentist—he had never seen so many rotten teeth.

THE COMBINATION OF THE GORILLA VODKA, A SMOKE-infested plane, and lack of sleep rendered unpleasant George Graham's first encounter with the mirror the next morning. Black coffee with warm milk and a roll helped some. The pickled herring and greasy sausage on the breakfast buffet held all the appeal of what they were: dead fish and animal entrails.

At 9:30, he got into the black Chaika in front of his hotel. Whir, whir, whir, whir, clunk! and it started off, to deliver him without mishap to the local police headquarters. His host, his host's boss, and two other officials, whose exact function he did not catch, were waiting to accommodate him.

A young woman served what looked like coffee, except that she poured the cup only half-full. Graham started to drink it, but his host motioned him to wait. In a moment, she came back with a second pot of boiling water to dilute the tea, which the others then mixed with copious amounts of sugar. They smoked nonstop.

He learned next to nothing.

They had received the bill of lading for Peter the Great he had faxed to them. They had also received a copy of the $2 million Baron's Bank check payable to Cameron Aker III. They had never heard of the corporation that wrote the check and were, regrettably, unable to obtain any records about its origin since it was incorporated under the former Soviet Union and the records were in disarray. They were sure he would understand.

Art theft is a major problem and, unfortunately, much

of the art being illegally exported from Ukraine has been cleverly forged. They do not have a special theft recovery unit like Scotland Yard, and it was all they could do to keep track of the most important pieces. This was all most regrettable, didn't he think?

"The Mother of God is, I am told, the most important piece of art in the Eastern Orthodoxy," Graham said.

"Ahh, it is," said the next-to-highest commissioner, "but it was loaned by Russia, not Ukraine."

Graham looked at him as if to say, "And…?"

"And, because Russia has recklessly put the icon in harm's way does not mean that we in Ukraine must immediately divert all of our investigative resources to try to find it. Russia has, my friend, stomped its boot on Ukraine for seven hundred years and now, through a foolishness that is difficult to comprehend, it has lost a treasure that originated right here, in this city in which you sit."

"I thought it came from Byzantium—Constantinople," said Graham.

The official shook his head vigorously. "It came to honor Saint Vladimir. It was consecrated here and resided here until Kiev was too weak to keep it. But it doesn't matter. We will surely help you look for the icon—we will even look ourselves. We just have limited resources."

"Thank you," said Graham. "What can you tell me about where the bull ended up?"

As expected, the second-highest commissioner responded with regret, "Again, my colleague, we have not much information. My associate," nodding to Graham's host, "can take you to a private farm about forty kilometers from here. We are told that the bull is there, but we have been able to find no evidence of who brought him or who owns him."

"Who owns the farm?" asked Graham, with as little patience as politeness would allow.

"A reasonable question," said the second-highest commissioner, "and we have checked." He handed a list of four names across the table. "These names are the four incorporators of the farm, but we can't be sure that they are also the owners of the bull."

"This is it?" asked Graham.

They nodded together.

Graham glanced at the list, folded it, put it in his inside suit coat pocket, and said, "Let's go see."

Graham decided that the Chaika whirred four times before it clunked into first gear, but after that, had discretion as to how many whirs it needed before it clunked into second, third, and fourth gears—if it chose to do so. But the land was flat and the day beautiful, if hot, and as they proceeded eastward across the plain, he could see some evidence of the black earth and the ground "stretching into the distance where the hills meet the sky," just as Chekhov described.

When they got to the farm, he was astonished. The collective barns alone covered at least ten acres. Two long, low buildings with grey corrugated tin roofs stretched parallel to a wide interior yard where four feed silos were nested together. At the end of each of the long barns was a structure that looked like a single-wide mobile home tacked on sideways. They stopped in front of one of these structures, his host indicating that it was the office.

The most remarkable feature of the huge assembly of buildings and silos, however, was the absence of any animal life whatsoever.

"Where are the cows?" asked Graham.

"We shall see," responded his host. "Some of these collective farms, since they are no longer run by the state, have been sold to private businesses that do not have capital."

"Capital, my ass," said Graham. "Somebody paid two million bucks for a single bull."

"Perplexing, is it not?" said his host as they entered the office.

The office was nearly as empty as the barns and feed yard.

His host and the lone attendant conferred in Ukrainian. The host turned to Graham and said, "There is not much activity here. The herd was shipped out for slaughter last week, and they are awaiting a new herd to fatten for market."

"They didn't send their $2 million bull to market," said Graham. "What about him?"

More Russian or Ukrainian or whatever tongue they were speaking. Head shakes. Exclamations, which in any language sounded like swear words.

Turning back to Graham, the host said, "He swears that no such bull as the one you describe has been here. I told him that we had traced the delivery to this farm, but he says he knows nothing."

"What about his superiors?" asked Graham, thinking that he should not have to direct such an inquiry to one so used to hierarchy.

"I already asked. No one with more authority will be here until the next herd arrives."

"Where can we find someone?" asked Graham.

"I already asked. He does not know."

"Can I look around?" The question was conveyed, and the answer delivered with a shrug.

"I take it that means yes," said Graham as he steamed out the door, not knowing what he was looking for, and having even less assurance he would find it.

As he walked the length of the barn on the left, seeing empty stall after empty stall, he concluded that this farm had seen even less action than the caretaker admitted. The weeds were high, and the smell of cow flop muted enough to suggest that animals had not been here for months.

He wandered to the end of the left-hand barn, across behind the silos, past the loading pens and the discarded waste of old feed pallets, rusting machinery, and plastic buckets. He had veered right and started along the other expanse of barn, when he stopped and turned, as if his auxiliary dinosaur brain had finally relayed a message of importance. What he had seen was a green Georgia-Pacific stamp on a piece of plywood that was splintered and leaning up against the side of a large shipping crate.

One side of the plywood piece was discolored with urine and manure and straw and feed that had been stomped into the wood by the feet of a very heavy animal. But the underside of the plywood, on which the Georgia-Pacific stamp was so clearly legible, was new, and in the middle, where a nail protruded, was a small scrap of green polyethylene like that of which a garbage bag is made.

Graham knelt down and examined the stringers that were exposed on the floor of the pen. Instead of being evenly spaced, an area in the middle was framed in like a window, except that it was covered by the bottom sheet of plywood and had been covered on top by the floorboard that had first caught his attention. The dimensions were roughly a yard by two feet. Small strips of Styrofoam padded the inside of the cutout.

His host was looking at him and finally said, "We have a Georgia—one of our fellow republics southeast of here."

"Yeah, it's a big, devious continent over here," said Graham.

CHAPTER 12

Professional Help

After extracting a promise from Freddy at the Metropolitan Museum that he would leave the name and number of an expert who could positively identify what she did not describe to him, but he surely guessed, Lara spent the remainder of the afternoon at her desk, accomplishing little. She fended off one call from the relentless Wanda Chin, who wanted to know whether rumors that the museum would permanently close were correct.

She hoped not.

Estelle and her daughter now controlled the Aker Foundation, and Lara had consulted with Vincent Buckley, Aker's lawyer, who assured her that the replacement lawyer (that is what he said, but it was obviously a Freudian slip)—the replacement trustee—would be named, and Lara's wishes that it be someone with knowledge of the visual arts would be honored ("if possible"—Buckley never gave unequivocal answers).

So now she had changed into a party dress. It was a Caribbean number with bright reds and blacks and greens and yellows and ruffly sleeves and sequins and a ruffled skirt. In it, she looked very nice, indeed. The event was the annual Akerhill benefit auction, fundraising doo-dah that was obligatory for stroking the big contributors, establishing a continuing presence in the community, and maybe, for a change, getting a little favorable press. Some might have thought it unseemly to have a party while Cameron's carcass was still warm, but Estelle liked parties, and Washington (this was near enough) didn't pause for any death below a president. Most agreed Cameron was a turd anyway.

The nearby Hunt Club was all hosed down, its veranda sporting round tables with green and white striped umbrellas. Proud horses, oblivious to the expensive blood coursing through their veins, grazed behind white fences.

As the ambassadorial corps from Western Europe, Japan, New Zealand, and Great Britain arrived in the largest-model car of their respective countries, Lara thought how little she enjoyed these efforts. But then, she mused, she was down on protocol generally. Akerhill was now a curiosity, and publicity was publicity.

After cocktails and Washington political talk and for the thousandth time, "No, I haven't a clue where the icon went," and "Yes, Cameron was a difficult man, but he doesn't deserve to be dead," they sat down at the round tables, set for ten as is the custom in Washington, boy-girl, boy-girl, for the dinner catered by the company that had catered the one these people had attended the night before, and the night before that.

Since Lara had done the seating charts, she was surprised to find that the man to her left was a stranger. She leaned toward him to see his place card. There was none, so she extended her hand and, with her most professional smile, said, "I am Lara Cole, I don't believe we have met."

"We haven't," said the man, "but I changed the place cards so that we would have this opportunity."

"How thoughtful," Lara said. "And it isn't even your party. You probably are going to tell me why we should have this opportunity?"

He was blonde, like Robert Redford, and had unpigmented moles on his face, like Robert Redford, but somehow the rest of the package didn't convey. His head seemed large for his wiry frame and, since he was seated, Lara could only guess at his height—probably around five ten.

He was dressed in a standard issue Washington business grey summer suit with white shirt and nondescript necktie. He spoke with a slight accent, but Lara had never had an astute enough ear to associate pronunciations with geographic origin.

He inquired about the icon, casually at first, but with increasing insistence and specificity like an interrogation. He wanted to know how Madam Kopulskaya, the director of the Tretyakov Museum, reacted to the loan of The Mother of God. He asked Lara to describe the wood cradle holding together the back of the icon, and his inquiries about the location of missing pigment on the front were too precise, too aggressive to be either casual or innocent.

She confined her answers to monosyllables and kept turning toward Vincent Buckley, who was seated on her right, to escape the conversation. Each time the man would draw her back, at first by the insistence in his voice and then by grasping her elbow. Her first opportunity came when the waiter served the salmon mousse in dill sauce. ("Fish course first" decrees the canon of good social breeding.)

Lara used the interruption to acknowledge Vincent Buckley, who had been overhearing the conversation with an amused smile. "You've got a live one," he said.

"Who is he?" asked Lara. But before Buckley could

respond, the man on her left tugged at her sleeve and, as she abruptly turned toward him, said, "You know nothing about icons. Am I right?"

"You are wrong."

"I am right, otherwise you would have never agreed to house The Mother of God in your tiny museum, much less failed to protect it in accordance with its significance and value."

That was too much. Lara reached over, tilted his plate toward him, and scraped the salmon mousse into his lap in three quick swipes. She replaced the plate, turned to her own, and with the same fork, took a bite. "Good mousse, don't you think?" she said with a beatific smile.

———————————

Driving home, Lara mused that never in her life had she done anything like that. And, she never learned the name of her dinner partner, who departed so abruptly after his salmon surprise. He's probably the new trustee, and the first thing he'll do is find a new director.

As the headlights swept her front porch, they reflected two luminous yellow dots. When she got closer, the dots turned into the eyes and then head and obnoxious voice of Igor the cat.

"What are you doing outside, Igor?" she said, and then stopped as she saw the front door ajar.

She hurried back to the car, fumbled around in the glove box, dropping the maps onto the floor, until she found a flashlight, turned it on, and found that the battery had expired. She dropped the flashlight on the seat, slammed the door, and said to herself, "Might as well find out."

Her couch was turned over; the books were pulled from the wall shelves. The refectory table was on its side across two chairs, broken by the force of the upsetting. The kitchen pots and pans and dry goods were all over the floor, and every shelf, cupboard, and storage space had been emptied.

Above, in her bedroom, the mattress was pulled off the box springs, and the trapdoor into the attic storage hung open.

She picked up the phone which, to her surprise, was still working, and dialed the sheriff's office. They would send a car immediately. She asked if they would please call the FBI. They could handle a burglary, thank you. Insulted.

Lara fumbled in her purse, hands shaking, and extracted with some difficulty the business card George Graham had given her. It had a blue blob on the left side that looked something like the Rotary emblem and was inscribed "George C. Graham, Special Agent, Federal Bureau of Investigation." In pen, he had written "24 hour" with an arrow toward the number.

The FBI operator said someone would call her back shortly.

Just as two Rappahannock County sheriff's cars, sirens blazing, came squirreling up the gravel road, skidding to a stop and almost colliding, the FBI desk called back saying that George Graham was out of the country, but his assistant would respond, if she desired.

"No, just tell him, please, that my house has been burglarized."

By 1 a.m. the inventorying and fingerprint dusting and questioning had been completed, and Lara gratefully accepted the offer that the deputy "cast an eye" on her driveway for the rest of the night.

Nothing was missing, at least, nothing she could identify. The intruder(s) wore gloves, as the smudges on the windowpane where they had broken the clasp showed. Lara offered no opinion or explanation for why her house should have been so abused, but for the rest of the night, as she lay stroking Igor's head and staring at the ceiling, she reiterated her determination that, in the world of intrigue, she desperately wanted to maintain her amateur status.

At three o'clock, as she was sliding into something close to sleep, she sat bolt upright, and said out loud, "The answering machine!" She leaped out of one side of the bed—prompting Igor, his ears pinned back in surprise, to leap out the other—and rushed down the circular staircase into the kitchen. The answering machine was upside down next to the sink. She turned it over. The red light was blinking, two pulses.

She pressed the rewind, counted the clicks, and heard:

"Oh, hello. It's Mother. I was just wondering how you were. Call when you get a chance. Oh, it's—what time is it?—it's 6:30. I love you."

Six-thirty where? Her time zone or mine?

The machine beeped and, after some static, the voice said, "Freddy here, Lara. The person you want is Michael Solak. He is a Russian by birth but was educated in the United States. He works for a conservation laboratory associated with Columbia and loosely with the Met. He knows his stuff, you know, all those high-powered electron microscopes and spectrometers that keep me in the poorhouse? He is one of the few people I know who calls art by its first name. I talked to him and he is in all morning tomorrow, so you could call him." He gave the number and the address.

She would do better than that. She would catch the

first shuttle to New York and plant herself in his office. She needed an ally, someone who could give her a reliable opinion, and she was not going to be able to make that determination over the phone.

What she could not know was whether those who had tossed her house had seen the blinking light and listened to the message, or whether he had called after the intrusion. If they rewound the tape and listened to the messages, it would not be blinking, she thought. But then, maybe they know how to make the machine blink after they have listened to the tape.

She went back to bed and wondered, as she had before some college exams, whether simply lying down without sleeping recharges your batteries. At 5:30, as the eastern sky began to lighten, she got up, found the extra Mr. Coffee pot that she had kept for no reason, brushed the glass off the burner, and ground the coffee beans. She dressed quickly, poured the brewed coffee into a traveling mug, and headed for her car. The atmosphere was heavy, and the birthing yellow light outlined quarrelsome, overlapping thunderheads. Like Tiepolo. I used to have time to appreciate this, she thought, as she slammed the car door. She stopped at the end of the driveway to acknowledge the deputy who was sitting there in his patrol car.

"You OK?" he asked.

"Fine," she said. "I'm going to the airport."

"We'll keep an eye on the place."

She headed in on Highway 66 toward National Airport and the LaGuardia Shuttle. By the time she reached Nutley Street, her leg was asleep from the ill-fitting car seat, but if anything was more dangerous than offending art thieves, it was pulling over to the shoulder during rush hour. The system of red and green neon Xs supposedly told you when you could drive on the shoulder and when you could not. Confusion reigned, and if you stopped on the shoulder, no matter what color the Xs, the chances of getting cleaned out by someone going sixty miles an hour were excellent.

She wiggled around in her seat and was able to keep enough feeling in her leg to make it to the concrete parking structure at National Airport. Forty-five minutes later, she was looking at the Capitol and the Jefferson, Washington, and Lincoln Memorials as the plane rose over the Potomac.

HAD LARA BEEN ABLE TO LASER INTO THE WHITE HOUSE as her plane rose over Washington, she would have seen President Sorensen and her advisers grappling with the same problem that engulfed her. They knew that in a multifaith country such as ours, supplicants seek a personal relationship with God. Believers in Russia, through the Orthodox liturgy, seek a collective audience. The loss of The Mother of God, particularly for political gain, had caused both religious and political whiplash, and Kiprensky was feeling the heat.

But his problem was far more complicated. Ukraine, as the original, and it felt, legitimate owner of The Mother of God, shared the insult. Ukrainian-Russian hostility was centuries old. When the czars made Ukraine a protectorate in the seventeenth century, the czar of Moscow claimed obeisance from Great Russia (his own people), Little Russia (a pejorative for Ukraine), and all the other Russians (everybody else he could dominate). Ukrainian nationalism was suppressed ruthlessly by Stalin in the thirties, and five million Ukrainians died for it. During War II, some Ukrainians sided with Germany against the Soviet Union, and after the war Polish-Ukrainian nationalist guerrillas resisted into the early fifties.

The Tretyakov Gallery in Moscow took rare eleventh century mosaics from the Museum of Ukrainian Art in Kiev and gave them some second-rate nineteenth century oils in return. Ukrainians saw it as a reprise of earlier appropriation of The Mother of God—a sign of "Russian Imperialist Thinking."

A third major complication for Kiprensky was the Orthodox Church. With sixty million members, it could bring some heavy-duty pressure to bear, and the church had served notice it wanted back all religious objects, from cathedrals in the Kremlin to icons and vestments confiscated during Soviet rule. Kiprensky had played a masterful game of throwing enough bones to the church to keep its support, but he was getting squeezed on this one.

"Ladies and gentlemen," said President Sorensen, "you have obviously done your homework, and I appreciate it. What, may I ask, do you suggest I do?"

No one said anything until the president nodded and said, "General?"

"Our man has returned from Kiev and reports what you already know: that Ukrainians don't like the Russians. But he also found evidence that a wooden pen used to ship a bull from Virginia to Kiev—a bull that was owned by Cameron Aker—may have also concealed the stolen icon, which means that somebody in Ukraine has it."

"If we had known that Aker and Kiprensky had a little gunrunning business on the side, I'm sure we wouldn't have ever endorsed the icon loan," said the president. "Aker provided the money, and Kiprensky shook loose some assault rifles and grenade launchers and other small, untraceable military paraphernalia, and they made a bundle. No jets or missiles; just non-flashy but thoroughly lethal contraband."

Ironically, they wouldn't have learned that Kiprensky was involved if the US hadn't established an FBI office in Moscow to share crime detection techniques and develop "speaking partners" with the Russians. After the icon flap, a thoroughly disgusted Russian policeman confided that Russia's noble leader was up to his elbows in organized crime. Whether Aker's death was tied to gunrunning, the icon theft, neither, or both, no one could say.

If, however, Ukraine had The Mother of God, the problem was explosive, literally. They had 1,800 nuclear warheads and were the third-most powerful nuclear presence in the world. They had started dismantling their SS-19s and probably took apart all 780 warheads. Then they were supposed to disable the SS-24s, each of which carried ten warheads. The US paid them exactly $1,086,956.50 per missile, but while they were supposedly making the world safe, they were working feverishly to develop software to program and target them instead of taking them apart. Russia could be that target. Countries had gone to war over far less lofty symbols than The Mother of God.

The room was silent. The president leaned back in her chair and looked around the table from face to face. Finally, she said, "Nothing. Nothing is what we are going to do. This is not a bold and innovative strategy. I just have no idea what is going to happen next, and I would hate to make it worse."

KIPRENSKY DIDN'T KNOW WHAT TO DO, EITHER. HE KNEW Aker was dead, but not why. He knew the icon was gone, but

not where. He knew his end game to rally the Russians had
worked—they were rallied, all right—but against him for
having loaned the icon. He had expected to be able to turn
their anger by finding the icon, but the Buyer had checked
out and, he concluded, double-crossed him.

All this merely got Kiprensky's juices flowing. Not
knowing what to do didn't mean doing nothing to him.
He would keep the board spinning. He had an appetite for
a game of nuclear chicken.

SEATED ON THE SHUTTLE TO NEW YORK WITH WHAT WAS
euphemistically called a "breakfast snack," Lara took out a
pad of yellow paper. She needed to make sense of what was
happening, and for her, that meant, writing it down.

Her first heading was "What Has Happened." The list
looked like this:

a) icon gone

b) Cameron dead

c) real(?) icon in its crate at museum

d) Sounder's office burglarized

e) Russian president wants hostages

f) US refuses

g) my place tossed

h) WHAT NEXT?

Next, she wrote "What Is My Objective?" Under that, her
list said:

a) avoid getting killed

b) learn whether the icon I have is the real one

c) return it to the Tretyakov (if real)

d) to hell with all of them if it isn't

She put down her pencil because her hand was trembling.

Was she really in danger of getting killed? How could she know? She could not bring herself to believe that Cameron had stolen the icon from himself, but why else would he be dead? If he unknowingly stole Wilson Porter's fake, in a way, it served him right—well, no, it didn't—nobody deserves to be killed. But if whoever wanted the icon would kill for it once, surely, they would not hesitate…

If she were really afraid—she stopped.

"I am really afraid," she said to herself. "But I am not so afraid as to take the craven road out. That would be to call up George Graham and say that I've got something in a box in the basement of my museum. Turn it over to the government, use it for a political football if you want, but make it public so whoever is willing to kill for it won't kill me.

"Somehow, that strikes me as being as practical as it is unrealistic," thought Lara. "I didn't borrow the icon for it to become an implement of political terrorism, although it looks like Cameron did. And if I have one moral obligation, to myself and to the Russians and to the world of art, it is to get that icon—the real one—back to the Tretyakov in one piece, as promised."

"Would I give my life to do it?

"That's a damn dumb question.

"Well, would I?

"How should I know?"

And at that point, her unquiet mind slipped back to the convent and what, to this point in her life, she had considered the hardest thing she had ever done:

Two reasons, Father. First, I can't feel God. The more I pray or fast or wait, the greater the void in my soul.

But can't you see, Lara, you are the one who is keeping God out. You fail to deny yourself and, until you listen, until you surrender, God can't fill your life.

I haven't got a life, and that's the second reason. God gave me an intellect and passions and put me in a world with people and problems and opportunities. Can it be His will that I turn my back on them to serve a church I am increasingly coming to resent?

Child, child. Christ founded the church to show men by prayer and confession and sacrament that they could wipe away the mortal sin that has infected us all.

Sin—or divine retribution for it—holds less terror for me than it once did. I've thought about it, and I'm willing to risk trying to live my life as an adult rather than to be a perpetual child in your church.

You are not thinking clearly, Lara. You must rest. I will see that you are relieved of all your studies and duties for a time.

If I have no faith, I have no sanity, either? Is that it?

You are confused, my child.

On that, we agree. Goodbye, Father.

LARA PONDERED WHY NEW YORK CAB DRIVERS ALL SEEMED to be able to speak our native tongue and find their destinations, while Washington cab drivers can do neither. Once, she was told, a passenger found himself deposited at the Washington Monument, his cab driver believing that that was what the locals called The Washington Post. The trip from LaGuardia across the Triboro Bridge and into Manhattan was not unduly slow and, at a quarter after ten, she was sitting in the waiting room of the Institute for Verification and Restoration. It was not exactly a reception room—more a large desk for a secretary, a folding chair, and walls and walls of trade journals, papers, and mailing envelopes. She had hardly sat down when a musical voice coming rapidly from her left called out, "You are Lara Cole. I was told you would call, and here you are. I am Michael Solak."

She reflexively rose from her chair and was about three-quarters of the way up, turning toward the sound, when he came into her field of vision. Twice before this had happened. Once was a mistake she had married, and the other was a man who got off her bus, looked through the window, and locked eyes with her, sparking an unmistakable burst of electricity. She had often wondered how her life might have been different if she, too, had gotten off that bus.

But this glance was off the Richter scale. She looked at Michael Solak, later thinking her mouth was probably open, a word of greeting frozen, or rather, fried, by the energy generated between them.

Then, shaking her head as if she had cracked it on the underside of a cupboard, she mispronounced her name as she followed him back down the hall at his speed walker's pace.

She declined coffee and sought to reconstruct herself as she removed a yellow pad from her briefcase.

"What did Freddy tell you?" she asked.

"Only that you were a former employee—actually, a colleague is the word he used, and that you needed some expert authentication."

"A colleague. That's sweet of him. I worked for Freddy as the lowliest of curators, but I learned a great deal. I now head a small museum in Northern Virginia that you probably never heard of. It's called Akerhill."

"Of course I have heard of Akerhill." Somehow, by the very manner in which he said it, she felt no obligation to explain or apologize for any of Akerhill's recent travails—at least, not at this point in the conversation.

Lara said, "Before we proceed, I must tell you that my query, my dilemma, is somewhat delicate. I hope you will understand my need to interview you before the nature of my need I explain."

What's the matter with me? I sound like I'm translating from the German.

But Michael Solak nodded, spread his hands generously, and said, "I would not expect otherwise. The work that I do, particularly when it involves the authenticity of an artwork, could not be more confidential. Millions of dollars and professional reputations are at stake. Please inquire."

In response to Lara's questions, he reeled off a string of degrees including a PhD in organic chemistry, another PhD in art history, membership in scientific organizations in the United States, Russia, Great Britain, France, and Greece, and thirteen years of experience in authentication and restoration of works for the world's major museums.

"I can disclose the names of none of my clients," he said, "but in a recent case, a West Coast museum suspected it had been swindled in the purchase of a highly publicized and expensive artwork."

"This was recent?" asked Lara. "I didn't hear about it."

"That is exactly the point. I determined the work was authentic, and no scandal arose to blemish the reputation of either the auction house or the seller. Without discretion, I have neither reputation nor credibility."

"Are you a restorer yourself, Mr. Solak?"

"Yes," he replied. "How it should be done—I give advice on that. But I no longer actually apply brush to canvas."

"How do you advise?"

"The restorer must leave a visible record. He should work with materials unlike those used by the original artist so those who come after can distinguish immediately who did what. Likewise, the restorer may never intrude into the aesthetic or the structure the artist has created, either by gratuitously adding or taking away. All restorations are exactly that: re-storing—putting back the visual gift the artist originally conveyed."

Lara realized she had not heard a word he said. She was staring at Michael Solak, and her subconscious saw his mouth moving, but her brain was addled by the unabashedly sexual energy this man's very presence exploded in her.

He paused only briefly, and then said, "Look, Ms. Cole, I can talk to you about my expertise more meaningfully in the presence of great art. Let me first take you to lunch, and then I will demonstrate to you, I hope to your satisfaction, that I am both trustworthy and knowledgeable. We will go to the Metropolitan Museum; do you agree?"

"That would be lovely," she said. And then thought to herself, I'm supposed to be in charge here, but I feel like I'm on my first date.

With bad timing and no conversational flow, she added aloud, "Of course, I will take you to lunch, Mr. Solak. I appreciate your willingness to spend all this time."

He smiled with crinkled eyes and a lovely lilting mouth with straight upper teeth and slightly canted lower ones, the kind that are supposed to come on airline pilots, not nuclear-powered art experts.

A short cab ride deposited them in front of the Metropolitan Museum. They walked past the domed lobby, the grand staircase, and the antiquities to the elevators, where he showed a pass and they zipped up to the fourth floor. He gently took her arm only long enough to direct her toward the patrons' dining room.

He was greeted by name, and they were seated next to the windows facing Central Park. It was early; the dining room had just opened.

"I can pay here, can't I?" asked Lara. The time for such a question had long since passed, and the directness of his look, although he said nothing, so disoriented her that the entire left side of her brain went south.

"The crab cakes," he said. "The crab cakes here are exquisite, and the sweet pepper mousse."

"I'm used to the crab cakes from the other side of the Chesapeake," said Lara. "I think I'll have poached salmon."

"Also, a good choice," he said.

"And I will start with slabs of foie gras on artichoke hearts and bitter greens," she said, attempting, through food, to coax back her reason.

"I will have," said Solak to the waiter, "the warm goat cheese and walnut salad on red oak leaf lettuce and the crab cakes. Wine," he said, looking at Lara, "a glass of chardonnay, perhaps?" She nodded. He asked if they had any unchilled. "It's better that way," he said.

The lunch was delightful, the food incidental. She ate it,

and it was probably good, but she could recall afterwards none of the flavors or even the act of eating. Neither could she recall the ministrations of the waiter, or whether any other diners occupied the room.

Lara and Michael were locked in a conversation about art and current affairs and New York and Paris and St. Petersburg that brooked no intrusions and held no pauses. It was a wonderful lunch, with coffee and a shared dessert that arrived without consciously being ordered, and a bill that he had paid before she could muster protest from the still out of commission left hemisphere of her brain.

Lara visited the women's room to regroup after lunch, but she floated through it all in a blur and next found herself standing, perhaps too close, to Michael as he was looking up at Peter Paul Reubens's painting of himself, his wife, Helena Fourment, and their son, Peter Paul.

"This is oil on wood," Solak said. "The painter is looking at his wife, and she at the son. But an X-ray of this piece shows that, when it was originally painted, Reubens had them both looking at the child. He overpainted his own face so that he was looking at his wife because he felt it better balanced the painting. Such a change, when we detect it, is a badge of authenticity. The artist is not afraid to change his work to make it better."

He gently touched her elbow again, and they arrived before a Breughel. "Here, the gleaners are harvesting, a painting that all of us studied in school, but look at the background; the trees are all blue. What that tells us is that the yellow varnish that made the trees green has deteriorated with time. Sometimes, because we know what the painter intended, our brains will supply the right color, even if it isn't there. I would not, as a restorer, reapply a yellow resin. The painting could be ruined if I didn't get it right."

They moved again, Michael greeting some of the guards by name.

"I was involved when this institution downgraded its only painting by Hieronymus Bosch to the school or studio of Bosch, because, I am convinced, the master himself did not do the painting. It's like being a detective, where we compare every other known example and look for clues that either confirm or challenge the authenticity. We did the same, a few years back, with a Goya that, regrettably, isn't.

"Joseph Mallord William Turner," he said, a few galleries later, "is a restorer's nightmare. Turner would finish a painting, varnish it, and then decide it needed something more—more color, stronger figures, whatever. He would then add what struck him as necessary and varnish over that. Years later, we have two or three coats of varnish which have yellowed differently, but to scrape them away is to scrape away pigment.

"So, what do you do?" asked Lara.

"It's like the oath that medical doctors take: 'First of all, do no harm.' The restorer's art is a gentle one, just as the authenticator's virtues are subtle. One hundred beautifully restored or accurately authenticated artworks would not make up for a single irreparable mistake."

Lara took his arm and addressed him informally, without invitation or hesitation, "Michael, let me tell you about your project for me. Where can we talk privately?"

"I know the place," he said. She almost ducked to avoid the disabling power of his eyes.

They emerged on a balcony that commanded one of

New York's most spectacular views. To the south, over the multiple hues of green foliage, was the Plaza Hotel and the noble buildings flanking Central Park. To the west, they overlooked the lake and playing fields. "The Sentinel Towers on the building across the park—that is where Peter Jennings lives," said Solak.

Peter Jennings has nothing on this guy, thought Lara.

AS THEY TALKED, LARA LEANED SLIGHTLY INTO HIM, their shoulders touching. She both consciously willed it and couldn't help it. This was miles from a high school come-on; for the first time since The Mother of God had interrupted her life she had an ally—a confidante.

"You know of the theft—how could you not know of the theft?"

He nodded.

"It is probable," she said carefully, "that it was stolen, not by religious zealots, but by somebody else, maybe for political reasons."

"I can think of many groups that might see the value in having it, either for itself, or for the leverage it would provide them," he said.

"Like who?" asked Lara.

"The Orthodox Church, for one. They have reclaimed, or at least made demand for all of their churches back, and with that goes well over a million works of art that are presently in Russian museums, or at least under Russian control. To have The Mother of God would be like recapturing Jerusalem—a great religious victory."

"Who else?"

"The Russian foes of President Kiprensky. To lend it and lose it is an act of consummate stupidity unworthy of a leader. Ukrainians. They have claimed the icon since their independence in 1991. Their president vowed never to relinquish his country's claim to the artworks that had been taken by the dominant hand of Big Brother Russia. If they could turn up with it, it would be a symbolic victory of tremendous popularity in Ukraine."

"Anybody else?" asked Lara, feeling as if she needed a scorecard to tell the players.

"Well, if I am Kiprensky, and I am trying to get concessions from the United States, maybe I send them a very good fake Mother of God, arrange for it to be stolen, and scream bloody murder. It is a desperate strategy, but not beyond reason."

"And I am the stooge that brings the fake to the United States," she mused.

"Hardly a stooge."

"I worked for Cameron Aker, and he is dead. My house was ransacked; Sounder's headquarters was, too. I think that whoever has the icon is displeased with the merchandise."

"Sounder?"

"Reverend Sounder and the Constants of Leo who were protesting the icon's presence in the United States."

"I still don't understand," he replied.

"You need to know a couple more details. I had—have, an assistant director named Wilson Porter, a man who just graduated from Cooper Union and has more talent than he could ever imagine. At first, he was just messing around, and then, when he sensed that the icon might be in danger from these modern-day iconoclasts, he set out in earnest to duplicate it, and he succeeded to a degree that I think even you would find remarkable. Then, when things got really dicey at the museum, he substituted his icon for the real one."

"Amazing," said Solak, "and the Wilson Porter icon was stolen?"

"It was, and it may have gotten Cameron Aker killed. But Wilson—Wil—was so enthralled with his rendition of The Mother of God that he signed it on the back. If he had wanted for the thieves to come after him, he couldn't have figured out a better way to ensure it. I told him to disappear, which he has, and hopefully he will stay hidden."

"Do you know where the real one is?" he asked.

"I know where the one that I borrowed from the Tretyakov is, but I need you to tell me whether it is the real one."

"This may seem like an elemental question, Lara, but why don't you just give the FBI the icon, and take yourself out of harm's way?"

"A reasonable suggestion," she said, "and one I have asked myself plenty of times. But I always come back to the guilt-laden feeling that it is my duty to return The Mother of God to its lender."

"Even at personal risk to yourself?"

"That is why I need you. If Russia sent a fake in the first place, then all these hoodlums deserve each other, and I would be more than happy to turn over what I have and let them fight it out. But if the icon is real, then my obligation is to get it back to the Tretyakov."

"Why?" he asked. "You know it's typical for local congregations to carry the icons around in religious processions. In Romanov-Borisoglebsk, the congregation carried a sixteenth century Christ the Savior icon around on a rainy day and it was seriously damaged.

Who knows what happens if the church gets back The Mother of God?"

"If I give it back to the Tretyakov, and the Tretyakov gives it to the church or to Ukrainians or Tartars, for that matter, it is out of my hands. But my life and my values and my integrity all say that I will protect the art, and I don't give a rip for the politics," she said, her eyes misting and voice starting to quaver. "I believe in beauty and spirituality and human achievement and, as far as I can tell, politics cannot accommodate any of those."

He drew back slightly, and then brushed her cheek with his fingers. "I will help," he said simply.

"Not so fast, Michael, being around me may not be healthy; being with me and The Mother of God is likely to be downright dangerous."

"Ahh," he smiled, "I am a scholar and an academic and a scientist. Why should I fear danger?"

"It's not funny, Michael. One man is dead, several crimes have been committed, and whoever wants the icon won't respect you just because you're smart and educated."

"Lara," he said, seriously and quietly, "I am compelled to help. When do you need me? And where?"

She noticed that he had small freckles underneath his eyes, and those wonderful eyes had small yellow rivers through the iris. "Not tomorrow; I have to make some preparations. Day after tomorrow at Akerhill."

CHAPTER 13

Examinations

"He nailed the icon into the crate. Can you believe it?" George Graham said to Lara from across her table/desk.

"He stole it from himself, using that passkey, triggering the basement stairway alarm, and then just walked through the garden door and back to his house carrying Russia's patrimony under his arm. He wrapped it in a plastic garbage bag to keep the bull from peeing on it. Then he nailed that sucker inside the double bottom of the crate that held the bull. So, he sold a tired bull and a priceless icon for $2 million. My guess is that something about that deal got him killed."

"He was a wheeler-dealer," said Lara, "but I never figured him for a thief. Everybody just assumed he had the touch for where money could be made. Wasn't he friends with President Kiprensky?"

"I'm a long way from understanding what's happened," said Graham. "Let's assume the bull is just cover for the icon—to get it out of the country undetected. And let's assume I'm right about it going to Ukraine. Aker is, then, not only screwing his old buddy Kiprensky, but giving it to Kiprensky's political rivals."

"Couldn't somebody kill him because of the bull?"

"Timing isn't right," said Graham. "The bull didn't have time to perform. I suppose they could have learned they paid too much, but that doesn't seem like a murder motive to me."

"Kiprensky is making all sorts of demands on the US because of that theft. Cameron would have known that would happen if he stole the icon," said Lara.

"Would he?" asked Graham.

"Absolutely. Cameron may have been a moral midget, but he understood politics."

"Hmmmmm." Graham stared at the tent he was making with his fingers and, after a while, mused, "Maybe Kiprensky needed a crisis to divert the home folks from their other problems. Would Aker play along with that—borrow the icon, then steal it for Kiprensky?"

"I can't read his mind, Inspector. But it's in character. He would have loved the action."

Graham tented his fingers some more and was silent. Then he said, "I can't figure the Ukrainians. If Kiprensky and Aker have a scam going, why does Aker send the icon to Kiprensky's rival?"

Lara shrugged.

"If Kiprensky found out Aker sent it there, he would have a solid motive for killing him, but I'm the only one who knows where it went…except for the Ukrainians who actually have it."

Then Graham said, "I need you to describe what this Buyer looked like."

"How could I do that?" responded Lara. "I didn't ever see him."

"But you said you saw a $2 million check."

"Well, it didn't have his picture on it. Aker showed me this $2 million check with some scribbled signature on it, and then made me a proposition I had no difficulty in refusing."

Graham smiled slightly. "What bank?"

"Baron's Bank," said Lara. "It was a cashier's check, but I am almost sure it was Baron's because I remember the lettering being blue."

Graham got up and paced beside the table. "I hung around Kiev for a couple of days after I found Peter the Great's crate at the collective. My escort was annoyed as hell when I found that crate, but I keep thinking to myself, if they didn't want me to find anything that was traceable to the bull, why would they take me to the farm where he was delivered?

"Granted, there weren't any cattle around when I got there and I was just plain lucky to find the Georgia-Pacific stamp that screamed 'Made in America,' but why risk it? I am paranoid about getting set up, particularly when they had a little man tailing me after my host and I parted ways."

"Sounds like things have not changed much since the Soviet days," said Lara.

"I wasn't trying to sneak around. I told them I wanted to look at St. Sophia and some of their museums. The churches are something else; singing is out of this world. Each church has this high screen with icons of the saints and biblical heroes. Packed. People were spilling out onto the sidewalk."

Lara listened to Graham, thinking how unlike her image of an FBI man he was.

As if he had read her thoughts, he said, "Well, daughter," and the term surprised her, and maybe him, too, but he went on, "I've been sitting here telling you about my trip, and you haven't been telling me much at all."

"I'm sorry," said Lara. "I just don't know anything about Cameron's business affairs."

"Well, what else do you know?" asked Graham casually, but with an edge to it.

"Nothing," said Lara, hesitating just long enough that he knew she was withholding.

"Sure?" he said.

Lara nodded, feeling her ears start to redden, but he didn't press her.

"I brought you something," he said. And he handed her a small pendant. "It came from a street vendor and cost me the equivalent of $1.13, so you don't need to trouble your conscience about accepting it."

On the pendant was an icon of Mary and Jesus painted on the front. On the back was an 11th century inscription translated into English:

> Oh, womb, dark and black,
> you have coiled like a serpent,
> hissed like a dragon, roared like a lion:
> now sleep like a lamb.

Graham said, "I read that, and I thought if we could put some of that reverence back into childbearing, we all would be a whole lot better off. This is a charm to ensure healthy birth. I figured you might need it someday."

She smiled and said softly, "Thank you."

After goodbyes, Lara returned to her chair, fingering the amulet. Then, as if a tiny railroad man in her brain had thrown the switch, she bolted from her chair, ran through the great hall and out to the parking lot, catching Graham as he was starting his car.

"I remembered something."

He waited.

"The other night at a museum benefit dinner, this man sat next to me. He was not invited, or at least he was not invited to sit there. He came on really strong about the icon and why we were displaying it, and he asked a lot of very specific questions about how it looked on the back—as if he were trying to confirm a description. He kept at it and was so rude that I scraped salmon mousse into his lap."

Graham, still with his hands on the steering wheel, said, "And you want me to protect you?"

"No. I don't even know his name, but Vincent Buckley, Cameron's lawyer, was seated on my right and I had the feeling Buckley knew who he was."

"What did he look like?" Graham asked, listening as Lara described a blonde man, unpigmented moles on his face, large head, wiry body.

"You may need my protection, Sweet Pea. You were sitting next to the Buyer."

SAINT PAUL'S STRUGGLE WITH DOUBT AND FAITH DID not describe Reverend Bob Sounder's life. Sounder was a man of few maybes. God was either worshipped or scorned; glorified or blasphemed; honored or despised. When doubt picked at the corners of his mind, he prayed to the Lord to confirm his course, systematically discounting all negative thoughts.

Yet, for all of his charismatic leadership and public presence, Bob Sounder was an intensely personal man who spent a great deal of his life praying. It wasn't that he was incapable of seeing both sides of an issue, but rather that once he decided God's will, he followed that course with absolute focus and unwavering devotion.

That the United States government was persecuting him for his religious beliefs was, in his mind, beyond question. That the administration of President Sorensen was trafficking in blasphemy was likewise certain. What he needed guidance on, however, was the extent to which he ought to use the government and all its trappings against the government itself in this battle.

Elvin Massey had told him that retrial was likely, and although subsequent evidence suggested that the investigation had turned away from the Constants of Leo, Sounder would not have been surprised if the government were to seek an indictment against him for the murder of Cameron Aker complete with trumped up evidence and false testimony.

Sounder sought God's will. He did not want to be a reluctant prophet like Jonah, always seeking to avoid delivering God's message. If a celebrated murder trial was the vehicle, Sounder was ready. If disengagement from the political world was God's will, he would return to his preaching. So he prayed—on his knees, at his desk, and when he awoke to go to the john in the middle of the night.

After three days (there was theological significance in the number), he was sure God would use the government and the courts for God's own counteroffensive against the iniquities of this heathen administration.

Sounder had no illusions about the human failings of some of his troops. He knew Gary Simms was ambitious, and Elvin Massey a mean street fighter, more interested in victory than the cause. That did not bother Sounder a bit, as long as he was sure he was doing God's will. God could use the talents of these men.

So the Constants of Leo launched its offensive under 26 US Code Section 1983. The United States government, under the color of law, had deprived Sounder, Simms, and the Constants of Leo of their civil rights by breaking into their offices, persecuting them for their religious beliefs, harassing them, and causing them to endure criminal charges without basis in fact.

Massey saw the best defense as an aggressive offense. Sounder saw God as working in strange and wondrous ways. Gary Simms saw a dynamite opportunity for publicity, and Wanda Chin was there to help make it happen.

The Washington News-Gazette featured a front-page story that quoted Sounder saying: "Church and state are supposed to be separate in this country; religious belief is protected, and this lawsuit will remind President Sorensen, that in her arrogance, she has trod on the beliefs of the little people."

He loved to speak for the little people. God protected the meek (which he wasn't) and the dispossessed (which he wasn't), and the least of the brethren (which he didn't think he was, either). But he certainly felt enfranchised to speak for these groups, and Chin's story made it abundantly clear that he had hauled his pulpit into the courtroom.

The Constants of Leo appeared, the same day, in Lafayette Park directly across Pennsylvania Avenue from the White House. Already there they found the "Peace Protest" and the "Stop the Censoring of Mail" protest and the "Return Our Servicemen from Overseas" protest and the "Justice for Janitors" protest.

What distinguished the Constants of Leo was God's drums. Their beat was something between a funeral dirge and a high school marching band—constant, imprecise, unrelenting—God's psychological warfare against President Betty Sorensen—a multifront offensive.

Three hours after George Graham left Akerhill, a bright blue Pontiac Grand Am four-door pulled into the parking lot. In Lara's mind, 100 percent of that model car belonged to Messrs. Hertz and Avis, and, in this case, she was right. She did not typically spend her afternoons watching the museum's parking lot, but the prospect of seeing Michael Solak had put her in a state of abnormal excitement. So, when he emerged from the bright blue Pontiac, it was all she could do to return to her desk chair and assume a position of studied indifference.

He was announced. He entered her office. She rose slowly and strode around her table/desk offering her hand. He ignored it and enclosed her in a bear hug. She hugged back.

She wanted to say, "I will now throw you to the floor and ravish you," but instead, settled for, "Did you have any difficulty finding us?"

"None," said Solak, "nor did whoever was following me."

Lara swore, resenting the monotonous predictability of impediments in her life of late.

"I caught a man eyeing me on the plane. Nothing obvious, but it was the kind of thing I remember my parents describing when I was a little boy in Moscow. Then, as I was merging onto the Parkway from the airport, a white Ford practically ran over two taxicabs to merge in behind me. I kept watching my rearview mirror as I drove on Highway 66, and there was the white Ford.

"I turned off at Marshall, went into the town, and pulled into the first service station I came to. The white Ford cruised by, but I didn't get a good look at who was in it.

"I got back in and, instead of heading back to the freeway, I went on through Marshall, and there was the white Ford with two men in it, one being the fellow from the plane. I turned back around, not much caring if they knew I had made them and drove on out here."

"So, who are they?" asked Lara, feeling tired.

"I'm new to this," demurred Michael, "but they could work for any of the groups I told you about who would benefit by having the icon. It is unlikely they are friends."

"Agreed," said Lara. "Let's get to work."

On the way downstairs, she encountered head guard Wesley Foster, introduced Michael as a friend from New York, and said: "I have an uneasy feeling that whoever stole the icon may be back, so if anyone comes around looking suspicious, shoot him."

"I don't have gun," said Foster, squinting to tell if she was serious, "except for that crooked-barrel .22 we used to shoot at the squirrels."

"Why don't you call the sheriff and ask him to send a deputy up here for a while?"

Michael removed The Mother of God from her nest in the padded, humidity-buffered box, and with the tender ministrations of a lover, slit the tape, unwrapped first the plastic and then the kraft paper, and stood silently gazing on her face as Schliemann might have beheld the mask of Agamemnon.

Reluctantly breaking his gaze, he stepped back, opened his briefcase, and extracted a pair of white cotton gloves. He gently lifted it by the edges and rotated it around so he could view its vertical boards joined across the back by a wooden cradle.

He examined the joinery, particularly the ends of each board where the grain was exposed.

"Sometimes you can tell more by looking at the back of a painting than you can from the front. The most difficult fakes to detect are the older ones, and this is clearly old. At least the materials are. Do you mind if I spend some time just looking?"

"Of course not, Michael." Lara sat on a high stool, leaning forward with her elbows against her knees and her hands cupping either side of her face. "Do you mind if I watch you?"

"I could think of nothing I would like more. But I can only form an impression today. To be certain, io have an opinion upon which I would stake my reputation, I must examine it in a sophisticated lab where I can use an X-ray, electron microscope, and spectrograph. After I have done all of that, I assure you, I will have an opinion."

GEORGE GRAHAM'S ASSISTANT ENJOYED BEING CALLED in to report on her research. She felt like an honor student getting to recite without having to raise her hand. She explained how the Russians were struggling to control an extralegal system they had set up when they were still the Soviet Union. The KGB procured export licenses through dummy corporations and then trucked raw materials out of the country, where they sold them at a 300 percent profit. The money, deposited in foreign bank accounts, was supposed to fund leftist groups but, in fact, much of it went into personal bank accounts of KGB operatives and export officials. Leaders can decree political and economic principles, but can't erase the seven deadly sins, and greed is on that list.

"Now, after the implosion of the Soviet Union, the ex-KGB officers are driving big Mercedes and living in the mansions the Communist Party used to own. The former export officials are doing the same jobs they used to do, getting even bigger bribes, and the Russian and Ukrainian economies are hemorrhaging from the outflow of raw materials. Since everything is up for grabs in the new economic disorder, the erstwhile true believers have expanded into exporting weapons, chemicals, stolen autos—practically anything of value.

"Cameron Aker spent a lifetime making connections with people in the Soviet Union. He financed and traded with the 'favored firms' who did business with the KGB, and Pavel Kiprensky was, and apparently still is, in it with greedy enthusiasm."

"What about the bull?" asked Graham.

"Nothing in my research suggests that bulls were ever a highly sought-after commodity. Anyway, the bull was imported, not exported. Do you want my guess?"

Graham nodded.

"The bull was worth fifty-seven cents a pound at your local dog food factory, not $2 million. But he provided the pen so the icon could safely be sent to Ukraine. The Mother of God is what they were after in the first place, and that is what the $2 million was for."

"I'm confused," said Graham. "They got the icon, so why is Mr. Cameron Aker III dead?"

"Here are some options. Kiprensky has him killed because Aker was a double-crosser, either by stealing the icon in the first place, or by stealing it and selling it to Ukraine. Or the Orthodox Church did it. Unseemly business, I agree, but during the days of the Workers' Republic, the Orthodox Church was thoroughly infiltrated by the KGB. If some of those nasty church-types wanted to flex their political muscle, they could send over thieves to steal the icon. That way they wouldn't have to wait around until Russia gave it back, because that is never going to happen, and once they got it, they could either trade it back to Russia, sell it to Ukraine, or keep it to pacify the believers. Under any scenario, that would be worth a couple of million dollars."

"Doesn't tell me why Aker is dead."

"Unless he was conspiring with them and they snuffed him to shut him up. But I have a couple more ideas. Russia tried to dissuade Ukraine from becoming independent. President Bush picked up the chant and urged them to stay part of the Soviet Union and not to pursue 'suicidal nationalism.' William Safire called it 'Bush's Chicken Kiev Speech.' It was not too popular with the nationalists in Ukraine.

"Ukrainians are still annoyed with the USA and think The Mother of God should have been in Ukraine the whole time. Why not just steal it from the United States and even two scores at once? Aker could have been a party to that plan, too, and he would be just as dead."

"What about those four names on the incorporation paper I brought back from Ukraine—the farm owners?"

"Zippola on numbers one, two, and three. Number four is Boris K. Golchev. Boris worked for the Soviet Embassy in DC for two years. He was KGB almost certainly. He served in the Soviet Army but comes from Ukraine, and the CIA's dossier shows he is close to the mayor of Kiev."

"You have a picture?" asked Graham.

Graham looked at it, swung his feet down to the floor, and said, "Tell you what, you hustle on down to Legal and get yourself a warrant, and then you go over to the headquarters of Baron's Bank and run Boris K. Golchev and Cameron Aker III through their system and see if that $2 million check didn't go from one to the other."

BETTY SORENSEN FOUND NO COMFORT IN AGENT GRAham's findings. Her strength, and an unusual one it was for a politician, was problem-solving. Although she might not appreciate the maleness of the comparison, she was like a tackler who blasted head-on into blockers figuring that, at worst, someone else could make the tackle and, at best, the runner would be felled by the flying bodies.

But this situation didn't lend itself to interference-busting because there were too many possibilities, and it was not becoming any clearer why the icon was gone or who had it.

Kiprensky had promised he would seize the American Embassy in Moscow and take his own hostages. He was getting crazier (and more dangerous) by the hour, and she wanted desperately to give them all a face-saving exit.

"Do I tell Kiprensky we think the icon is in the hands of Ukraine, his not-so-friendly neighbor?"

"It might keep him from seizing our Embassy," said the chief of staff.

"I doubt it. I can't give him enough hard evidence Ukraine really has the icon. What have we got? One FBI agent found a crate with American wood and a piece of garbage bag nailed to it. If I were Kiprensky and heard that, I would believe that the US thought me pretty dumb."

"What do we have to lose by telling him?"

"Well, suppose," said the president, "that Kiprensky believes it and invades Ukraine? Isn't that exactly what we want to avoid?"

"Sure, we don't want war, but the foundation of your personal diplomacy with Kiprensky is sharing all relevant information that concerns the safety of Russia and the United States. If you don't tell him, and it turns out to be true, not only have we missed an opportunity to extricate ourselves, but we have lost his trust."

The president gave the chief of staff a quizzical smile and sat for a long while, knitting a long, finely sharpened pencil between her fingers, gazing at it without really seeing it. She knew that in diplomacy, especially with Kiprensky, trust was a brittle branch.

Finally, she said, "I'll call him. Have the Embassy in Moscow shred documents and get every nonessential staff member out of there. Hide them somewhere, smuggle them out of the country, do what you have to do."

"How about the Embassy Marines? Do they go down shooting, or open the gate and surrender?"

"Tell them to lock and load. Full battle dress with every available weapon ready. If Kiprensky wants an incident, he is going to have to buy it with blood."

CHAPTER 14

First Run

———◦⟡◦———

M ichael Solak had been looking at the icon for over an hour. Lara's infatuation gave way to hunger. She got off the stool, stretched, and went to the refrigerator where Wilson kept his eggs, bagels, and other assorted emergency foodstuff, including a rancid half-gallon of milk.

"You aren't supposed to have food in the conservation laboratory, anyway, are you?" she said to Solak.

"Never. More artwork has been damaged by careless conservators knocking a Pepsi over onto the work they are trying restore than by thieves."

"I have some crackers and peanuts in my office," she said. "Why don't you take a break?"

The crackers were stale, but the can of party mix peanuts was unopened and, in her refrigerator, a half bottle of pinot gris had escaped the ravages of late afternoons with too much to worry about and too little to do. The museum was still closed, but the security force was there and, since it was just past five o'clock, the guards were turning on the night alarms. A sheriff's car was parked in front, the deputy and one of the guards leaning casually against it, talking in a way that allows men to avoid all subjects of serious emotional content.

Michael was pensive, as if he had just had an audience with God.

"The portrait artist only has two expressive vehicles: the eyes and the hands. What is so stunning about The Mother of God is that her eyes say so much. It makes you think she really is inspired by God—that she can show sorrow and hope and tenderness and steadfastness and virtually every other noble sentiment at the same time."

"What else can you tell me?" asked Lara.

"So much of the form of these icons was prescribed by the church. The red, for example, is the color for redemption and the impending sacrifice of Christ. That is why Byzantine emperors wore red at Easter."

"Michael, you are not telling me what I want to know. I am not going to sue you if you are mistaken, but what do you think? Is it real?"

He teased her for a moment with his eyes, and then he said, "You saw me shine the harsh light on it from the side—the raking light? That was to check the surface for signs that it had been recently made or altered, and I didn't…"

They both looked up at the sound of screeching tires in the parking lot. The white Ford sedan, as described by Michael, was back, this time with a second car that had slewed in behind the police cruiser.

The sheriff and the guard were standing dumbly, staring at the barrels of half a dozen weapons, including a nasty repeating shotgun with a pistol grip.

Lara and Michael sprinted for the basement.

Frontal assaults are not unknown in the museum world. Thieves dressed as policemen tied up the guards and made off with $200 million worth of Old Masters from a New

England museum. But that was secretive and at night. This assault held no subtlety at all.

After tying the sheriff and the guard with duct tape, the men proceeded to the front doors, ripped them open with a fusillade of close-range shotgun blasts, and encountered head guard Wesley Foster in the museum foyer.

A "nine" is a favorite Washington, DC, street gun. Graceless and ugly, its elongated grip holds a fifteen-round magazine that discharges such an indiscriminately lethal pattern of flying metal, that aiming is almost unnecessary.

Foster, with no thought but to protect the museum, charged the man with the nine. The magazine was empty, and Foster dead before he took his second step. The Mother of God brought none of her legendary armor to his aid.

In the basement, with the unmuseumlike explosions and shouts above them, Michael and Lara were furiously wrapping the icon, first in the kraft paper and then in the plastic. Lara fumbled with a roll of masking tape, the only adhesive available, and slapped on roughly torn strips to hold the plastic together.

After Michael, hands shaking to the extent he could not unstick the tape from itself, had ruined three pieces in a row, Lara bumped him aside with her hip and finished the taping just as the sound of the fusillade that ended Wesley Foster's life reached them.

"There's a way out. Can you carry this without dropping it?"

Solak was white as he grasped the icon, blinking vigorously and working his mouth like a fish against aquarium glass. With limited options available, Lara decided he could.

She blasted her way through the garden door, the alarm screeching to an uncaring audience. Half looking over her shoulder at Michael and half expecting a bullet from the intruders, she zigzagged through the garden, then the gate to the lawn extending to the Aker house, and in the kitchen door without a knock or invitation.

She knew that all the museum windows were shaded to protect the art from hard light, but even if the shooters hadn't seen them run through the garden, they would be on their trail promptly.

The kitchen was empty, but the house wasn't. From down the hall a shriek caused both Lara and Michael to flex backwards, until it was followed by another shriek and a moan in a different octave, the unmistakable sounds of lovemaking in full flower.

Lara's shoulders relaxed and settled. "Maybe I have underestimated Estelle," she said.

"Your car and my car are both at the museum," said Lara. "They know we were in there and if they are determined enough to have blasted their way in, they certainly won't stop until they find us."

Lara thought of the barns and asked, "Do you ride?"

"I'm a Russian, but not a Cossack. Anyway, the icon is a bit big for saddle bags. We should leave it here."

"Absolutely not," said Lara. "It doesn't leave my sight."

Michael was trembling, pale, and out of breath. He bent over and drank directly from the spigot of the sink.

Lara quietly opened the door that led from the kitchen into the garage. Cameron's Mercedes 560 two-seater was there, just waiting to be taken. The keys? Where did he keep the keys?

That was easy. A wooden board with horrid tole painting and five hooks along the bottom held various sets of keys, one of which had a Mercedes emblem on it.

"How do we get out of here?" asked Michael, regaining some of his color.

"We run the gauntlet," said Lara. "There is only one road, and it is the gravel driveway that goes by the edge of the museum parking lot, through the museum gates, and out to the access road."

"And you want to do that?" his color again vanishing.

"You didn't like horses, you don't like cars, you have a helicopter, maybe?" she asked, the tension spewing from her.

"I'll put the icon in the car," he said, taking the keys.

The sound of climax number two came drifting down the hall from Estelle's bedroom. Definitely misjudged her, thought Lara.

An elegant green leather purse with shoulder strap and gold clasp sat on the kitchen counter. Lara opened it and extracted the wallet that held Estelle's driver's license, cash, and credit cards. She looked at the picture on the driver's license and shrugged, thinking, "Well, we are both women," put the wallet back in the purse, and slung the strap over her shoulder as she closed the kitchen door from the garage side.

Michael had the cloth top down and was wedging the icon into a back seat that was more of an afterthought than a space for humans.

"I couldn't secure it in the trunk. If I wedge it into the back seat behind us, it shouldn't move, even if you do some dangerous driving. You are driving, aren't you?"

"Born to drive," said Lara. "Let me adjust the seat before you wedge the icon in."

Michael found some leaf bags to cushion the precious cargo. "The way you have got it, Michael, I can't use the rearview mirror. It sticks up behind my head."

"Can you see well enough with the top up to drive?" he asked.

"I guess. I can use the side mirrors. Let's get out of here."

"You want to open the garage door or drive through it?" he asked.

Then, without waiting, he hit the garage door opener button. She backed out and put the car in the S gear, which, in German, she hoped meant "schnell."

By the time she reached the ninety-degree turn where the gravel driveway abutted the museum parking lot, she was doing forty. The two intruders in the parking lot instinctively raised their weapons but did not fire.

Lara swung the wheel to the right and floored it. The tires on the left caught traction causing the car to fishtail wildly, screeching, and spitting gravel. The automatic weapons spit right back as the car headed toward the iron gates.

The boom of the shotgun was more frightening than the pellets that rained off the metal body and cloth top. The car was traveling away and was too far for the shotgun to be effective, but the other weapons shredded the back window and punctured the rear deck of the Mercedes.

Michael saw the men scurrying for their cars and turned forward again as the closing pistons swung the huge metal gates toward them.

Lara, emitting a high-pitched, continuous, and inhuman wail, hunched over the wheel and kept the accelerator flat to the floor in what is not textbook soft track technique. The car hurtled from side to side and into the opening, no wider than the car itself, hitting the right side of the gate, bouncing the car to the left and Michael into Lara's shoulder, hard…careening against the left side of the gate and miraculously ejecting the car out the other side.

Sixty was surely as fast as any car had ever gone on the gravel road between the gate and the paved access highway, and when Lara reached the end and turned ninety degrees right, her four-wheel skid into the pavement almost rolled them. She laid a strip of rubber twenty feet long as she accelerated, slammed on the brakes at the stop sign but didn't stop, shot across the overpass, skidding recklessly into the oncoming lane and was on the access ramp of I-66 eastbound toward Washington.

She realized the tachometer was in the red, eased the accelerator from ninety mph, and shifted from S to D. The short hair on the back of her neck was standing straight out, and her lips were sealed back into her teeth like a racehorse. Solak leaned slightly back in his seat, let go of the door grip, and massaged Lara's neck.

"We're getting there fast," he said.

"We're getting where?"

"I thought maybe you knew."

"I can't see them in my side mirrors, but they have to be back there. Washington is better for losing them; there are more people to mix with."

Michael looked back at the shredded rear window.

"We're sporting a bunch of bullet holes, and both sides of the car are bashed. That makes us kind of obvious, doesn't it?"

"We're going to Washington, Michael. Half the cars there have bullet holes in them. Anyway, we have got to ditch this car since they've seen it."

She thought to herself, I sound like a gun moll when all I am is one museum administrator who is scared enough to wet her pants.

They were silent for a few minutes as they flashed by the slower-moving cars. Then Lara said, "We'll go to National

Airport. We can park there, take the Metro into town, and get lost. Then we'll figure out what to do next."

Michael closed his eyes, leaned his head back, and mumbled, "Dostoevsky said beauty is mysterious as well as terrible—God and the Devil fighting for the heart of man. I'm getting pretty good exposure to the terrible side and am not thrilled about it at all."

Thirty-five minutes later (certainly a record for a trip Lara had made dozens of times), she screeched into the multilevel cement parking structure at the airport, drove past the crosswalks without regard for pedestrians, and turned abruptly into a parking spot.

She sat for a moment, both hands on the wheel, head down. Michael was out of the car instantly, but Lara's door was jammed shut from the collision with the museum gate. He helped her out on the passenger side and put down the top to remove the icon.

As he lifted it out of the car, he uttered an exclamation in Russian. A dull grey mass of lead was embedded in the wood of the icon just behind the headrest.

The Mother of God, the Great Palladium, had done for Lara what it declined to do for Wesley Foster: it saved her life.

THE BACK OF CAMERON AKER'S MERCEDES WAS A MESS. They could conceal the shredded back window by leaving the top down, but a bullet had carved a furrow ending in a jagged hole along the back deck and three other bullet holes adorned the left fender, the rear license plate, and the back of the trunk lid. The longitudinal furrow on the left side had removed the door handle, and on the right side, the gate had raked a groove from fender to fender, denting the right wheel well and pushing it dangerously close to the tire. Even in Washington this car would be reported within a matter of hours.

Michael said, "Let's bail out, Lara—just take a cab to FBI headquarters and give them The Mother of God."

"Then I would try to live with myself for the rest of my life. Yes, it might eventually get back to Russia, and yes, it is probably the real one, and yes, I have no legal obligation to risk my life. But, Michael, I am not put together that way. I have to know if the icon is real, and if it is, get it back to its owner. I promised myself when I left the convent that I was in charge of my life from then on, and I am responsible for this icon."

Michael looked perplexed.

"No time for either history or philosophy, Michael, but you don't have to come along."

She tore a small piece of masking tape off the plastic wrapping and placed it over the embedded bullet in the back of the icon. Michael made no reply, but he picked up the icon and nodded.

"There is a subway stop about two hundred yards from here," she said. "If we are lucky, they will think we flew somewhere."

Lara bought two $2 tickets from the fare machine. She and Michael huddled against the dividers of the aboveground platform, not knowing from what side searching eyes might be looking.

They boarded a Yellow Line train; Lara studied the station map and then came back and sat with Michael.

"We change at L'Enfant Plaza, take a Blue or an Orange Line Train to Metro Center, get off there, and get lost in the crowds. When I came here for a conference years ago, I stayed across from the Treasury Building. Great location, but not what you'd call upscale.

"Let's get one of those huge suitcases that the Japanese tourists pull around, put the icon in the suitcase, and maybe we will look a little less like fugitives."

Michael nodded and smiled. The train had gone underground and now was emerging onto the bridge that would take it across the Potomac at Fourteenth Street.

"I was thinking," he said. "This train is called the Metro. In Eastern Orthodoxy, a leader outside the seat of the church is a Metropolitan."

"I'm glad you are keeping your sense of historical perspective, Michael, but the Fourteenth Street Bridge is also the site of a celebrated plane crash."

At the Metro Center station, they emerged from the subway, Lara clutching her fare card with fifty cents still left on it in one hand and Estelle Aker's green Italian leather purse in the other. Michael carried the icon, looking like the bearer of a jumbo-sized pizza. Heavy. Every two blocks he had to stop, resting it on his shoe top as he regained his strength.

They walked west on F Street and entered The Shops, a seemingly endless multi-floored mall of the kind that gave Lara an instant migraine. She consulted the directory and found a luggage store.

While Michael lounged against the wall, his oversized pizza leaning against his leg, Lara went in and reemerged within minutes, motioning him to join her.

"Nothing is big enough," she said. "The clerk looked in the catalog, but the biggest made is only thirty-four inches." Michael held the icon up to the biggest suitcase. It was Cinderella's ugly sister trying to don the glass slipper.

They walked another block west and into the once nicer lobby of the Hotel Washington. She got a room, using the name, credit card, and signature (she hoped) of Estelle Aker.

The room, on the eighth floor, southwest corner, was large and artless with a king-size bed and a spectacular view of the Washington Monument.

They had escaped immediate death, but this sterile room lent no comfort and did little to relieve their fugitive status.

ESTELLE AKER ANSWERED LARA'S CALL AFTER THE FIFTH ring with a noncommittal "Hello."

"Estelle, it's Lara."

"Oh, hello, Lara, it's nice to hear from you, dear."

"Estelle, I borrowed your purse. The green one that was lying on the counter in the kitchen?"

"That's all right, dear, I have lots of purses," Estelle said, in a dreamy monotone.

"No, Estelle, what I am saying is, I borrowed your purse with everything in it, I mean your wallet and your credit cards and some money, and I would like your permission to use your credit cards for a while."

"Oh, my," said Estelle, sounding befuddled by such a curious proposition.

"People are chasing me, Estelle. They may be the same ones that killed Cameron."

"Yes, Cameron's dead," she said. "The police just left. All this shooting is very distressing."

"Estelle, I also took Cameron's car. It's in the garage at National Airport. It has some damage."

"I never drive Cameron's car, dear."

"I'll be back in a few days, Estelle," said Lara, not knowing whether she was communicating or simply talking into the phone.

"Take your time, and enjoy yourself," said Estelle.

As Lara replaced the phone, a huge stack of towels entered the room, and when they fell onto the bed, Michael Solak's cheshire grin appeared as he kicked the door shut with his heel.

"We need some padding for the icon. I couldn't find any service carts in the hallways, but I found where they keep them, and I stole in like a thief in the night and brought back these towels."

"Michael, you are proud of yourself," said Lara. "Is this the first thing you have ever stolen in your life?"

"Fifth Amendment," said Michael. "I know my rights."

"I have to make one more call, and then there is a small matter we seem to have forgotten. I was starving when you were examining the icon. That seems eons ago, but my mind and stomach have turned again to food. There used to be an outdoor restaurant on the top floor: it was this place's best feature."

She called information, got a number, dialed it, and said to the dispatcher, "This is Lara Cole, you had a deputy watching my house a few nights ago? I'm out of town, and my cat is in the house and needs to be fed. I know it is not what you normally do, but would you be so kind as to have the deputy swing by? The key is under a rock just to the left of the stairs. The cat food is in the kitchen."

"You'd be surprised at how many cat calls we get here, Ms. Cole," said the dispatcher. "No pun intended. Glad to do it."

Only after Lara had hung up did it occur to the dispatcher that he was talking to a material witness to the most brutal murder in Rappahannock County history. Too late. Caller identification was a feature this rural sheriff's department did not yet have.

THE DEPUTY EDGED HIS CRUISER INTO LARA'S DRIVEWAY, lights illuminating her front porch. He left the engine running, the police radio on, and walked up the flagstone path, nervously fingering the butt of his revolver. Generations of life in Rappahannock County had produced nothing like that afternoon's assault on Akerhill Museum. Wesley Foster, dead. Another guard shot and in the hospital, and a deputy and a third guard chagrined and chastened, but glad to be alive with nothing more than skin burns from the duct tape.

As he approached the door, he heard insistent, even hysterical yowling. He found the key and inserted it in the lock as the screeching continued. That was one discontented cat.

Holstering his gun, he found the cat food, which Igor began to eat as it poured from the sack.

"Wet food," he muttered, looking in the refrigerator and finding a can of Kitty Delight covered with tin foil. He was achieving hero status with Igor.

He changed the water, believing that animals, like humans, preferred cool to tepid. He then left Igor to his feast, replaced the cushions on the couch, and decided that a total cleanup was beyond his responsibility. He pushed open the screen door and sat down on her front step. It was a Northern Virginia evening of unsurpassed gentility and beauty.

The crickets and the cicadas vied for airtime. He wondered whether they were calling to one another or just showing off, but the cacophony did nothing to interrupt the otherwise tranquil night with its occasional bird call and rustle of wind.

The low humidity over the last couple of days gave a lightness to the air, although it probably was still at least sixty-five degrees, and he thought to himself, I have lived here all my life, and my daddy and his daddy before him. I love these rolling hills and broadleaf forests and rock-walled fields. I love to hunt and farm and, God help us, live in peace with my neighbors.

He knew it was outsiders, with their military weapons and disdain for human life, who had assaulted the museum and obliterated the tranquility of this bucolic county. The worst that had happened during his years as a deputy was the occasional murder of passion or somebody poisoning a neighbor's dog with anti-freeze.

The deputy's reverie continued until a mosquito landed on his neck, at which point he locked the door, got into his car, and drove to the station.

LARA AND MICHAEL SHARED THE SAME EVENING THAT had comforted the deputy. From the balcony of the Hotel Washington, they could see the roof of the White House and, beyond it, the Second Empire architecture of the Old Executive Office Building. The flags circling the Washington Monument swayed gently in the almost-still evening air, punctuated regularly by the noise of jets on approach down the Potomac to National Airport.

Commercial plane traffic stops at 10:30 p.m. for noise abatement, except when it doesn't. Like so many other paradoxes in Washington, no credible explanation exists.

Michael chose a Virginia pinot gris about which, Lara suspected, he knew nothing but pretended he did. It probably had what the wine aficionados would declare a "full bouquet, good legs, and a dry but fruity taste."

To Lara, it could have been the cheapest screw-top, and it would have been sublime in the company of Michael Solak, who was kidding her about her I-may-get-run-over-by-a-bus-tomorrow attitude toward culinary restraint.

"I run, and I worry, Michael. Nobody in my family is fat; we just eat whatever we want and burn it all up."

This exchange was provoked by Lara's tournedos of beef preceded by an artichoke and fennel salad with tomatoes, niçoise, and anchovies dressed in olive oil, lemon juice, oregano, and thyme. He approved of the salad, not of the entree.

He, on the other hand, perhaps just to tease her, ordered a Mediterranean lamb stew cooked with fennel seeds, white wine, onions, carrots, celery, raisins, and toasted pine nuts.

"Lamb is the very definition of fat, my friend."

"Not this lamb stew," said he. "They skim the fat off the top (something he could not possibly know since he had never been here in his life). And this pinot is clearly better than the one we didn't get to drink in your office."

She was arguing with a chemist, and didn't much care to best him, anyway, so she said, "But you ordered two main courses."

"Not so, the scallops and tri-colored peppers are on the appetizer list."

They laughed and looked at each other and raised their glasses and loved the evening that was so gentle and serene and that also held the men who wanted to kill them.

The food came, and was eaten, slowly and secondarily to their conversation. Indeed, as they finished their main courses, they were the only diners left on the patio.

Their waiter broke away from the small clutch of other waiters and bus boys who were chatting by the cash register, waiting for these last two diners to depart, and offered, with little enthusiasm, dessert or coffee.

Lara shook her head and, directly to Michael, said, "I would like to go to our room now." Her look was eloquent.

In their room, their dessert was a souffle of love: light, and rich, and smooth, and even. To each, the other's body was new and fresh and unknown and breathlessly exciting.

For the souffle to succeed, the temperature and texture and timing all must be perfect and with Lara, his ministrations were overwhelmingly exact.

She lay, for what seemed to be time suspended, in his arms as they caressed and rubbed and explored, without haste or pause until they slowly disentangled, and slept—the sleep of peace and human fulfillment in a world hurtling toward disaster.

CHAPTER 15

Random Trashing

P avel Kiprensky was livid. The international chess board he had so carefully crafted was changing shape and, for once, he was not the manipulator. Cameron Aker was not supposed to be dead. His role was simply to make the icon disappear from the museum and reappear at the Russian Embassy from whence it would return to Moscow in the diplomatic pouch, to be "recovered" in a manner and at a time most politically propitious.

The icon disappeared all right, presumably by Aker's hand, and was now out of Kiprensky's control—a situation that could cause him political heartburn of substantial proportion. With Aker dead, he had no means of tracing it, and Betty Sorensen had just told him it might be in Ukraine. Big trouble.

Then she had the temerity to suggest that she knew about his harmless little sideline selling Russian chemicals and weapons with Aker's assistance. She just dangled it out in conversation, casually, as she passed on to another point. It was a negotiating ploy of which he would have been proud, but as the target it really pissed him off. He didn't care about their tight-assed Western morality, but how much did she know? He didn't want to be exposed as the father of the icon heist.

Time, he thought, to regain the initiative.

⸻

LARA STOOD AT THE BATHROOM MIRROR, TOWEL wrapped around her, using an eyebrow pencil she had found in Estelle Aker's purse. She looked at herself critically, raising one eyebrow and then the other, and decided the rest of her face would have to fend for itself.

Michael came up behind her, wearing jockey briefs and a watch. He kissed the back of her neck and said:

"For life, too, is only the dissolving of ourselves
Into the selves of all others…"

"That is a poem of Yuri Zhivago," he told her, "the lover of your literary namesake—a character not half so lovely as you."

She turned and, putting both her arms around his neck, kissed him, a long and involved kiss, and as she withdrew, she shuddered and laid her forehead against his chest.

"It was nice last night," he said.

"It was wonderful." Then, knowing the luxuries of time and reverie were not theirs, she said, "Why don't you order some room service coffee and rolls or more if you want—and then let's get out of here."

"But we should think about this," he protested. "They don't know for sure we have the icon."

"You don't think our racing out of the museum was some admission on our part?" she asked.

"Sure, that we didn't want to be beaten up or killed, but

they can't know for sure that we have it."

"Who else could?"

She thought, then answered her own question, "Well, Wilson, and Sounder, and—oh, my God. Estelle. They surely will squeeze her."

"But you said she is an airhead."

"I don't know if she is or isn't," said Lara, "but when they start beating on her, odds are she is going to tell them that I have her purse, and they will start looking for a credit card trail, which means, my friend and lover, that we really don't have much time."

THEY WERE ALREADY LOOKING. THE BUYER'S ASSOCIATES had traced Wilson Porter to Montgomery. They were white, not Black, and their chances of penetrating the communication network of the neighborhood where "Willy" was staying were zero.

Willy, (not Wilson or Wil in these parts), his peripatetic energy needing some outlet, had organized an icon-painting class for ten- and eleven-year-olds in a neighborhood Baptist Church basement. The results were as remarkable as the instructor. He taught the kids to draw upside down, with their eyes closed, with their subdominant hand, and once they developed a sense of freedom with line and color, their icons became vehicles to express their hopes and dreams and problems. He did all that the first week—like God's Creation, kind of. If numbers are evidence of success, Willy started with seven and now had seventeen, eight of them boys.

But Willy didn't show up for class the day after Akerhill Museum was attacked. The Buyer's associates, who qualified as the Man in this Montgomery neighborhood, had come around and, more effectively than any sophisticated electronic network could perform, the neighborhood got the word to Willy to vanish. And that was precisely what he did.

REVEREND BOB SOUNDER'S NETWORK SHOULD HAVE been so good. Sounder lived in Arlington, fittingly enough, off Seminary Road. The neighborhood was dignified, not lavish, the houses built in the sixties and seventies, with broad lawns and shaded sidewalks.

They found him at home, eating dinner with his wife. They tied and gagged her—duct tape again—threw her in the master bedroom and proceeded to beat and choke Sounder until his eyes refused to blink, but he told them only that the Lord was his Sword and Shield and if he had the icon, he would have destroyed it.

They did not care for either answer but they left him, blue and bruised, fighting for breath on his dining room floor.

The young man who was servicing Estelle Aker, in a chivalrous act of stupidity, leaped up when they burst into her bedroom. For his trouble, he got a chest full of silenced lead that kills every bit as effectively as noisy lead.

Estelle told them, weeping and choking, that she didn't know her husband's business, she didn't know where The Mother of God was, she didn't know where Lara Cole was, and she did know that Lara had her purse. They found that to be some progress and perhaps, because Estelle was prescient enough to have written down the numbers of her credit cards on her Rolodex, the Buyer's associates thanked

Estelle by leaving her with her life and a very large bruise on the back of her skull.

The Buyer got right to work. He was a driver on the information superhighway, and he was looking for those credit card purchases that would lead him to Lara Cole. It was not her he wanted, although she would surely die when he found her. His quest was a holy one: to return The Mother of God to Ukraine.

AFTER SHE SIGNED ESTELLE AKER'S NAME TO THE HOTEL bill with hardly a twinge of conscience, Lara found a cab (the doorman was occupied talking about the Redskins) and, as it drew up, Michael walked quickly to the curb with the icon, now padded with hotel towels inside the paper and plastic. Into the trunk it went, and they were off to Union Station.

"There may be some people we would like to avoid waiting for us at Union Station. Can you drop us off somewhere other than the front?"

"Not s'posed to, lady," he said.

Lara was ecstatic, not at the response, but that it was in English, a rarity for DC drivers.

She opened Estelle's purse, extracted a twenty, held it between her fingers as she leaned across the seat.

"There are lots of things we're not supposed to do. How about finding a way to get us in another door?"

He reached back without looking, stuffed the bill in his trousers, and said, "Maybe."

He turned right on K Street, and then right again onto Massachusetts Avenue, and stopped at the light just to the west of Union Station. When it changed, or actually just before it changed, he hurtled diagonally across the intersection, traveled an eighth of a block the wrong way on First Street and up the ramp to the parking structure behind the station.

Halfway up the ramp, he turned right, passing the queue of waiting taxicabs, and screeched to a halt saying, "Fare is six bucks. Take the escalator down, and you are in the station."

She gave him the money and, immediately after they retrieved the icon from the trunk, he slammed his car into reverse, backing to the end of the queue and erasing the ire of his fellow liverymen.

Not wanting to use Estelle's credit card to advertise their destination, Lara exhausted most of her cash: two sixty-eight dollar one-way tickets on the 8:36 Metroliner to New York.

The icon was too big for the overhead racks, but they put it up there, anyway. The conductor was already in a foul mood, and as he ripped off the stubs and stuck them above their seats, he said, "Check your bags next time, Buddy," to which Michael responded, "Yes, sir," and the conductor's mood was in no way improved, since the anticipated shouting match was stillborn.

Lara spent the first twenty minutes to New Carrollton looking over her shoulder and then through the glass door to the next car, expecting momentarily for someone, she didn't know who, to emerge. Then she decided there was nothing she could do about it if such person did arrive, and she would be better off making another list.

She borrowed a sheet of perforated notebook paper from the young girl who was sitting across the aisle, put down the tray on the seat in front of her, dug a gold Cross pen out of Estelle's handbag, and began to write.

As she did so, Michael turned to her and said, "This is a Metroliner. Metro again. It's a very good sign."

"You are unrealistically romantic," she said. "Keep that high voltage smile to yourself so I can concentrate."

Ten minutes later, her list contained only four items:

1. Stay alive.

2. Determine authenticity.

3. Return it if real.

4. Give it up publicly if not.

As Lara stared at the list, the reptiles of her mind scratched at her youthful wounds.

Am I doing this to prove my courage, my independence? Will I vindicate myself by getting killed? Have I escaped God's pressing hand, or does He still have me pinned with guilt and indecision? Am I reckless because I have nothing left to lose, foolish because I am self-deluded?

In a single thrust of resolution, she flushed her mind of the past and forced her attention back to the list.

"Look at this, Michael."

"Staying alive, I approve of that. Determining authenticity, I can do that. Returning it if real—I don't know about that. Give it up publicly if not—what does that mean?

"It relates to number one—staying alive," said Lara. "If you determine it's not legitimate, then we hold a press conference at the Met, get Wil Porter up here and have him tell his story. You pontificate and then invite any doubters to see for themselves. If we publicly give it up, whoever is chasing us might stop."

"Lara," he said softly, "Number three and number one

are related too, but inversely. If it is real, the more you try to return it, the greater difficulty we will have staying alive. Why couldn't we have the same press conference at the Met, say it is real, and let Madam Kopulskaya come get it?"

"No, no, no, no!" said Lara. "That puts it right back in the hands of the politicians. Who knows whether they would let her actually take it back to the Tretyakov, or if it would be any safer in her hands than in ours? Anyway, if I just bring it and dump it at the Met and say, 'Come and get it,' how am I going to live with myself and my obligation to the art world?"

"What obligation to the art world? Nobody is requiring you to get killed."

"You're right. It's my own conscience, my own ethics, my own sense of duty," said Lara.

"What it is…What it is, is that you are being stubborn, and being stubborn can get you killed."

"I'm not, Michael." She paused. "OK, I'm being stubborn, but you, more than anyone else, should understand what The Mother of God means in the religious and aesthetic history of the world. When you have the power to restore her to her original location, are you prepared to leave this all to chance? I'm not. This is one time when I won't chicken out."

He sat back and, looking straight ahead, said, "I've been thinking about that, too. Repatriation is a tricky game. Russia has had it, but Ukraine claims it, and I suppose the Turks could make a pretty good case that it should be in Istanbul. I have been trying to sort out, in my own mind the risks, the intelligent choices." He sighed. "My mind used to work that way, Lara, but you have changed it. I am going to do what you do, and that is all that really matters to me."

"Do you think it is The Mother of God?" she asked, embracing his arm.

"An X-ray could show that it is held together with consistent-pitch screws—post-industrial revolution screws. I could find, upon quantitative analysis, that the paints are synthetics, unknown in the twelfth century.

"Maybe my analysis of the organic materials will show molecular chains inconsistent with any known materials in Byzantium at the time the original was painted…"

"But what do you think?" she pressed.

"What is my intuition, my gut, my hope? To all three, the answer is, you are sitting underneath The Mother of God, and we both better hope that she can protect us because for every one she saves, another gets killed."

As George Graham reviewed the assaults on Estelle Aker and Reverend Bob Sounder, and the mayhem that had occurred at Akerhill Museum, he had the sickly feeling that those presently dead and injured were only a way station on the road to Armageddon.

His assistant bounced in, looked at him as he sat, tie knotted up to his collar, feet on the floor not on the desk, and respecting this unusual body language, she muted her own exuberance.

"We still don't know where Wilson Porter is, but if we can't find him, chances are pretty good that Boris Golchev can't either."

"We are sure Boris Golchev is the Buyer?" asked Graham.

"Yep. Aker's lawyer says he was the uninvited guest at the Akerhill party. Estelle Aker, in her one non-hysterical interlude, said she told her assailant that Lara took her purse." She looked at him. "Yes, I got the numbers of all of her credit cards. I'm not a rookie, you know." He nodded but did not speak.

Then he tossed aside the picture of Wesley Foster's ruined body. "She is going to get herself killed."

"Estelle?" asked his assistant.

"Lara," he said. "She may think she is A. J. Foyt screaming out of the museum like that, but I doubt that she would do it just for kicks. If she were worried just about staying alive, she could have faded into the forest until they got tired of searching for her but instead, she goes squirreling by a regiment of automatic weapons, takes half a dozen slugs in the back of the car, and what for?

"In fact," he stood up, "if the real icon was stolen, what is any of this about? Why raid a museum after the only thing in there that is really worth stealing is already gone?"

"You think it is still there?"

"Was," he said. "She knew it. Boris Golchev knew it or suspected it. I didn't know it, and I wasn't smart enough to get it out of her when I talked to her.

"Now she's got some idealistic notion that she is going to be a hero and save the art world. She is going to get herself killed."

His assistant waited.

He put both hands palm down on his desk and leaned over the scattered array of pictures and reports. Then, without raising his head, he said, "Run all the credit card numbers through the system. I want immediate notification—I mean, immediate notification—whenever any of them is used. Don't let them cancel the cards or put a hold on them. Just notification. You got it?"

"Yes, sir." And she was gone.

CHAPTER 16

Preparations

The train pulled into Penn Station at Seventh Avenue and Thirty-Second Street, and Lara winced as she got up from her seat. Michael looked at her with concern. "Sore buns," she said. "I can hardly walk."

"How come?"

"From you-know-what last night," she said.

"Sorry."

"Totally worth it," she said and walked off the train like an arthritic crone.

Wrapped in its kraft paper and plastic, and padded with hotel towels, the icon was so unlike the attaché cases and shoulder bags everyone else was carrying, Michael looked and felt obvious—like everyone knew he was up to no good.

Outside, in front of Madison Square Garden, a man was grabbing tourists by the elbow and saying, "Give me five dollars, and I'll tell the cabbie where to take you."

Only in New York, thought Lara.

She found a cab without such "help" and gave the driver their destination: the Metropolitan Museum of Art, Fifth Avenue and Eighty-Second Street on the east side of Central Park. He nodded, slammed a cassette into the tape deck, and pulled into traffic as the syncopated rhythms of reggae pelted their ears.

As he headed crosstown, the driver was lurching and singing with the repetitive choruses of the music. He turned north and by midtown, was clapping with the music—not while stopped at a light, but while he was going forty miles an hour through traffic.

Michael was sitting back, unconcerned; Lara jerked forward and said: "Is that Marley?"

"Yah, Mon."

"Well, let him sing and you hold the wheel."

He turned, broad smile fading as he saw she intended no joke.

He held the wheel for five more blocks until the pulse of the music overcame him, and he began rocking in his seat, then clapping, and Lara, resigned to her fate, lay back against the cushion and thought this might just be the most dangerous thing they had done so far.

On Michael's directions, which he screamed over the insistent and, he thought, compelling beat of the reggae, the cab passed the entrance of the Met and turned into the loading area where the cabbie was set free to service fares who better appreciated the musical arts.

<hr />

MICHAEL GREETED THE GUARDS AT THE LOADING DOCK, but also dutifully fished a picture ID from his coat pocket and clipped it on. It didn't say he was staff, but it didn't say he wasn't, either.

Lara signed the book and asked the guard if she might use the phone. Several minutes later, Freddy arrived, suave and elegant in a light grey and black minutely checked summer suit, gleaming white shirt, and maroon paisley tie that said, quietly but emphatically, "I am expensive."

Freddy greeted Michael with a professional nod and Lara with an enthusiastic kiss on either cheek. "You didn't tell me you were coming, my sweet."

"I am not into advertising these days."

"And you brought me a present," said Freddy, eyeing the package that Michael was holding protectively. "Let me see it."

"How about we go inside?" said Lara.

In the unpacking area Freddy could no longer restrain himself, and with uncuratorial haste, he swept the scraps and moldings off a carpeted table with one elegant forearm and attacked the package like a four-year-old at his birthday party.

When it was open, he gazed upon the face of The Mother of God with unrestrained delight. He clapped his hands and, with little bounces, said: "It's wonderful. I've always wanted one of these!"

"It's not for you, you avaricious pirate," said Lara.

"Why else would you bring it here?" he said, the very picture of innocence.

"Michael has to use your laboratory, that's why. We have been chased, shot at, trashed in the press, and sentenced to hell because of this icon. You are the one, Freddy, who preached to me about the integrity and nobility of a career in art. So you had better lend us your equipment for a few hours while we figure out whether this is really worth risking our lives for."

"While we're at it," she said, grabbing both of his well-pressed lapels, "you better give me a receipt so I can get this icon out of here if it's real."

"I am so disappointed," he said in mock surprise. Then suddenly serious, "Who else knows you are here?"

"Only you and the guards, and hopefully, not the killers who have been chasing us for the last two days."

"Give me a couple of minutes," he said, "and I will go to the lab and 'prepare the way for you.' Consider me the John the Baptist of your stay here."

Lara had not seen the basement conservation lab since its total renovation, and befitting the institution of which it was a part, it was world class. Gone were the Bunsen burners and dark, slate topped tables reeking of spent chemicals. The walls and carpeting were quiet earth tones and the working spaces broad, flat tables with binocular microscopes and fiber-optic halogen lights that looked like extraterrestrials.

Lots of computers. These accessed the programs for the micron microscope and gas spectrograph, the heart of this high-tech center. Ironic, she thought, we need all this high-tech gear to tell us whether something is old.

Michael greeted his friends enthusiastically, went to the table Freddy had designated for him, and was all business. He stared intently at the icon as if she would, if he looked long enough, reveal the secrets of the universe.

Freddy had instructed the conservators to give this one a wide berth, but their curiosity was clearly going to be hard to restrain. These were people whose profession it was to be curious and, as they walked by adjoining spaces, they lingered and looked.

Lara sat behind Michael at the workstation, practicing Estelle Aker's signature until she was satisfied she could fool a clerk. She then made herself another list, not worrying that she was becoming compulsive, and concentrating every bit as intensely as Michael. She dug out a New York Yellow Pages from a bottom drawer and placed call after call. She conferred briefly with Michael, reconfirming the details they had discussed on the train, assuming, of course, that his investigation concluded that the real Mother of God was with them.

They kissed, apparently not a typical maneuver in the eyes of one curious scholar, and then Lara, with Estelle Aker's green purse in her hand, left the room.

She intended to take a cab, but as she emerged from the Met a bus was pulling into the stop, so she dashed on just as the door was closing. She tried to recall, from the spy novels, how one determined if one was being tailed. She remembered nothing.

She got off at Fifty-Sixth Street, glancing furtively as she stepped down and then, as rapidly as she could walk, headed crosstown until she found a café with tables on the sidewalk. She sat down, turning in the direction from which she had come. No one seemed to pay any attention to her at all, least of all a waiter. Most places, waitstaff serve customers. In New York, they exist to insult, not to serve.

She bolted up, walked briskly around the block into Bergdorf's, out the other exit, crossed the street mid-block, nearly getting run over by a cab, and darted into a store that sold worn-looking jeans at extraordinarily high prices.

After two more jogs and waits, she admitted to herself that she could spend the rest of the day in this frenetic pantomime and still not know if somebody was watching her amateur dashes.

SHE PULLED OUT HER LIST, WALKED TWO BLOCKS, AND twenty minutes later emerged wearing a blond, curly wig. Although it didn't make her look exactly like Estelle Aker, it was closer than her short, dark hair.

Next, she tried to get a cash advance on Estelle's bank card, only to realize she didn't know the four-digit PIN. There is another way, she thought. She went into a bank and got a $5,000 advance on Estelle's American Express Card. Easy.

At another bank, she drew $1,000 on Estelle's Mastercard and another $1,000 on her Visa.

Spreading her business around, she wrote a check for $3,000 to cash on Estelle's Baron's Bank account. Amid the seemingly interminable wait while the teller cleared the check, Lara imagined steam rising from Estelle's wallet and thought: Ten thousand. It better be enough.

Eating! She grabbed a polish on rye from a street vendor, spilled mustard on the front of her shirtwaist dress, and tried, with little success, to spot it off. Not to be distracted, she thought.

She found a travel agency before a luggage store—the next two items on her list. The travel agent, talking and pounding away on her computer simultaneously, told Lara much more than she wanted to know.

"We used to have to call the airlines directly, but we hardly ever do that anymore because we can call up all sorts of information on our computers, which includes discounters that buy up fares, and they used to have to buy the whole airplane—ha, ha—not the plane itself, but all of the seats, but they don't do that anymore so they come up just the same as the regular fares except they are less sometimes and you probably want to save money, I mean, who doesn't, and besides there is an Aeroflot, which is not an airline a lot of people think of because they are sort of a low-service outfit, you know, in fact, it's funny, my brother took an Aeroflot flight from Tbilisi—that is in Georgia—I know you are thinking of our state, but it is a whole different country somewhere near Russia, and the flight took off and there were people standing in the back—can you believe it? And he got up to go to the bathroom and when he came back there was an old man sitting in his seat and it was all he could do to get the guy out of it, and it's high season now, so, you know, we may have some difficulty..."

Lara waited.

Finally the jabber ended, and the serious talk began. She had three options. Well, two, really. There was a discounter's fare that cost $150 less than the seat KLM was offering on the same KLM plane. The other option was the dread Aeroflot, and it was $100 less than the discounter's fare, $753, except it went through Moscow.

Moscow was where they wanted to end up, but it wasn't part of the plan Michael had suggested, and the thought of sitting there on the ground in Moscow and potentially being snatched or seen gave Lara the creeps.

"How does the KLM flight go?" she asked.

"Oh, it's an airplane," said the cheery travel agent, winking at her own wit. Then, looking at the screen, she said, "You go to Amsterdam, change planes and take a 737 direct to St. Petersburg. It is a good connection, only an hour layover in Amsterdam."

"When does it leave, and when does it get there?" asked Lara.

Squinting, she replied, "Leaves 6:50 p.m. tomorrow and arrives St. Petersburg at 3:05. Also p.m.

"You have your passports?"

Lara had thought of this. Of course she didn't have her own passport. It was back at her house being guarded by Igor the cat. But one of her calls had been to her ex-roommate, Barbara Stiles, who was approximately the same size, coloring, and gender as Lara. Barbara had graciously agreed to lend Lara both her passport and her identity, with no questions asked, particularly after Lara agreed to stay overnight at her apartment.

"Yes, I have a passport. My name is Barbara Stiles," Lara fibbed, hoping no identification would be required.

"You'll have to show your documents when you check in," said the woman. "And the other party?"

Lara had anticipated this as well and was beginning to feel semi-smug. "Yes, he is a Russian. His name is Michael Ivanovich." Indeed, those were Michael's first two names, and they had decided that, rather than place either of their names on the passenger manifest for inquiring eyes to see, when they got to the check-in counter they would simply say the travel agent had left off his last name.

One must be a risk-taker to engage in international intrigue, thought Lara, warming to the task.

"How will you pay for these?" asked the agent.

Lara was way ahead of her, again: "Oh, I cashed a check so I could buy traveler's checks, so I'll just give you cash" which she did, $841 twice plus landing fees and other extortionary add-ons, and she was out the door with two tickets for a flight leaving in a little more than twenty-four hours.

Next, Lara engaged in some power clothes shopping. Underwear, two dresses, jeans, and a T-shirt, a sweater, a pair of running shoes, and two pairs of sensible heels. She bought a shoulder bag that could double as a briefcase, a light trench coat, because she was, after all, acting like a spy, a fold-up umbrella, and some makeup. She also bought deodorant, which she now badly needed, toothpaste, and a toothbrush.

It was 5:15. She was running late, and the traffic was getting very New Yorkish. When she reached Lincoln Center, she went first to the offices of the Chamber Music Society, and then to the Metropolitan Opera, where she talked to old friends—fundraisers working late and furiously as always. They were able to grant the favors she requested.

CHAPTER 17

Second Run

P aintings out of their frames looking forlorn and abandoned, gilded chairs without seats, and terracotta grave warriors standing headless in mute procession all waited, like patients in an emergency room, for the exquisite ministrations of the Metropolitan's restorers. Michael ignored them. As fascinating as he would have normally found them, they weren't his business.

He had glanced at the curator's report, titled "Report Study," provided by the Tretyakov when he was at Akerhill. It gave confidential details they used to authenticate The Mother of God. Curators who have lived with a great work of art can usually identify it on sight much the way they identify their own children. But for an outsider such as Michael, those peculiarities, like a birthmark or a scar, could be known only through a detailed description such as the curators' report.

It told him, for example, the radioactivity of carbon-13 in this particular painting so he could determine whether the chain of amino acids in its egg yolk was consistent with an egg laid eight hundred years ago as opposed to one bought yesterday at Safeway. Of course, the report accompanying the icon would match it. He needed to decide, independently, if the icon was what the Russians said it was.

He put aside the Tretyakov's report.

First he performed the simplest of tests. He took the precise measurements of The Mother of God and compared them with published descriptions. The cleverest of fakers might, at the outset of his deception, blow his cover by a slightly missed dimension.

Next, he removed a very small sample of paint, using two tiny needles. No expert ever damages an artwork. The paint sample must be taken from a place it will never show and be as small as possible while still allowing analysis. He used a jeweler's loop to aid in the surgery.

One part of the sample he encased in resin that dried immediately. He sliced the resin and examined it under a binocular microscope to determine the purity of the pigment. The other part of the sample he pulverized and inserted into an X-ray diffraction unit to record the wavelengths of the inorganic pigments.

After X-raying the icon and finding that it had no unexpected foreign objects or overpainting, he used an infrared spectrometer, electron microscope, gas chromatograph, and mass spectrometer looking for chemical markers that would tell him if the materials used would have been available to its Byzantine creator.

He was methodical and when he was done, he was persuaded.

⸺◈⸺

PAVEL KIPRENSKY ORDERED THE AMERICAN EMBASSY surrounded by T-72 tanks, each with its gun depressed, pointing into the ground twenty yards in front of it. Tracked, armored personnel vehicles also joined the encirclement, their troops in full battle dress, the obligatory cigarette hanging from the corners of their mouths, and the bored but alert expression soldiers universally assume.

Kiprensky explained to the world via CNN that he was surrounding the embassy for its own protection since the outrage of the Russian people at the loss of The Mother of God was such that he could not otherwise guarantee the embassy's safety.

The guns on the tanks were pointed inward. He was never accidentally ambiguous.

Betty Sorensen watched the announcements from the Oval Office and thought to herself that Kiprensky didn't give anything away to Reverend Sounder in the showmanship department. Five hours later, she herself was on worldwide television saying, in her kitchen porch way, that the United States was doing everything it could to recover the icon, and its loss did not affect our abiding friendship with Russia, the republics of the former Soviet Union, and their brave and noble citizens. (She had apparently exhumed Leonid Brezhnev's speechwriter for those phrases.)

Showmanship comes in different packages. Here was Mother Sorensen kissing our scraped elbows and fixing chicken soup to make the world safe again. Then, without breaking character, she was warning Kiprensky with steely confidence, that retaliation would be swift and definitive to any who harmed her children.

The Buyer, now known to the FBI at least as Boris Golchev, watched both of these broadcasts. Kiprensky, with whom he had dealt over the years, was entitled to no more honor than the next thief. Stealing the icon from him caused Golchev not the slightest moral hiccup. But like many ideologues, Golchev was short on perspective, and when he found that "his" icon was not the real Mother of God, his righteous anger cost Cameron Aker his life and was now focused, with white hot intensity, on whoever had the real one.

That person, he knew, was Lara Cole, the arrogant woman who had deposited food in his lap. He would enjoy meeting her again and separating her from both the icon and her mortal existence. It would be an even greater pleasure to see The Mother of God in the Mother Church in Kiev—an object of worship, not a pawn on an international chessboard.

He meditated for the next thirty minutes, coming humbly before his God while looking at an icon of Peter and John, painted on the side of a pocketknife he always carried.

Just before 6:30 p.m., Lara telephoned Michael at the conservation laboratory of the Metropolitan Museum of Art.

"What do you know?"

Michael replied, "The medieval banker, Jacob Fugger, when traveling in Italy would send his man servant ahead to taste the wine. If it was good, he would write on the city's lintel post the Latin word 'est'—it is. The wine of one town was so superior that he wrote 'Est, Est, Est.' It is still the name of the town, and it is also my answer: Est, Est, Est.

Lara ignored the pedantry and simply said: "I'm relieved, although I've been thinking that our lives might return to normal faster, and indeed, last longer, if it weren't."

"Est, Est, Est," replied Michael. He was pumped.

"OK, here's what I've done, then," said Lara. "I've hired six underemployed singers from the opera to spot along your route home so we will know if you are being followed. You go up Eighty-Third to Fifth Avenue, then to Ninety-Sixth, right?"

"Right."

"I've described you and what you have on. They'll fan out along the route. Give them forty-five minutes to get in place and leave through the main exit at exactly 7:30."

"Got it."

"But that is only half," continued Lara. "We'll repeat the same drill in reverse tomorrow morning. Leave your apartment exactly at 9:00 a.m. and walk to the museum. We'll have the same route salted."

"What if somebody tries to grab me?"

"I guess you run like hell."

"Kisses to you," he said and rang off.

What a strange expression, she thought, liking it a lot.

No one bothered Lara as she made her way to Barbara Stiles's apartment at One Hundred-Tenth and Riverside Drive, nor did she think she was followed. Perhaps she had missed her calling as a CIA operative.

Barbara greeted her at the door with a hug and then stepped back, holding her by both arms. "Lara, it is so, so good to see you. I was afraid…I was afraid you wouldn't ever want to see me again; and when you called—well, I was just overwhelmed. But," she hurried on, "I want you to know that what happened in the past won't happen again. I wish it could be, but I accept that it can't and I'm…" and then she hugged Lara again for a long time.

"If you can hug me in my current state of disrepair," said Lara, "you are a true friend indeed."

"A bath!" exclaimed Barbara as if she had discovered the Mother Lode. "I'll start it while you put your things away. Your bedroom is just where it was before."

⸺⸻◆⸻◆⸻⸺

LARA SET ABOUT CLIPPING OFF THE TAGS ON THE DRESSES, underwear, jeans, and shirt she had bought. Barbara called out cheerily that her bath was ready.

Lying with her head back against the porcelain, Lara realized both how tired she was and how, with the adrenalin rush of the day, she had forgotten that her buns were sore. Sorer tomorrow, she thought. The second day is always the worst. Barbara knocked and opened the bathroom door, carrying a glass of white wine. "Tonic from the doctor," she said, looking at Lara, turning, and leaving reluctantly.

Barbara had prepared a vegetable moussaka and tossed salad that, to the food-deprived Lara, tasted sublime. The tablecloth on the familiar table, with the candlelight and real black rooster Chianti, made the meal a remembrance of things so ordinary and safe, and now so distant.

Instead of dessert, which Lara couldn't have eaten anyway, Barbara presented a neatly wrapped package that held her passport, driver's license, voter precinct card, and a work ID.

"The work ID is an old one," she said, "but it doesn't have a date on it, and I thought it would bolster the package. I'm sorry I can't give you my Mastercard, but I need it. The driver's license is useless since I sold my car six months ago."

"I am so grateful," said Lara. "You have been sweet enough not to ask me any questions about all of this, but what I am doing is, to the best of my knowledge, not against the law, either in the United States or Russia—at least it shouldn't be."

"Russia!" exclaimed Barbara. "It's fantastic. I was there, well, let me see," and she grabbed her passport, flipped to the back page, and looked at her visa. "A year ago April."

Lara was stunned.

"Shit. Shit. Shit. Shit. Shit. Shit."

Barbara stared at her.

"How could I have been so stupid? Of course, you need a visa to get into Russia." She whammed the heel of her hand into her forehead, shook her head because it really hurt, and moaned: "It's blown. I am a dumbass. Jesus! What a fool."

Two hours later, having explained her stupidity to the ever-sympathetic Barbara, Lara lay awake in the solitude of the bedroom. She had not called Michael. They had agreed that the chances of his phone being tapped were substantial; and when one of the singers reported that he had been followed, the impressed silence seemed prudent.

She couldn't sleep, beating herself up repeatedly for her negligence, and even more for her pride and baseless assumption that she could play with the big boys of international intrigue.

BARBARA PEEKED IN, AND LARA SAID, "I'M AWAKE."

"May I come in?"

"It's your home, Barbara."

"I'll rub your back and help you go to sleep."

"OK," said Lara, turning over on to her stomach. After she had rubbed Lara's back and neck, and even her sore buttocks, Barbara said softly: "I love you, Lara."

"You're a good friend, Barbara."

"That's not the answer I wanted to hear, but it's the best I'll get, and it's OK."

"FIVE THOUSAND DOLLARS ON AMERICAN EXPRESS AND a couple more on Mrs. Aker's other cards," said George Graham to his assistant. She's building a war chest. For what?"

"Nothing on the airlines," she replied, "and I can't imagine they would leave the country any other way, unless they were going by car or train to Canada."

"Where does that get them?"

"I can't see it either," she said.

"So we got him going to the museum, but we haven't a positive ID on her in New York, right?" he asked.

"Right."

"And if we grab him now, we don't necessarily get her, so we've got to give him enough slack to lead us to her."

"And the icon," she said.

He looked at her as if she had just told him his name.

His assistant couldn't figure out how his green and white seersucker suit never seemed to get dirty. He wore it every day during the summer, and every day it looked as if it had been washed and pressed the night before. But he hadn't loosened his tie again, and that, in his reverse body language, was a sure sign of stress.

"You don't build a war chest just to hang around," he said. "She's got to be getting ready to take it back. Otherwise she wouldn't have put herself in danger in the first place. The irony of it is that the damn Russian who is rattling sabers over there may not even want it back because it screws up his tantrum."

"So...," said his assistant, resuming her usual role as provocateur.

"So she dodges and strains and somehow gets past all the authorities, and then the Russians arrest her and no one ever hears from her or sees the icon again. Meanwhile, we sit here with our thumbs up our ass, clueless as Elmer Fudd."

He brooded and she paid no prudish never mind to his language.

"Surveillance on JFK, LaGuardia, and Newark. Cover all the Moscow flights. I'm talking about people on the ground—lots of them. Check and see if she has a passport—him, too. We'll go to New York first thing in the morning to get a search warrant for Solak's apartment. You had better ask for a little divine help, too."

BORIS GOLCHEV'S INFORMATION WAS JUST AS GOOD, AND his conclusions, except the hoped-for good health of Lara, were the same. His associates in New York, while searching for Michael and Lara, also had to watch for the police and FBI who were looking for them, too.

One small inconvenience (actually, this whole episode was becoming a huge inconvenience) was that one of the men who had so rudely interrogated Reverend Sounder had gotten himself caught by the Arlington police. He claimed diplomatic immunity, which is a stretch for a strangler in any country, but he had the bad judgment to claim it through Ukraine, which was an uncomfortable connection to be sure.

The embassy disclaimed any knowledge of the man, but that wouldn't wash for long, since he was listed as an agricultural expert, had registered with the American government, and was known to those in the Department of Agriculture with whom he had been liaison. Even more reason to bring an immediate and satisfactory termination to this chase.

In one respect, Golchev's information was better than George Graham's: his men had spotted Lara and Michael going into the Metropolitan Museum, so they knew where the icon was. All they had to do was get it out. Why not just steal a few Van Goghs while we are at it, he thought. How could it be in a less accessible place?

If she got it in there, she could get it out, so the key was to capture Lara Cole and persuade her to cooperate by whatever means necessary. Then he could smuggle it back to Ukraine, and the mission would be salvaged. No obstacle would prevent him from honoring the symbol that connected earth with heaven.

COFFEE WAS ALL LARA COULD MANAGE FOR BREAKFAST. Fifteen minutes after nine, a singer called to confirm that Michael was followed when he left his apartment, but they could detect no effort to interdict him. Lara had sent Barbara out to walk around her block looking for obvious watchers. She saw none.

So, in one of her new dresses, a salmon-colored muted print with buttons up the front of the bodice and a full skirt, Lara left Barbara's apartment. She had on her running shoes, and with her large satchel over her shoulder, she looked like thousands of other New York workers striding to work with their office shoes in a bag.

She asked the taxi driver to let her off two blocks south of the Met, and she checked, first from the east side of the street and then from the Central Park side, to see if anyone appeared to be watching. How could she tell? Everybody looked suspicious now.

Well, I can run two blocks, she thought, and that is exactly what she did. Carrying her shoulder bag with both arms over it, like fullback John Riggins going through the line, she ran, dodging oncoming pedestrians and baby prams and dogs on leashes, not looking back to see if anyone was following, if anyone cared, or if anyone even noticed.

By the end of the first block, she thought how can I be winded when I jog three times a week? Two men, seated on a bench next to the park got up quickly as she thundered along. She saw them, made a cut to the right that would have made old Riggo proud, only to see another man discard a cigarette and move toward her path. This time a baby carriage was her blocker, and she didn't turn to see the upset when he crashed into it. She would feel guilty some other time.

She stumbled when she hit the downslope of the ramp for the loading dock. She took four strides with bended knees, recovered her balance, and bounded up the steps and into the museum. She signed in, as if she had every right to be there, and headed for the conservation laboratory in the basement, her breath still coming in harsh gulps, and her brand-new dress showing some very sweaty stains.

Michael was there, sitting with the conservation director, drinking coffee, and laughing as if it were just another day at the office. He saw Lara, grinned broadly, and rose to embrace her, but she pushed him away. "Michael, I am such an idiot. All of these preparations, and I don't have a visa. I can't get into Russia. I've got Barbara Stiles's passport, but her visa has expired. I am such a DUMBASS."

He sat back down.

"You two might want to be alone," said the director and he picked up some papers from his desk and left, shutting the door behind him.

"The last time I tried to get a visa, it took two weeks, and that was the equivalent of the speed of light by Soviet standards. Now, with Russia, how could things be more efficient? I'm screwed—we're screwed."

After seeming to inventory the top of the director's desk, Michael said: "There are two possibilities. Plan B is that I take the icon myself. I don't need a visa because I have a Russian passport. But Plan A is better, and that will require me to see some people today. Maybe I can't get a visa in a day, but why not try?"

"Because you were followed here," she said, "and the minute you step outside, at best they will follow you and at worst grab you and pull out your fingernails until you tell them what is going on."

"You have a point."

They sat, she on the edge of the desk, he where the lab director had been.

She said, "The truck will arrive at 11:00, assuming everything goes as planned."

"So I get in the truck, the back of the truck, and it takes me out of here. Simple. But I need some money to grease the wheels of Mother Russia's bureaucracy."

"How much?"

"Two thousand. Maybe it will take less. If it takes more, it can't be done."

"We need a meeting place and time," she said. "If you can't get back here by three o'clock, go directly to JFK and meet me at the KLM international counter. I will have the icon—unless I don't—and then I suppose there isn't much sense in going."

She looked at him and thought she should make some declaration about how, in spite of the agonies of the last several days, she had never been more fully alive. Partings seldom yield pure truth, and she was unable to articulate the tones of her heart.

They clung to each other.

THE DAY BEFORE, LARA HAD GIVEN ANOTHER SOMETIMES opera singer, well, a spear carrier really, $500 and now, using a Metropolitan Opera van with appropriate lettering on the side, he stopped by a pawnshop on Forty-Seventh Street. The proprietor had assured Lara when she phoned that he had both a double bass and a cello in fine playing order, and that they would be a bargain at any price. If the sort-of singer could obtain them both for less than $500, the change was his. He did well for himself.

Still double-parked in front of the pawnshop, blocking the street, as is the duty of all New York City delivery trucks, he carried the double bass and the cello to the back of the truck where he put each in a sarcophagus-like case bearing the inscription: "Property of Lincoln Center Chamber Orchestra." The case for the double bass was eighty-eight inches tall, forty inches wide, and twenty-five inches deep, tapering gradually at the top so that it looked something like a burnished aluminum container for a stand-up mummy. It had wheels on the bottom. The cello case could have been the mummy's adolescent child.

Precisely at 11:00 a.m. the singer/spear-carrier/teamster backed the Metropolitan Opera truck into the Metropolitan Museum's loading dock, the guard raised the door, the two instruments were unloaded, and Michael Solak slipped into the rear. The driver didn't know about this part, but he earned $200 more for it. It was easy money and certainly no sweat for one accustomed to the stage.

⁂

A DISPLAY MAKER IS TO A MUSEUM WHAT A MILLWRIGHT is to a mill. He can fix anything, find anything, arrange anything, and fulfill the most fanciful requests of deranged exhibit designers. He is a boatwright, a cabinetmaker, and an artist of consummate skill. Freddy had assigned his best display maker to fulfill Lara's every whim.

The display maker's creations are seldom acknowledged by museumgoers, but they are the musical score of a movie, the staff of a successful politician, the band of a rock star. Without them, the main course is dry, lifeless, and naked.

In the conservation laboratory, Lara wrapped the icon back in its brown paper and plastic and sealed it with packing tape, sticking the rest of the roll in her shoulder bag, just in case. Then she realized she couldn't carry the icon by herself and asked the display maker to lend not only his talent but also his brawn.

When they reached his workspace, she pointed to the cello and said: "That is window dressing. The action is with the big guy." The double bass case opened with multiple latches revealing a well-used, but apparently serviceable instrument, complete with bow. The case was generic, with adjustable rubber shoulders that could slip into place to hold the instrument firmly, taking into account that double basses are not uniform in size or curvature.

"It's like remodeling a bathroom," he said. "First you have to do demolition," and with an economy of movement, he stripped out the foam padding. Then, with a flurry of measurements and angles and calculations and more measurements, he said, as he whistled through his teeth, "Measure twice and cut once."

His saws screeched, and his drills whined, and with wood and velvet padding, he created a cocoon for the icon. He slipped it in, turned four padded arms to hold it in place, and said, "Now comes the hard part."

He launched into another whirlwind of measurements, whistling through his teeth like a neglected kettle, this time on the double bass itself and then on the case and then the instrument again. With a pencil and tape he made a number of marks on the resonating box of the double bass, loosened the strings, picked up a drill, and cut a half-inch hole in the top of the box just below the neck. "Burr hole like a brain surgeon," he said.

Then, with an electric reciprocating saw he flashed Lara a maniacal grin and said, "Kill your baby for ya, lady?" He inserted the saw blade and began cutting the back off the bass. He cut the sound box all the way around, completely removing the back. He measured again, nodded, and affixed a rubber bumper all around the remaining portion of the sides. He then tightened, but did not attempt to tune, the strings and laid the instrument, or what was left of it, in the case, affixing four more padded arms to hold it firmly in place. He turned to Lara and said: "They open the case, you are OK. They lift out the bass, and your mail goes to Siberia."

CHAPTER 18

Trying to Fly

F reddy came striding into the workshop. He wore a tan suit with a broad, faint, chalk stripe in white. The pant legs broke fully in the front and hung perfectly straight in the back to the top of his Bally cordovan tassel loafers with paper thin soles. A blue tab collar shirt, navy and white geometrically checked tie, and a pocket silk emerging with casual forethought from his breast pocket completed the ensemble—a Park Avenue haberdasher's dream.

"I have spent the last forty-five minutes fending off the parries of a great big FBI agent named George Graham, who, as we speak, is sitting in my office upstairs. He has threatened to shut down the place and search, room by room, artifact by artifact, until they find you, and I have no doubt that he means it."

"You didn't tell him I was here, did you?"

"I didn't have to tell him you are here. His troops saw you sprint in here like a mule deer with a cougar on her tail. All I could say, and I kept saying it over and over, is that the Met is a big institution—several city blocks worth—and I had no idea where you were. Right now I am supposed to be going to the bathroom. You had best remove yourself before he really does close the place down and search it inch by inch."

"Freddy, you are such a sweetheart." She stood on her tiptoes and kissed him on the cheek. "All you have to do is give me a Met truck that will haul me and these two mummies to the airport, and you can go back to your rarified world of stealing art from the auction houses."

WHILE SHE WAS SITTING ON THE WHEEL WELL OF THE museum's step van, she mused that the two vehicles that had assisted her this morning were both Metros—the Metropolitan Opera's and this one. Maybe Michael was right—the hard shining light of the Metropolitans of Great and Small and All of the Other Russias were watching over them and giving them succor. She shivered. To trust in religion was contrary to everything her imperfectly understood life had taught her.

She was way too early. It was five and a half hours before their flight and instead of hunkering down in the bowels of the museum, she was exposed in an airport with few hidey-holes and probably lots of FBI and foreign assassins searching for her increasingly famous face. Plus, she had these two huge instrument cases in tow, and she couldn't handle them by herself. Skycaps had taken them to the KLM desk, but it was too early to check in and passengers had to have their luggage with them when they did. Michael wouldn't be here for two hours, that is, if he made it at all.

She made friends with one of the KLM employees, a blond Dutch boy of the "I will dispatch my duty but under no circumstances will I smile" school by playing the helpless female in distress gig, and he allowed as how he would be working until five o'clock, and since she had graciously opened the cases to show that they actually contained musical instruments, he would watch them for her while he assisted other passengers. She thanked him and told him he spoke better English than she.

Lara skittered off to the United Airlines Red Carpet Club lounge, where she talked her way in with some razzmatazz about having applied for a card but it must have miscarried in the mail and yes, she would gladly fill out another application. After she had gone to all that trouble, she discovered that Estelle had a card in her purse. I truly don't know who I am supposed to be these days, she thought.

She poured herself a cup of coffee that rattled on the saucer as she walked to the most remote corner of the lounge. There she pretended to read a magazine for the next two hours during which time she went to the bathroom four times—pregame jitters—and reviewed in her mind for the fortieth time "The Plan," or at least its remaining elements. "The Plan" goes out the window the moment the battle begins. Somebody famous said that—probably a dead guy.

Michael's plan took them to St. Petersburg, where they would be met by his friend from the Russian State Museum, whisked through customs (hopefully having bribed the appropriate officials), and the experts at the Museum would verify that the icon was legit. With the comfort of that second opinion, they would then take the train to Moscow and, in a glorious public event with all sorts of world press, present it to Madam Doctor Kopulskaya, who would test it, embrace it, and celebrate its return.

That was "The Plan."

KIPRENSKY WAS NOT ABOVE RESORTING TO THE TRUTH; sometimes circumstances encouraged it. Nor did he feel any shame in being found a stranger to it. Truth telling was just not very high on his personal list of virtues. What he told Betty Sorensen in their latest phone call was that Aker should have sent the icon, through the Buyer, back to Russia. The Buyer (Golchev was really a rat, didn't she think?) had failed to complete this last stage of the return, that is, he had absconded with the icon.

If Golchev had just disappeared, he, Kiprensky, would have one set of options. But according to his sources, Golchev was looking for the icon, too, which meant that perhaps they—Presidents Kiprensky and Sorensen—could work together. What troubled Kiprensky's devious mind, however, was the thought that President Sorensen might know a whole lot more about where the icon was than she let on. He didn't buy her grandmotherly bullshit for a moment.

Ah, what fun it was to play the total annihilation card. He had it in his arsenal, and she did, too, but he was willing to lay it on the table and she wasn't.

She should agree, he suggested, that this was no time for recriminations. If she would just find the real icon, which must be around somewhere in the United States, and return it to him, he would not be forced to obliterate her Moscow Embassy. Maybe, just maybe, if she cooperated, the world would not have to be destroyed.

He was, he insisted, a reasonable man.

KLM FLIGHT 642 WAS SCHEDULED TO LEAVE FOR Amsterdam at 6:50 p.m. Michael arrived at the airport at 5:46 p.m. Lara knew, because she had looked at her watch every five minutes from 3:00 o'clock on. At 3:30 she had put on the blond wig, abandoned the Red Carpet Lounge, and spent her time trying to decide whether she was less conspicuous standing beside the two mummies or trying somehow to blend into the airport shuffle. She chose what was probably the worst of her options: she did one and then the other. By the time he arrived she was a mass of undifferentiated anxiety.

"Got it," he said.

She grabbed him. "What did you have to give?"

"Don't ask, but it cost less than you might think."

"What?"

"I'll tell you on the plane."

Lara handed the agent her ticket and passport, without having looked at the newly acquired visa.

"Good afternoon, Ms. Stiles," said the agent.

Lara started, realizing that she almost didn't react to her name. She smiled and shook her head, saying, "I don't like to fly." He continued to look at her quizzically, holding the passport photo.

Oh shit, she thought, he is going to say it isn't me, but instead he said, "You have changed your hair" at which point Lara whipped off the wig, and mumbled something about being completely discombobulated, which wasn't far from the truth.

"Flying is safer than driving," said the agent apparently dismissing all thoughts of trickery from one who couldn't find her ass with both hands.

Lara's theory about checking in was that if you don't pay any attention to the pursing of lips and tapping of keys as the agent searches for your reservation, everything will be fine. After five minutes of tapping and grimacing, it was clear that everything was not fine. The agent was explaining Lara's problem to the person on the other end of the phone: "I have an oversized piece of luggage, eighty-eight by forty by twenty-five, tapered, not rectangular."

He listened.

"I know what the tariffs are. I need to know if it will fit."

He listened some more. Then he turned to Lara and said, "Ms. Stiles, what is this thing?"

"It's a musical instrumental—you know, like when you see the symphony orchestra, and these people standing in back are sawing away on what looks like a Jurassic violin?"

The agent looked confused.

"A jazz combo. The guy who stands in back plucking the big tall wooden thing with strings?"

His face brightened, he nodded and returned to his call: "Two hundred and forty kilos of volume at $2.50 a kilo. That's fine, but it's a 737 from Amsterdam to St. Petersburg, not a 747 like we're flying across the Atlantic." He listened and said, "I knew you would get it sooner or later."

He waited.

Michael waited.

Lara, or whoever she was, waited.

The ticket agents of various nations waited, on alert for Lara or Michael or both.

The other end of the phone came back to life, and Lara's

agent said, "Are you sure?" Listened some more, wrote down a couple of names, said "Thanks," and hung up.

Lara stood like a criminal in the dock waiting to be sentenced.

"It's too big," the agent said. "The cargo door on a 737 is 34 inches by 48 inches, but according to that man's chart, the maximum length is 76 inches because the plane body is so narrow, they can't turn it once they get it in the door."

Lara's self-loathing had reached its nadir yesterday when she had realized her visa oversight. Now she regarded herself a moron too foolish to function. She had no energy even for expletives.

The agent said, "My cargo department suggests that you send your instruments through a freight forwarder like Emery or Airborne. It would be cheaper for you, too."

Michael asked if they could step out of line for a moment to talk.

Surely they could.

Tears worked their way into the corners of Lara's eyes. She was exhausted, physically and emotionally, and her brain simply could not cope. Michael put his arms around her and nuzzled her ear, just holding her for a moment. Then he said, "The only reason for these monster cases is disguise. It is like Hannibal building structures on top of his camels so they would look like elephants to the Romans. Maybe we weren't smart enough, but there's no sense in donning sack cloth and ashes. (The religious reference didn't do much to cheer Lara.) The only option I see is to ditch these cases and carry the icon on the same way we did between Washington and here.

Lara sniffed, drew a long breath, and decided she couldn't just curl up and die. She would see this clambake through to the end. She elbowed her way back to the ticket agent who was just finishing with an ordinary customer with ordinary baggage and ordinary traveler's anxiety and declared that they would use freight forwarders and therefore had no bags to check.

The agent activated the obligatory smile and said, "The smaller fiddle is no problem; it fits within the size guidelines."

"No, never mind," said Lara. "They can keep each other company." The ticket agent thought that was cute.

He handed Lara back her ticket and passport and reached out to Michael for his ticket. He gave him both the ticket and his passport. He looked at both and then at Michael. "The passport says your name is Solak, but the name on the ticket is Ivanovitch?"

"That's right," said Michael, with a thousand-watt grin. "My first two names are Michael and Ivanovitch. Apparently, the ticket agent made a mistake. The first two names on the passport are on the ticket, and the ticket is fully paid for, so it shouldn't be a problem."

But it was a problem, so he called his supervisor, again. And waited, again.

Finally he nodded, finished the ticket, and handed it back with his passport saying that he had changed the passenger manifest to reflect Michael's correct name.

Bugger.

Michael rolled the larger instrument case into the handicapped stall in the men's room where he removed The Mother of God. Lara hailed a passing skycap with a hand truck and said, "Would you mind taking my cello out to the arriving passenger pickup? My ride is meeting me there?" She handed him a fiver and said she would be along shortly.

Michael came toward her, walking fast, carrying the icon wrapped as it had been before. She picked up both of their bags—the one she had bought yesterday and his athletic bag that couldn't contain much more than a few changes of underwear and perhaps a clean shirt, and they headed for the metal detectors that blocked the concourse.

He carried the icon through the people arch since it was too big for the conveyor belt that X-rayed the carry-on luggage. The officer with the handheld metal detector waved his wand around it, paused at what was undoubtedly the bullet lodged in the back of the wood, and passed them on with a casual wave of his hand. It didn't look like a weapon, beep like a weapon, and as far as they were concerned, it was none of their business whether it was a legitimate carry-on.

At the gate, a seemingly belated poster warned: "Travel to Russia is not advised by the United States government. The safety of citizens traveling in Russia cannot be guaranteed. Any travel to Russia, until further notice, should be deemed at the traveler's own risk."

"I suspect our ticket agent would have told us that, too, if he had not been distracted by our luggage."

"One more hurdle to cross," said Michael.

"Jump. You jump hurdles," said Lara. "But it is not too late to chicken out, if you want."

"Never," said Michael. "And when is any traveler anywhere really safe anyway?"

He told the flight attendant at the gate that he had a very large carry-on object that was also fragile, but she waved him down the jetway, saying that they were already beyond pushback time: "Talk to the attendant at the door." The steward at the door thought it might fit behind the last row and seats. They already knew the drill.

GEORGE GRAHAM KNEW THAT WITH THE COMPLICITY of a good part of the art world of New York, Lara and the person she was with had eluded both the FBI and Boris Golchev's lethal associates and were on their way somewhere. It took a little longer to figure out where. The bomb squad had been alerted to two abandoned pieces of luggage. The cello case was hand X-rayed and found benign; the double bass case was also not a bomb, but the curious configuration of the case suggested it had held something the owner wished to conceal, and with some detecting, that led them back to the KLM desk and ultimately to a Barbara Stiles who was traveling with Michael Ivanovitch Solak, a person traceable to the Metropolitan Museum, and bingo, they had their fugitives on their way to St. Petersburg.

The FBI confiscated both instruments as evidence—of what they were not entirely sure.

By the time the detecting had been done, the passenger manifests examined, the names researched, and the conclusions drawn, i.e., that Barbara Stiles was Lara Cole, their plane had landed in Amsterdam and presumably they were already in the air on another flight to St. Petersburg.

One encouraging byproduct of their fruitless attempt to prevent Lara and Michael from leaving the United States was that they had snared three more of Boris Golchev's operatives, two of whom closely matched the descriptions of the assailants who had murdered Wesley Foster at Akerhill.

The passenger manifest showed no record of either Barbara Stiles or Michael Solak checking luggage, but the specially rigged double bass case spoke volumes, not only of their ingenuity and determination, but of their increased vulnerability—not to mention the vulnerability of the icon—since they were carrying it without benefit of disguise.

George Graham didn't exactly hold it against Freddy for his complicity in assisting Lara's escape; he simply made it clear that if Lara ended up dead, Graham would personally knock Freddy senseless before he charged him with enough federal offenses to put him away for at least four score and seven. He then required Freddy to stay with him for the rest of the evening while they tried in vain to catch up with Lara.

That is how it happened that Freddy was sitting with George Graham in the New York offices of the FBI at midnight. The FBI director, having been briefed by Graham over the phone, was at the White House with Betty Sorensen, her chief of staff, and assorted other presidential advisers, of whom the chairman of the National Endowment for the Arts was not one.

They had adequate time to warn Kiprensky that Lara and The Mother of God were headed his way, but the question was: should they? No one was keen on trusting Kiprensky, who could make both Lara and the icon disappear, or hold her as hostage, or claim the icon was bogus, or any number of other scenarios that they could neither predict nor control. Of course, he could welcome The Mother of God back and end the crisis, but it was now clear that he would do so only if he could gain from it either politically or financially. He was a rapacious bastard, they all agreed.

They knew from Freddy that Lara intended to return it to the Tretyakov Museum in Moscow and that Michael had positively authenticated it. So why were they headed for St. Petersburg? None of their moves to this point had been random, except when they had no option but to flee.

In Moscow the tanks were still just sitting around the US embassy. If Kiprensky were really serious, he would have cut off the water and power. The president rubbed her eyes. She hated these all-night sessions sitting around trying to figure out the least unacceptable alternative to insoluble problems, but that was her job, and by god, she would do it.

"I'll call Kiprensky," she concluded, "but I am not going to tell him everything that we know. I will ask questions and see if we can figure out what he is thinking. In the meantime, we had best get our agents on a plane to Moscow about as fast as we can. Moscow is likely where the action will be. I'll tell Kiprensky they are coming."

When the FBI director called Graham from the White House to tell him he was going to Moscow, Graham turned to Freddy and said, "I hope you brought your toothbrush. Since you know what this Solak guy looks like, you are going to get a maybe not so free trip courtesy of your Uncle Sam."

BORIS GOLCHEV KNEW MOST OF WHAT GEORGE GRAHAM did, but he was a few hours behind. Only when airline personnel changed shifts at 7:00 a.m. was he able to secure the passenger manifest. Then he had to do some sleuthing to confirm that Solak must be Lara's helper and that the two of them had flown to St. Petersburg. He also learned that he was increasingly shorthanded, as his men (and women) were being picked off by the American authorities. Annoying. But this business had now shifted to Russia—not his home country, but a place where there was no lack of personnel dedicated to recovery of Ukraine's most sacred object.

He faxed all the information he had, including photographs of Lara and Michael, to his associates in St. Petersburg and Moscow, and hoped that they would be able to catch up with and separate Cole and Solak from the icon, and if necessary, from their lives. Then he would attend to the increasingly urgent business of disappearing. He had learned much from the *Dukhi* of Afghanistan.

MICHAEL WAS EXPLAINING TO LARA THAT AIRLINE travel was enhanced by a few sleep-inducing shots of Stoli. He also regretted not having had the leisure to quaff a few before their departure. Russian lore has it that sitting down ensures a successful trip. Lara assured him that she had done enough sitting for both of them to have a most prosperous journey.

She was still twitching in her seat, trying, from the backs of the heads, to determine if any passengers constituted a threat. If anybody on the plane was after them, he or she would have gotten a plenty good look as they paraded the wrapped icon down the aisle to its resting place behind the last row of seats. Since they were about the last ones on and the doors shut immediately, anyone wishing to do them harm would have had little opportunity.

"What makes you think we can even get into Russia," Lara asked.

He smiled enigmatically, the warmth of the Stoli having loosened him up, "I have friends."

"You mean like your friends wherever it was that you got the visa? And by the way, is it real or forged? And how much did it cost? You promised full disclosure."

"It doesn't matter if it is forged or legit as long as it works. It cost less than you might think. You, or rather Estelle Aker, paid $1,000 for the benefit of the agent at the Russian Consulate in New York. A forgery would have cost more. It will cost another $1,000, which I will deliver in cash to his father in Moscow. If I fail to deliver the second $1,000 within two days, he will alert the Russian authorities, and you will spend the rest of your life in jail there. Pretty good deal, wouldn't you say?"

"Your friends in St. Petersburg?" inquired Lara, "They just let us walk through customs without any questions?"

"You might be able to do that anyway without any bribes. You look like the innocent type to me."

"Oh, sure, carrying Russia's patrimony, wrapped in brown paper with a bullet smashed into the back—that wouldn't attract much attention, would it? By the way, I can't carry it—too heavy."

"We are supposed to be met at the gate and taken to the VIP lounge where I use Estelle's dollars for a little inconspicuous palm greasing. Then we are escorted to a van that whisks us off to the Russian State Museum."

"How much does all this cost?"

"When a museum director makes the equivalent of $60 per month, and a guard or customs official $20, a $2,000 bribe is enough to retire on."

She sat back with Estelle's purse and counted. "I've got $4,400, left so bribe accordingly."

LARA LIMITED HERSELF TO ONE GLASS OF RED WINE WITH dinner and fell asleep, her head on a pillow wedged against Michael's shoulder. She loved him and asleep or awake, every moment with him was a treasure.

They were met at the gate by several people Michael seemed to know, one of whom gave Lara a single rose wrapped in cellophane. The VIP lounge had far too many men and women in uniform standing around looking as if they had very little to do. Michael took her passport and disappeared, leaving her to shift her red rose from one hand to the other as the cellophane crinkled. Finally, he returned and picked up the icon with a tense, "Follow me."

To his back as he was hurrying toward an exit door, she said, "You didn't give me back my passport."

"I have it," he said over his shoulder, practically running into the man in front of him who had stopped abruptly. Just outside the door, a group of men were scuffling. An automatic weapon fell to the pavement along with part of a tooth. They were motioned into a small black van as two men continued to kick a fallen combatant in the head and ribs. The sound of boots on flesh, as much as the sight, prompted nausea that Lara only partly relieved by putting her head between her knees.

St. Petersburg is a beautiful city bisected by the Neva River that, in turn, surrounds a number of islands linked by broad bridges. The narrow spire of the Cathedral of Peter and Paul graces one island, the glorious Hermitage Museum, once the palace of the Czars, another bank, and on still another, Peter the Great's Kunstkamera Museum, where he offered tea and vodka to entice his countrymen to view the "rarities, oddities, and curiosities." Lara saw none of this from the back of the windowless van, nor did she see the glorious St. Isaac's Cathedral, the imposing Nevsky Prospekt Boulevard, nor Etienne Falconet's bronze statue of Peter the Great on a rearing stallion.

At the loading dock of the Russian State Museum several blocks off Nevsky Prospekt, she was kissed wetly on both cheeks by a large bear of a man with a full red beard and hair that spiked out toward all points of the compass. He had a galaxy of freckles, half glasses on a chain, and a deep, rumbling Russian laugh.

But his pleasure at meeting Lara evaporated before the effervescence of The Mother of God. His laboratory was not modern by the Metropolitan Museum's standards, but it was well-equipped enough to verify the authenticity of Russian art.

Here there were no secrets. Half a dozen of the bearded man's colleagues gathered around the table talking excitedly and making suggestions. Michael sat back against a wall, arms folded in a proprietary manner like a well-satisfied cook watching diners consume his creation.

Now familiar techniques were repeated. With two fine needles, the smallest bit of pigment was lifted from a crack on the surface of the painting and then analyzed under high-powered microscopes, run through the spectrograph, chemically tested, and compared against the computer's database.

⁂

THE X-RAY SHOWED NO UNEXPECTED OBJECTS SAVE FOR the slug from Golchev's henchman's gun, which they did not need an X-ray machine to locate, but it triggered much excited conversation after Michael explained how it got there. Lara did not need to understand Russian to glean that even men of their scientific sophistication believed totally in the icon's power to protect human life.

She is selective, thought Lara, and fickle.

Food arrived and Lara ate it. Then tea was served, and the curators and scientists and experts continued to investigate. Finally the bearded man conferred with Michael, they embraced, touching both cheeks and kissing on the lips (an old Russian custom back in vogue), and the procession retraced its steps back to the van. It was still light at slightly after 11:00 p.m. They would drive a few blocks down Nevsky Prospekt to the station where they would catch the midnight train for Moscow.

CHAPTER 19

Third Run

L ara stood with her small shoulder bag at her feet. The Mother of God leaned against a wooden bench. The Baltic sky was semi-dark with vapor swirling—a film noir setting near midnight on a train platform. In St. Petersburg. In Russia. In danger. Indescribably tired.

The Moscow Station is one of five major train stations in St. Petersburg, each handling traffic in a different direction: to Moscow, Finland, Poland, the Baltic, and East. She had changed to her running shoes, although to where she would run she had no idea. If she tried to flee, she could carry the icon about five yards by herself and then would probably drop it. No, she wasn't about to abandon it even to save her life.

Michael returned with tickets for a sleeper compartment. "I asked," he said, "whether they could produce a passenger manifest like an airline."

"And?"

"In typical Russian fashion, it is technically possible but practically not. Their computer is down and has been 'as long as the memory of man runneth not to the contrary.'"

"This is good," said Lara.

"Good but not great. Someone could bribe an official to

go through the list manually. It takes longer, but if we are not actually seen on the platform or on the train then we should be home free."

Lara was bone weary, and the more her energy flagged, the more susceptible was her mind to doubt—of her mission, her courage, her self-discipline, her sanity.

Harder must be the heart
Spirit the bolder
Courage the greater
As strength grows less.

Beowulf, she thought—a staple of her medieval studies.

As she followed Michael down the platform to their track, each face, every traveler, presented as a possible assassin. Her senses were fried; her judgment depleted.

The platform for track eight stretched seemingly for miles with trains on either side, their compressors kicking on and off as the conductors and baggage men smoked and talked in small groups. Michael stopped short of the car that held their compartment, thinking it wise to wait away from their destination. The platform was crowded. All around were luggage carts piled high with steamer trunks, suitcases, and garment bags. Handsome couples were talking in loud, animated voices.

LARA'S SINGULAR COMBINATION OF ANXIETY, EXHAUSTION, and disorientation prevented her, at first, from realizing that the conversations around her were in English. Not English-English, but American-English.

Lara learned from an attractive woman with dark curly hair standing next to her that she, and forty-nine others like her, had been the winners of the Mrs. America Pageants in each of their respective states. A promoter, whose father was Russian, had spent over two years preparing for a combined pageant of Russian and American women that had just taken place in St. Petersburg.

If Lara had tried to imagine a less likely scenario than encountering American beauty pageant contestants at midnight on a train platform in Russia while she was running for her life with an icon that was the equivalent of an atomic bomb...Its improbability, indeed, its utter absurdity, reduced it to the ordinary.

The curly-haired woman was from Idaho and explained that she and her fellow contestants had been in St. Petersburg for a week to prepare for the pageant. She had to bring the steamer trunk and six suitcases because she had dozens of costumes.

Was she sponsored?

No, this was something one did because it was "fun." From the diamonds on her fingers, it was apparent that money was no consideration. She told Lara that her husband had joined her for the last three days of the contest and now they were going to see Moscow.

"It's amazing, really," said the woman. "I came here with all of these costumes for every conceivable stage or lighting condition or even for whether on the given day I would feel prettier in green or blue, and the Russian women we met—you wouldn't believe it—were sewing their one and only costume on the afternoon before the pageant."

"Really?" injected Lara wittily.

"And makeup? They just didn't have any. I loaned them

my lipsticks and, finally, gave them some as going away presents, but I still have a ton of makeup. I have wigs—they thought that was the funniest thing—wigs at a beauty contest, but I like to look nice even when I am not on stage, and sometimes I am just too pooped from the stress of it all to fix my own hair."

Stress, thought Lara. I could tell you a few things about that.

The conductor's whistle signaled that the train was ready for boarding, and the fifty contestants, thirty-five husbands, Lara, Michael, and, she hoped, no others who cared about their presence there boarded the train.

The compartments were small, with a bunk on either side of the narrow center aisle. Against the window was a small ledge and above each bunk, a reading light and shelf for ordinary-sized luggage.

Oaths and grunts emanated from across the aisle as two of the husbands tried to wedge the huge trunk of Lara's new friend into their compartment. After much bitching about why it wasn't stowed in the baggage car (a well-founded fear of theft), they got it in, but it claimed one of the beds since it would not fit between them. Once the rest of their luggage had been crammed into the compartment, there was room for sitting, but no one was going to be lying down.

The presence of the festive Americans had relaxed Lara and lightened her mood. With their pageant over, they would see the sights of Moscow before returning to the United States. Even if the agents of Russia or Ukraine or the United States caught up with her, this group would provide a marvelous diversion.

In their own compartment, the icon was in the aisle between the bunks, like a puritan's bundling board. The train, more subtle than a jet engine's challenge to inertia, was gaining speed before they realized they had left the station. They locked the compartment door and pulled the curtains even though the danger seemed slight. Lara jumped at a business-like rap on the door, which then burst open without pause. So much for the lock. A woman with a tea cart inquired whether they would like tea. She handed each a steaming hot glass container in a metal base with a mug handle. To each she gave two cookies, two long lumps of sugar wrapped in purple and green paper, and a wish for a pleasant journey.

The compartment was clean, the sheets crisp and starched. Tea added a civilizing effect, wonderful in its simplicity. They sipped and chatted sitting shoulder to shoulder on a bunk. Shoulders touching is a great comfort—one they both needed.

The train was now going full speed, and while the countryside was still visible in the lingering midnight light, the rocking and the tea and the sense of well-being made Lara desperately sleepy. She took off her dress and underwear, thinking how unselfconscious she was in Michael's presence. Tomorrow she would analyze that. Having no night gown, she talked Michael out of a T-shirt, put her underpants back on, and climbed into a bunk.

Two hours later, Lara jerked awake at a scraping sound. She sensed a shape moving in the darkness by her head. She fumbled for the reading lamp and twisted the switch.

"Sorry," said Michael. "It's the tea." He was working at the latches on the window, finally pinching both simultaneously and letting a rush of warm, diesel-laced air into the compartment.

"Why don't you go to the bathroom like a normal person?"

"I just came from there. It has a quarter inch of green-yellow slime on the floor, a stench that surely can't be human, and a single hole over which you are supposed to accommodate nature. My choice is to whiz out the window, which I am about to do."

"Wait," said Lara, sitting up and scooting behind him. "I know about spitting into the wind."

Now awake, Lara felt the same tea syndrome as Michael. "I am going to the bathroom, smelly or not."

"You'll be sorry."

LARA WOULD BE VERY SORRY, INDEED.

SHE OPENED THE DOOR TO THEIR COMPARTMENT AND was reassured by the raucous laughter of the Mrs. America contestants' husbands, for whom the pageant was a continuous party. She turned the knob of the bathroom door at the end of the compartment, but it was locked. From inside came the unmistakable sounds of retching that would make the place even less hospitable than Michael had found it.

The magnitude of her mistake in venturing out was unrelated to bodily functions, however. It had everything to do with the man who was looking through the glass door of the next car. He slid back out of sight as their eyes met.

Lara fled back to their compartment, turning the worthless lock. "They are out there. Some man was watching me."

"When you were in the bathroom?"

"As I was trying to get into the bathroom. It was locked, and a man was watching me through the window at the end of the next car."

"How do you know he was looking for you?"

"Well, I didn't interview him, but it spooked me. I saw him pull back when I saw him. I know I am paranoid, but he looked the same as all of those other men who were chasing and shooting at us in the United States."

Michael did not answer, but he began pulling on his pants and shoes.

THE TANKS AND PERSONNEL CARRIERS SURROUNDING the US embassy made no attempt to impede traffic in or out. The battle-dressed Marines at the gate, on the other hand, inspected all vehicles meticulously, using mirrors to check for bombs underneath, and only when completely satisfied did they perform the rifle salute to invite entry.

The Marine guards and the nearest of the Russian tank crews had established a friendly camaraderie of fellow combatants who can joke and pass the time of day until told whether they are required to kill each other.

The White House had instructed the embassy to fetch George Graham from the airport. A standard Ford Econovan, government navy blue with the great seal of the United States on the doors, was waiting when he and the two other FBI agents arrived along with one bemused and uncharacteristically rumpled Metropolitan Museum director.

Betty Sorensen had talked not once, but twice to Pavel Kiprensky since the midnight meeting in which she learned that Lara Cole and The Mother of God were headed east. In the first conversation, she told Kiprensky that the United States was proceeding on the assumption that what was stolen from Akerhill Museum was not the icon loaned by Kiprensky's government.

Should Kiprensky be so inclined, he might station some agents at the St. Petersburg airport in time to meet the 3:05 KLM flight just in case someone might be there to harm Cole and Solak or their most precious cargo.

Kiprensky would seriously consider such a request, he said. She also advised him not to intercept them but to allow them to proceed. Again, he noted her request, although it annoyed him that he was unable to parse the truth from the bullshit in her statements.

In the second conversation Kiprensky told her that Cole and Solak had landed in St. Petersburg, that his Russian police had caught some hooligans who might have had evil designs on them, but those interrogations so far had been inconclusive. He said the icon was taken to the Russian Museum, that it and Solak and Cole had boarded the train for Moscow, and that in all probability both his agents and those of some other entity were watching them.

Sorensen hoped that she and Kiprensky could arrange a simultaneous press conference in Moscow and Washington to announce The Mother of God's return to the Tretyakov Museum, an event that she expected would happen as soon as the train from St. Petersburg arrived. Although Kiprensky was back up to speed, he had not had time to think through the various scenarios to find the one that would most benefit him, and thus he demurred to President Sorensen's suggestion.

She said sweetly, "Now, I know you may have some difficulty arranging a press conference on such short notice (his international clock showed that it was past midnight in Washington), but I have mine all set up here for three hours from now."

Christ—a press conference at 3:00 o'clock in the morning?

"So you can just figure I am going to go ahead and tell the press that we have returned the icon. If you can have yours at the same time, we both will be at the party."

She will stick it to me regardless of whether I join the parade.

"One other thing," she said, "no, actually two. I assume you will send your tanks back to the armory at the time of the press conference. The other thing is that three of my trusted FBI agents are there at our embassy, and they would be happy to coordinate with you should coordination be necessary. The head agent is George Graham. I would think your countrymen would be overjoyed, so you can have yourselves a fine celebration."

Kiprensky, having no useful reply to President Sorensen's artful maneuvering, did the next best thing, which was to thank her cordially and ring off.

WHAT LARA AND MICHAEL DISCUSSED AS THEY WERE hurriedly dressing on the swaying train could hardly be called a plan. A plan suggests careful fact gathering; sorting of options; assembly of men and materials; consultation with experts. Of those qualities they had bubkes. Assuming that the person Lara had seen in the next railcar was hostile, they had to stem their panic and avoid him. They also had to assume he was not alone.

Delivery of the icon to the Tretyakov remained the

primary objective. To that end, Lara, now wearing Estelle Aker's blond wig, stepped out of the compartment and hammered insistently on the door of the dark-haired Mrs. America contestant.

I didn't ask her how she did in the contest, thought Lara.

The door popped open and without ceremony, Lara pushed herself in, closed the door, and locked it. Just inside the door is as far as she got because their luggage and two fairly well inebriated humans exhausted the room's capacity.

Lara declined the proffered drink. She then explained, as cogently as she could to her impaired audience, what she had in mind.

This was not easy.

Initially, it was all jokes, first the husband and then the beauty queen singing snatches of "Strangers in the Night" punctuated with gales of laughter and other alcohol fueled witticisms. Finally Mrs. America (why not give her the benefit of the doubt) said, "Sure, dump out all those dresses and bring it over. I should have given them to the poor Russian ladies anyway. I'm going to get a whole new wardrobe when I get home because I'm a WINNER!" And she toasted herself with her empty glass.

Michael brought in The Mother of God and then returned to their own compartment because there simply wasn't room for all of them in Mrs. America's. With great difficulty, and sweating and cursing on the part of Mr. America, the icon did fit, slant from the bottom corner to the opposite corner on top, and the trunk did close and latch. Lara reopened it and used the gowns to pad the trunk which Mrs. America found hilarious.

"Padded gowns," she burbled. "If I could get by with it I would have won by acclamation. She showed absolutely no curiosity about what Lara was wedging into her trunk, but she did study Lara carefully as the packing and padding was going on.

"Sweetie, you need to do something with your hair and makeup. You are a very pretty girl with nice broad shoulders and good boobs, but you look like you cut your hair yourself in the dark.

"It's a wig," said Lara.

Gales of laughter. When she recovered, Mrs. America said, "I thought I could spot a falsie or a hip pad or a buntucker from a block away. I must really be three sheets gone if I can't spot a whole wig." She dissolved into another paroxysm of giggles that brought tears to her eyes and an affectionate punch on the shoulder from hubby.

"I've got it," said Mrs. America. "I can't sleep while this train is shaking around, so you are my pupil. I'll teach you how to get yourself together and the tricks of the beauty trade—like spraying Firm Grip on your butt before you put on your bathing suit—and then you and that cute boyfriend of yours can get married, and you can be Mrs. America next year."

My life determined at last, thought Lara.

Mrs. America, having decided to be entertained, was not to be denied. Other suitcases disgorged makeup kits and mirrors and wigs—everything but a Lancôme delivery truck.

Lara said, "Make me look as different as you possibly can. I mean different from the way I look without this wig."

"The wig is clearly not you," and then, as if she had farted in the receiving line, Mrs. America stopped and said,

"Where are my manners? I don't even know your name. Tell me your name."

This confused Lara. Barbara Stiles did not seem necessary for this company, so she said, "Lara Cole." And for the rest of the makeup session, she was called "Laura." Hubby even burst out with a few bars of "Laura, is a face in a misty night, footsteps that you hear down the hall..." before he slumped into the corner and passed out.

No question about it, Mrs. America wielded a mean eyebrow pencil, and her 100 proof condition did not affect the steadiness of her hand one iota. With shadow and rouge, she raised Lara's cheekbones and narrowed her eyes to look slightly Asian, maybe Tartar.

She then extracted an elegant mandarin collar dress of green summer wool from yet another suitcase (she seemed to have a filing system that allowed her to find exactly what she needed among the jumble of leather and metal that was her luggage).

Finally, she groomed an auburn wig with bangs and mid-back length. She styled and fussed and talked to herself and giggled, but when she was done, the effect was utterly stunning. Lara was a beautiful stranger—to herself and to Michael.

"Could you do something like this for Michael?"

"I don't have any men's wigs, silly."

"How about the blond one I took off," said Lara. "Could you cut it so that it looked like a man's style?"

Lara could not have been funnier if she had hosted the late show. Mr. America rallied and refilled wifey's glass with Stoli so she had to stop laughing to drink, and Michael traded places with Lara in the train car's barroom-beauty-salon-fine-arts-storage compartment.

CHAPTER 20

Close to Home

‍

S ix Ukranians, each armed with an automatic pistol and
flash grenades, awaited the train from St. Petersburg.
Twenty uniformed Russian police and twenty more in
plainclothes occupied the same area. The platform promised to be the scene of a carnage bloodier than the Tel Aviv
airport as soon as Lara Cole and Michael Solak were spotted.

They never were.

By anybody.

If the detraining passengers could have been invento-
ried, the waiting combatants would have found that not fifty,
but fifty-one contestants now filled the Mrs. America con-
tingent. With their baggage carts and bedraggled-looking
husbands in tow, the contestants flowed off the train as if
they were anointed not only with beauty but command of
the earth as well. Chartered buses collected the people and
luggage and whisked them off to the Hotel Oktyabrskaya,
which—until the Russians decided communism had been
but a seventy-five-year distraction—was the playland of
party officials.

Since Lara's new friend was, in her own words, "a winner,"
she received top-drawer treatment. Her suite on the seventh
floor boasted a foyer, living room, study, bedroom, two

bathrooms, and a refrigerator filled with precisely what she didn't need: more vodka.

Michael and Lara didn't exactly sneak into the suite. A woman who looked like Rosa Klebb in the film "From Russia with Love" sat at a small desk next to the elevators. Perhaps she would be called a concierge. Mr. America willingly surrendered the key upon Rosa Klebb's demand, and they followed her down the hall to where she opened the room and ushered them in with an expression that bespoke stern disapproval of frivolous Westerners.

Mr. America homed in on the bedroom and passed out on the bed without further ceremony.

Rosa ordered that the key should be left with her whenever they went out. She offered no other service.

Mrs. America, unlike her husband, was up for some more fun. While Michael dozed on the couch, she attempted to teach Lara a card game in which four cards were dealt to each player, four cards were face up between the players, and the two of spades, ten of diamonds, and all aces gave points. Mrs. America won four straight games, and Lara, pleading the need to use the bathroom, excused herself.

<hr />

THIS TIME PAVEL KIPRENSKY CALLED BETTY SORENSEN. It was just after 3:00 a.m. Washington time. He apologized for waking her, only to be assured that she was both awake and up.

"They didn't get off the train."

"But they were on it when it left St. Petersburg?"

"They were, and they were on it during transit. One of my men absolutely confirms that he saw the Cole woman. They just did not get off and a thorough, and I mean thorough, search of the train confirms that they were not hiding on it."

"Can you find them?" she asked.

"It's a big country," said Kiprensky. "Obviously we want to find them, but let me not deceive you. We want more than anything else, to recover The Mother of God, and if I can protect your countrymen in doing so, I certainly will."

Kiprensky was again being economical with the truth. His men thought Cole and Solak had lost themselves in the large group of Americans who were staying at the Hotel Oktyabrskaya. They would search there, room by room. The Buyer's men had concluded the same thing, but felt it prudent to wait outside the hotel until their targets showed themselves.

LARA WAS SO TIRED SHE WAS DIZZY. HER LEGS FELT heavy, and she couldn't feel her feet at all. When she came out of the bathroom, she found that Mrs. America had tired of being social, and the door to the bedroom was shut.

Michael was snoring on the couch. After an inventory of the most comfortable alternatives, she took a pillow from a small chair, pulled the desk chair up, and put her head down. She jerked awake sometime later, a small puddle of drool on the desktop.

My god, where is the luggage? The luggage never came to our room. Oh, Jesus, oh God, oh nooo. She dived on Michael, shaking him roughly. "It's not here. It's not here, Michael, oh Jesus, oh God!"

In fact, some of the luggage was in the room. Various suitcases were piled in the foyer where the bellman had dropped them, but not the trunk. Lara tried the bedroom door. Locked. Could it be in there? Lara hadn't seen it go by, but she had to find out.

She pounded on the door, realizing that she couldn't call Mrs. America by name because she didn't know it. No response. She pounded some more. Nothing. "Oh, Jesus," and this time she pressed her forehead against the door and pounded in pure frustration.

The only key was in the possession of Rosa down the hall, so Michael, again wearing the blonde wig that Mrs. America had so alcoholically coifed for him, strode out into the hall to verbally seduce her. It was easy. After she heard his first sentence in Russian, she beamed a rotten-toothed smile that they had, mercifully, been spared before. That this blonde-haired, white-toothed scoundrel was really a Russian just like herself thrilled her, and from then on they were allies, especially after he gave her twenty dollars that disappeared into her pocket with another revolting smile.

Rosa confided that the police were searching the hotel at that very moment, starting three floors below and going both directions. They were pigs. "The KGB was better. We knew they were corrupt. They knew they were corrupt. Everyone acted accordingly. These police hooligans are the same people, but they pretend they are not corrupt. For me, I take my corruption without the base alloy of hypocrisy," and she spat a gross loogie that lingered on the leg of her desk and fell to the carpet.

Rosa's key opened the bedroom door, but the trunk was not there nor were either of the Americas going to be roustable enough to aid in the search. Lara opened Mrs. America's purse to find her identification. Ruth Cummins.

Rosa called down to the lobby bellman's desk after Lara described the trunk and Michael translated. Nobody knew anything. Nobody would look around for it. Rosa shrugged. It was the way things were.

After Rosa left, blessing Michael with another clock-stopping smile, Michael agreed to go down to the lobby. It was expansive, and luggage of all description was piled around the departing or arriving travelers. Compounding Michael's problem was his impressionistic description of the trunk. He had only seen it briefly while Mrs. America was fixing his wig, and he really wasn't paying attention to it. Moreover, the lobby was swarming with police.

He wandered past the reception desk and sat briefly in an arrangement of low chairs as he scanned each pile of luggage looking for a match. Then he walked past the shops. Nothing. He asked the head bellman for help and got none. A twenty-dollar bill got him only a suspicious glare as the bellman pocketed it contemptuously and predicted that it would turn up.

What to do? He couldn't stay in the lobby much longer, particularly now that he had shown American money. He had made himself visible, and the curious would want to know more. Not knowing what else to do, Michael pushed through the glass entrance doors, and there it was, a green metal steamer trunk. One policeman sat on it while another, smoking a cigarette, used it for a footrest.

Michael said in English while he bent down to look at the tag, "I think this is my wife's trunk. Yes! See, the tag says Cummins."

Leaning forward, the policeman with his foot on the trunk responded, "And who are you?"

"I'm her husband. Most of our luggage was delivered, but not this trunk. I'll get the bellman to take it up."

"Perhaps you should first show us some identification," said the policeman, "Something with a picture of you on it. Then, you will be so kind as to open the trunk so we can inspect it?"

"It's just clothes; gowns for a beauty pageant."

"Then we will be all the more interested in seeing them," leered the policeman. "First the identification, and then the key," he said, holding out his hand and poking it firmly in Michael's chest.

Michael shivered in the summer heat at the same time he felt his scalp tingle beneath the wig. "I have neither. They are in my room."

"You will get them and come back here or we will break it open," said the policeman, flicking away his cigarette, foot still proprietarily planted on the trunk.

"WE'RE SCREWED," SAID MICHAEL, SWEATING AND PALE as he related to Lara what had happened. "Now we've got to run—get a cab to the Embassy.

"And leave The Mother of God here?"

"Lara, they will open it one way or the other, and when they do, we will both be arrested. You have no rights here. It isn't like the US."

"So we just take off and leave everything?"

"We have to. I blew it."

"No, we don't," she said. "I didn't come all this way just to run for cover. Anyway, if we run, Mr. and Mrs. Cummins get arrested because it's their trunk. If you can seduce Rosa Klebb, I can deal with a couple of Russian policemen."

Now Lara had Ruth Cummins's identification—purse snatching was becoming a habit—and she rifled through it as she rode the elevator down. The cigarettes surprised her. She had freshened up her lipstick and enough of Mrs. Cummins's makeup job remained so that she looked better than fine. As exhausted as she was, this coming encounter was sure to keep her awake. *Sisu*, she thought—the Finnish word for dauntless resolve—I'll get through this.

Regal and determined, she walked through the lobby, out the glass doors, and paused, taking the pack of cigarettes from her purse, putting one between her lips, and helplessly fumbling for a match. The policeman who had been leaning on her trunk obliged. She cupped his hand and looked into his eyes as he held the match, then thanked him, offering him a Salem.

She chatted first about the beauty pageant in St. Petersburg, casually mentioning that she had won. She liked Russia, she told him. "It is a masculine country—strong and virile." Her husband, she confided, was so inadequate; all he ever wanted to do was work, and after all, life was more than money. Would he like another cigarette? As he lit hers, she brushed her breast against his shoulder, sending sexual signals from all transmitters. This was her trunk. She nodded to it, smoothing her skirt. Perhaps he would help her bring it to her room? She would see that her husband was "out."

The policeman said something in Russian to his comrade who was still seated on the trunk. He apparently spoke no English, but whatever was said in Russian told him that the games were about to begin. He leapt off and the two of them, one carrying each end, followed Lara through the lobby.

The cigarettes were making her sick, which she quickly forgot when the elevator doors closed and the first policeman began feeling her behind and then put his hand in her crotch. She squirmed and said, "Not yet, not yet"—words he chose not to understand. By this time, the second policeman was fully enlisted in the enterprise, and as Lara freed herself, he cupped her breasts and squeezed painfully.

As they passed Rosa's desk next to the elevators, Lara gave her a look she hoped would convey distress. It only confirmed what Rosa already knew: Western women were sluts, and this one was particularly shameless. She spat again.

Lara rapped on the door, Michael opened it and the first policeman, with his free hand, jerked Michael's shirt front and propelled him into the hall. The second policeman tripped him as he came by and kicked him in the stomach, and Lara found herself in the hotel room, behind a locked door, with two aroused policemen, a trunk with the icon, and no defense.

The vodka. She took two bottles from the refrigerator and handed one to each policeman. Then she scurried to the breakfront for glasses only to find that neither of them needed one. One policeman was temporarily diverted, seating himself on the couch, boots up on the coffee table, taking long, satisfied pulls from the bottle. The other, however, attacked her from the back, trying simultaneously to fondle her crotch and unzip the back of her dress.

She tried to elbow him in the groin and missed. He spun her around and slapped her across the face, knocking her to the floor. He thought for a moment he had knocked her head off, and he stood there blinking at the red wig, trying to understand what had happened. His comrade was greatly amused, spitting vodka on the front of his jacket. He leaned over, picked up the wig, and put it on his head.

Which is what Rosa first saw when she opened the door. She barked an order that brought the first policeman to his feet, sheepishly holding the wig in his hand. She walked directly to the second, kneed him in the balls, and grabbing his collar as he doubled over, twisted his ear, and threw him out of the room like a sumo wrestler. Her stream of invective did not stop until both policemen were on the elevator. Then she turned to Michael, nodded once, and said, "So."

A MALE VOICE ANSWERED, "UNITED STATES EMBASSY."

"This is Lara Cole. I am a United States citizen here in Russia, and I need to talk to an official."

"What is the nature of your business, ma'am?" said the voice.

"I can't discuss that with you, but it is urgent and important."

"What I am asking," said the voice, "is, do you need help with a lost passport, do you seek transportation out of the country? Your answer will help me direct your call."

"Do you have a cultural officer?" she asked, not knowing quite why.

"One moment, please."

The voice that next came on the line answered in Russian.

"I am speaking English," said Lara, sounding as if she weren't. "My name is Lara Cole, and I..."

"One moment, please," the voice interrupted.

She heard some rustling as if the phone had been covered with the speaker's hand, and then another voice came on the line, saying, "This is George Graham. Sounds like you've been doing some hard traveling."

"You are the same George Graham that...?"

"The same one that you didn't tell everything you knew to. The one that brought you the amulet. The one who very much wants to save your precious and slippery young life. Where are you?"

"I'll answer in a moment," said Lara, "but I need your help."

"You have needed my help all along, Sweet Pea, but I am glad you finally know it."

"I am at Hotel—" and she paused and tried to find something that wasn't written in Cyrillic. "Damn," she muttered as she fumbled around, put down the phone, opened the desk drawer, and found a hotel brochure that was printed in English. "I am at Hotel Oktyabrskaya," she said, sounding it out. "The icon is here, but it won't be safe for long. The police are searching the rooms. Can you send a truck and some Marines with guns to get it?"

"That I can do," said Graham, "and we'll bring you here as well."

"Not exactly," replied Lara. "I have some business to do at the Tretyakov. You keep the icon overnight, help us set up a press conference for tomorrow morning, and then deliver it in all of its glory back to its home."

George Graham grunted. "I thought I had seen everything—or at least everything I cared to, but this really takes it."

"What?"

"We have been chasing you for God knows how long, trying to figure out what you were doing and why. Now you materialize but refuse to be rescued while proposing a plan that is exactly what Presidents Sorensen and Kiprensky are already trying to do."

"For timing purposes keep in mind that the Tretyakov

people will want to authenticate the icon when it gets there and that will take awhile."

The pickup would be in forty-five minutes. The first press event would be the delivery of The Mother of God to the Tretyakov, at 9:00 a.m. the following morning. After Madam Kopulskaya authenticated it she would tell the press, and then Presidents Kiprensky and Sorensen would simultaneously announce the return of the icon and restoration of good will. Michael would accompany the icon to the Embassy so he could say it had been constantly in his possession since he authenticated it.

Almost.

CHAPTER 21

Armageddon

———————◆◆———————

Lara was hoping that Mrs. America—Mrs. Cummins—would reappear to freshen up her makeup, reset the wig, or at least comb it as she had done on the train. A light knock on the bedroom door, then a heavier one and a peek into the room confirmed that both Mr. and Mrs. America would be out of commission for longer than Lara had to spare.

She returned to the bathroom, combed the wig as best she could, and secured it in place with bobby pins. Although she did not have the brilliance of Mrs. America's touch, she still would not have recognized herself passing on the street.

She got as far as the door and returned for the slip of paper on which Michael had written the address of the Tretyakov in Russian. It looked like all Hs and Ns to her, but she feared she would be unable to make herself understood without it. She swept through the lobby to the taxi rank, handed the slip to the driver, and without a word from either, he took off.

The front of the Tretyakov looks like a small dacha that has been grafted to a very large, orangish building. Above the three sharp gables, St. George, in grey stone relief, slays the dragon. But the outside matters little. Inside is the largest collection of Russian paintings in the world, hung in newly restored galleries. Its conservation laboratory is as close to state of the art as anything east of Berlin. Curiously, next to gleaming electronic equipment sit all sizes and weights of heavy metal irons that were used to press clothes before electricity. These, with their bulk, give up heat more slowly and can maintain steady pressure on a canvas to cure the restorer's work.

Lara realized when the cab pulled up that she had no money. At least, she had no rubles. She proffered a five dollar bill, the taxi driver grabbed it and sped off like a Scythian bandit. Apparently it was enough. She entered the museum, asked to be taken to the office of Madam Doctor Kopulskaya, and learned that Madam Doctor was not in.

She sat down and looked so helpless and dejected that Madam Kopulskaya's assistant, who didn't recognize Lara from her previous visit when the loan had been arranged, offered to help. The director, it seems, had had a bout of ill health. "Her life," explained the assistant, "is so entwined with this museum, that when The Mother of God was lost, she began to grieve, and her robust disposition has drained away day by day. We are all terribly worried about her.

"The worst sign of all is that she shows no interest now in the museum and will come in late, if at all, and leave early. In previous days she often would spend the entire night in the museum, happily working with her treasures and napping in her office."

Lara possessed the cure for both of them. "Tell Madam Kopulskaya that at 9:00 a.m. tomorrow morning, I will return The Mother of God, safe and sound, to her care. Tell her that she and I must make preparations together." With that, Lara removed the wig to reveal the person Madam's assistant remembered from the negotiations for the loan. She vowed that she would do everything she could. In fact, she would go to Madam's apartment and fetch her rather than call.

MADAM KOPULSKAYA AND LARA WERE MUTUALLY stunned at each other's appearance. Madam, who was grey-haired and vital when Lara last saw her, was now just grey-haired. Stooped and disheveled, she held the arm of her assistant as if her entire supply of energy was needed for the singular activity of moving one foot in front of the other.

As Madam gazed upon this creature in front of her, she received no signals of recognition. The long auburn hair and Asian eyes; the elegant dress and broad shoulders; this was a person unknown to her.

Lara greeted her, again removed the wig and explained, with as few words as she could, that she was being chased, that her life was in danger, and that she was, therefore, disguised.

Madam Kopulskaya was confused.

Her assistant gave Lara a look that was supposed to convey information, but Lara was not quite sure what. Lara followed them into a small apartment adjoining the director's office. There the assistant sat Madam Kopulskaya in a comfortable chair, indicated that Lara should sit on the couch, and began brewing tea.

Lara scooted to the end of the couch and took Madam Kopulskaya's hand in both of hers. Madam neither resisted nor consented. Then Lara started from the beginning.

"Cameron Aker was both my employer and a longtime

friend of Pavel Kiprensky. The two of them cooked up the plan for the loan of The Mother of God—you will remember how much political pressure Kiprensky put on you to make the loan happen? You were against it from the start."

A slight nod from Madam.

"Aker tried to steal the icon, perhaps to help Kiprensky gain political advantage, perhaps just because he was greedy, but Aker got killed because there is another group of people, perhaps from Ukraine, that want the icon."

Madam's aspect showed all the understanding of a dull normal.

Lara soldiered on: "The icon that was stolen was shipped to Ukraine in the pen that contained a bull—you know, a large animal—cows and bulls in the pasture—that kind of bull."

Shit. I wouldn't understand this, and I was part of it from the get-go, thought Lara, and she reloaded and started again.

"Never mind. The important thing is that what was stolen was not the real Mother of God. Do you understand?"

For the first time, Madam reacted: "Not real? But it was real. Valuable beyond price. Irreplaceable."

"No, no," what we borrowed from you was unquestionably real. What happened, though, was that a young man who worked for me was so concerned about the icon's safety that he made a copy and placed it on display, and it was that copy that was stolen."

"That is impossible," said Madam Kopulskaya, recovering with super-human speed. She squeezed Lara's hand and with blazing eyes, said, "The icon cannot be successfully copied. She is unique, not just to the world of art, but to all believers and to the soul of Russia."

Lara demurred, "I didn't say it was a perfect copy, but it was good enough to fool the thief. Meanwhile, the young man who made the copy had hidden your icon in its shipping box and, the whole time, it was in the basement of my museum. I have brought The Mother of God back to you."

———————

Now Madam Kopulskaya was on the edge of her chair, color rising in her cheeks and exclaiming, "Let us see it! I must behold it."

"It isn't here," said Lara, watching the woman shrink back—alternating between animation and flaccid morbidity. "It is here in Moscow at the United States embassy. It will be delivered to your museum tomorrow morning, provided you agree."

The assistant handed each a mug of stout tea with sugar, which Lara, at least, found to be an elixir. Lara explained to Madam that the presidents of Russia and the United States were prepared to cease hostilities provided that she, as director of the Tretyakov and protector of The Mother of God, expressed satisfaction that the icon is real and has been returned in good condition.

"You and your curators will have ample opportunity to inspect it when it is delivered here at 9:00 a.m. tomorrow."

Lara went on to explain that Michael Solak, an expert associated with the Metropolitan Museum in New York and another man whom she could only describe as huge, with red hair and beard from the Russian State Museum, would each state publicly that they had examined the icon and that it was authentic.

"Alexi! I know him," Madam Kopulskaya shouted.

Now she was excited. "We cannot wait until tomorrow to do this," she said. "It must be done now."

Her assistant, who was perched on the arm of Madam Kopulskaya's chair, said something in Russian. The two exchanged several sentences and then launched into a long discussion, with shaking of heads and nodding and what, to Lara, was a totally unintelligible but musical exchange.

Finally, the assistant turned to Lara and said, "Excuse us for leaving you out. Madam Kopulskaya and I have just been discussing details, and we agree there are many. We must prepare for the examination, notify the people who are important to this museum so they can be here, and order food and vodka. She agrees 9:00 a.m. tomorrow is satisfactory."

"But I will not sleep a wink all night," said Madam.

"I feel as if I have given up sleep permanently," Lara returned.

LARA CALLED GEORGE GRAHAM AT THE EMBASSY AND assured him that the Tretyakov would be prepared to receive The Mother of God the following morning.

"You are not going to be wandering the streets, are you?"

Lara had not even thought about where she would spend the night. Michael was at the embassy, and somehow he had been so much a part of her, that the thought of not being with him through the night was as disturbing as the realization that she literally had nowhere to go.

Madam's assistant, hovering around the office and unabashedly listening to Lara's end of the conversation said, "Here. You will stay here. I will make up the couch for you."

KIPRENSKY WAS NO AMATEUR WHEN IT CAME TO CROWD manipulation. The "outraged citizens" who had been surrounding the United States embassy melted away through the night and reappeared along the bridge and entryway of the Tretyakov. Ten deep they stood, except they neither shouted nor moved. They simply stood there, waiting, as Russians had become so accustomed to doing. This vigil was pregnant with expectation.

When, at 8:30, a Zil limousine led by a procession of black automobiles, all flying ecclesiastical pennants of the Orthodox Church pulled up in front of the museum, the crowd was not only quietly enthusiastic, but those with political insight knew that President Kiprensky and the Orthodox archbishop had cut some kind of nonaggression treaty whereby they both could benefit from the return of The Mother of God to Mother Russia.

The archbishop, followed by a resplendent flock of bishops and holy attendants, was greeted by Madam Doctor Kopulskaya, who by this time, with no sleep and only a large dose of artistic expectation, had recovered to animated, robust health. The mayor of Moscow arrived to embrace the glory of this political-artistic-religious shindig.

Lara, still wearing the auburn wig with almond-shaped eyes that by this time had rounded out a bit, stood as inconspicuously as she could, but kept being pushed forward by Madam Kopulskaya, who hugged her from behind with both arms around her middle. The notion that Lara might attract harm was one Madam was quite unable to grasp.

Television cables, lights, and cameras were everywhere. Interfax News Agency personnel, reporters, and still photographers were milling about, giving only modest attention to the velvet rope meant to hold them back from the front doors of the Tretyakov.

At precisely three minutes before 9:00 a.m., a ripple went through the crowd, and as if an announcement had been made, all turned to see a navy blue Ford Econoline van, with American flags fluttering from each front fender, round the corner and head up the block toward the museum entrance. It was escorted by six uniformed Moscow police on motorcycles, two in front, one on each side, and two behind. The precious cargo was unloaded and taken into the museum where the examination would commence without delay. Invited guests chatted and helped themselves to food and vodka. Lara marveled that any time of day or night seemed to be just the right time for a snort or two of firewater.

It took slightly more than an hour before two museum employees emerged from the laboratory into the lobby carrying an object draped in gold cloth. A third employee followed with an easel. The easel was unfolded, and the object, still covered with gold cloth, was placed on it. A microphone and five chairs to the right of the easel completed the preparations.

Next in the procession were Madam Doctor Kopulskaya, Michael, Freddy, the red-haired giant from the State Museum, and a small, stooped man in a black three-piece suit. Freddy had somehow managed to find a Park Avenue wardrobe far from home.

All but Madam Kopulskaya seated themselves. She stood at the microphone, adjusted her half-glasses, and began to read from a handwritten statement.

"I am an old woman. I am a skeptic. I am a lover of all that describes and celebrates what it is to be a Russian. More than that, I know that Heaven and Earth are bound by forces that cannot be described in words and are beyond the ability of any of us to understand. It is only through art—inspired art where the artist's hand is guided by unseen and unknowable forces—that we can better understand ourselves and approach God. This day surpasses all that have come before in my long life. I have died and this day been reborn. Behold, my countrymen, The Mother of God."

She turned and tenderly undraped the object on the easel. She looked at it for a long time, absentmindedly letting the drape sag to the floor.

CHAPTER 22

Endgame

For anticlimax, it was hard to beat the verification show that came next. First Michael Solak was introduced by Freddy in a curious routine where the introducee translated for the introducer, and then took the podium on his own behalf.

In Russian, Solak told the assembled group about the icon's curious odyssey to and from the United States. He explained that he had examined it at the Metropolitan Museum in New York and was persuaded without doubt (with all the murders that had been committed, he could have said "beyond a reasonable doubt") that it was authentic. He established the "chain of custody"—that it had been with him since his examination. Concluding, he reflected that the Palladium had lost none of her power and had, in fact, absorbed a bullet to protect life.

Next came the red-haired giant, who with admirable brevity and passion, launched forth a blizzard of Russian words summarizing the badges of authenticity he had found.

Finally, the old man in the dark, undertakerly three-piece suit, a senior curator from the Tretyakov, took the podium and, in a wandering and disjointed address, said that he was as sure as any mortal could be that the object which he most

291

prized was back in the arms of Mother Russia. That would have been a good place to stop and sit down, but instead he went on to question whether one could ever be sure of authenticity and whether, in fact, if one truly believed in an object, authenticity really mattered anyway.

He then mused whether, from the looks of the lead imbedded in the back of the icon, it could have come from a modern weapon. Perhaps he would have rambled on in this stream of consciousness indefinitely had not the crowd, with a combination of tears and lusty rich harmonies, started spontaneously singing a hymn of the Old Believers:

> **Oh, Mother of God....**
> **This is our salvation.**
> **We confess it in deed and word**
> **And depict it in holy icons.**

Moved either by the inherent religiosity of the moment, or the supreme political opportunity, the archbishop came forward and announced that he would parade the icon as a demonstration of thanks to God. Museum guards are neither trained nor prepared to respond to the most holy person in all of Eastern Orthodoxy directing that an object under their care be picked up, carried from the museum, and paraded through the streets, so when two of the attending bishops lifted The Mother of God off the easel, they stood motionless.

Madam Kopulskaya found no such paralysis. She placed herself directly in front of the archbishop and, in her fullest voice, protested that The Mother of God would not leave the museum where she had been housed for centuries. Each time the archbishop attempted to maneuver around her, she scurried again in front, but by this time the would-be procession had reached the front door of the museum and the crowd outside, seeing the archbishop leading The Mother of God parade, broke into wild cheering.

As they flowed out of the museum, crowd noise masked the first shots. The staccato report of automatic assault weapons reverberated off the façade of the Tretyakov and divots of stone flew from where the bullets hit. The two bishops carrying The Mother of God fell, crimson blood darkening their crimson robes.

The archbishop's bodyguards tackled and shielded him just before the first anti-tank rocket slammed into the US embassy's Ford van, lifting it off the pavement in an orange ball. The impact knocked Lara off her feet and back into Michael. Both were dazed by the blast, sitting, tangled on the stone pavement. Guns fired from every direction—from Ukrainians who were there to take what they could not steal—from police who were firing indiscriminately into the crowd—from soldiers disciplined only enough not to shoot each other. Only George Graham held his fire while he grabbed the back of Lara's collar slamming her flat on her back on the pavement.

Masses of people were either on the ground or running away from the museum. Two men, slinging their weapons over their shoulders as they ran, headed for the icon which lay, partly covered by the body of a bishop, near a marble statue of a male figure incongruently standing with arms folded. One jerked the robes of the dead bishop pulling him from the treasure while the other bent to pick up the icon.

Michael was on his feet, sprinting toward the two before George Graham could restrain him. He staggered as he reached them, hit by covering fire, but he dived on the man picking up The Mother of God, and they both tumbled to the pavement. Graham, kneeling, was sighting for a clear shot. The other, without hesitation, unslung his weapon and hosed down both Michael and his fellow Ukrainian with a close-range, lethal burst.

George Graham couldn't believe it. It was his disbelief at such callous disregard for life and loyalty that caused him to hesitate just long enough that the man swung his weapon, still spitting bullets, one of which caught Graham in the shoulder, knocking him back across Lara's legs.

The shooter's magazine was empty. He dropped his weapon and turned his full attention to The Mother of God, lying blood-spattered and face up on the ground.

Lara had never shot a gun in her life; Catholic boarding schools don't teach that. In fury, she wriggled free of Graham, wrenched his pistol from his right hand, pointed it at the man bending over the icon, and pulled the trigger until it locked open and would fire no more. Then she crawled, not to The Mother of God, but to Michael, whose eyes could no longer behold her.

She cradled Michael's head in her lap, oblivious to the bullets whizzing around and the cacophony of the massacre. She stroked his face, saying his name over and over, tears flowing down her cheeks and into her mouth as she repeated her mantra of desolation. He did not move, nor would he ever again. Bullets had ripped his heart from his chest.

———————————

For a moment, after the firing had stopped, the silence was so profound that it seemed as if cries of agony or despair would be so bleached, so hopeless that their very utterance would offend the air.

Then, like an unseen conductor dropping his baton, the world was filled with shrieks and oaths and whistles and sirens. The security guards who had been lying on top of the archbishop, shielding him with their bodies, dragged him onto his feet and into his limousine, leaving behind his tall, conical cap. They spared not a backward glance at either The Mother of God or the two dead bishop-porters.

Lara, her lime green dress blotted with Michael's blood, would not be separated from him and refused all offers of hands that would lift her or take Michael away from her. She willed that he not be dead; that they not be separated.

In the confusion, with the hulk of the Ford van still burning and the flames licking at the gas tank, The Mother of God, enigmatically holding her son, lay facing the sky, looking through blood and carnage with the same expression she had held for eight hundred years.

Lara didn't see the van lift from the ground again, but the whoosh of air singed her hair and blew her back, stopping Michael's name in midsound and drumming her head against the paving stones. Pieces of hot metal clattered to the ground around her, and then, again, the earth was unnaturally silent, and The Mother of God had vanished.

THE WHITE HOUSE DUTY OFFICER, WHO HAD BEEN watching the horrors at the Tretyakov live on CNN, summoned the chief of staff who already knew that The Mother of God had been at the forefront of another violent episode. The chief called Betty Sorensen. She had seen it too—the woman never slept—and was on her way to the Oval Office.

Boris Golchev, the Buyer, had the advantage of knowing what was about to happen, so he was watching from a hotel bar in Los Angeles and could hardly control his elation when he saw the van explode. It was all he could do to keep from cheering.

He had prepared himself, cleansing away all impure thoughts by lighting candles and bringing himself before God in contemplation of a rather second-rate icon. He bowed and held his fingers in a two-armed cross with three fingers below to represent the dual nature of Christ and the Trinity. Precision was important in faith and in works. The incense, the flickering candlelight, and his prolonged, single-minded focus transported him to the spiritual dimension in which God promised to consecrate a new Mother of God—a reward, of sorts, for his steadfast faith.

What he had just witnessed was better than he could have ever hoped. It was fulfillment of Ezekiel's prophecy to "bring forth fire and ashes" upon the wicked. The carnage and destruction had shaken the hem of Russia.

Kiprensky would fall.

Ukraine would be avenged.

CHAPTER 23

Solomon's Solution

L ara awoke in the embassy infirmary. Her singed hair had been clipped back bluntly, and the lacerations in her scalp disinfected and sutured. She began a mental inventory of where she might be, why she was there, and whether she was still in possession of all of her parts. Her head wasn't working very well, in part because her mind did not want to remember.

Her reflexive call of "Michael" brought the nurse who, as Lara became increasingly agitated, increased the sedative drip in her IV, sending her back to sleep.

Her second awakening was much the same, but she stayed awake for a while, weeping and wishing she could really escape this nightmare. George Graham came in, his right arm and shoulder immobilized in plaster. With his left hand he held hers, neither saying much. She sort of remembered Freddie being there, too, and that he said something about The Mother of God disappearing and nobody knowing for sure where it was, and that he was catching a flight home, and then he vanished.

Three days later an Air Force plane flew them home, along with the remains of Michael Solak. Lara insisted on sitting with the casket for the entire flight. Her "bankrupt heart had no more tears to spend." Graham came back and sat with her for a few minutes every hour or so. Remains, thought Lara. It is supposed to be the stuff that stays after the soul has departed. But what remained for her was not the carnage of the last moments, but the fullness of the life that she and Michael had lived under such trying and brief circumstances. She had known the very essence of another human being.

He had died protecting beauty and had liberated in Lara the knowledge that beauty is essential to human survival. That knowledge would live in Lara. Michael would live through her.

<hr />

UKRAINIANS WERE GETTING THE HANG OF WESTERN press conferences. With great fanfare and a professionally designed backdrop for his briefing, the Ukrainian president announced that the real Mother of God was not, as claimed by the Russians, in the Tretyakov Museum. Basing his arguments in part on the ramblings of the Tretyakov's elderly curator, he proclaimed that the real icon did not have a bullet in it; that the real icon had, through circumstances he was not at liberty to disclose, been returned to its original home and rightful place in Ukraine.

He displayed the icon, that, in the lights of the briefing stage, looked remarkably presentable. He announced that The Mother of God would take her place among the most treasured icons on the altar screen of the St. Sophia Church in Kiev and would be there for all Ukrainians and all believers to venerate.

It was, he said, "a great triumph for Ukrainian people, the Orthodox faith, and for all those who believed in cultural integrity."

He then challenged Russia to display The Mother of God that had not been seen since the slaughter in front of the Tretyakov Museum. "They claim to have it in their laboratory, restoring it from the rude treatment it had received in its last battle. Russians have no truth in them," he proclaimed.

"If they had The Mother of God, they would show it right now. The longer they wait, with their 'restoration sham,' the more the world will know they have been preparing an imposter."

IN EARLY OCTOBER, ALMOST TWO MONTHS AFTER THE shooting in Moscow, the humidity broke in Northern Virginia, restoring crisp nights, glorious, sunny autumn days, and the dying anticipation of Lara's favorite season. George Graham knocked on her office door, unexpected and unannounced. She looked up from her table/desk, smiled broadly, and said, "Have you come to arrest me?"

"No, but I thought I might take you to lunch if folks eat out in this part of the country."

"Did you hear?" asked Lara.

He shook his head.

"Estelle. She is giving the two million dollars Cameron got for the bull to the museum. It will be used to fund a program in memory of Wesley Foster, and it will support an educational program for kids to be run by your hero and mine, Wil Porter."

For the next few minutes they were like schoolchildren as Graham recounted to Lara the ceremony in which the handiwork of Wilson, Wil, Willy Porter had been enshrined in the politically correct and most venerated stable of useful art in the super-high church of Ukraine. In accordance with its international importance, it would be perpetually guarded by soldiers.

As they headed out for lunch, Lara said, "Wil Porter accomplished what King Solomon could not. He effectively split the baby, literally and figuratively, that is, assuming the Tretyakov really did recover The Mother of God while we were out cold on the pavement. The world may never know the answer, which means that The Mother of God has acquired another layer of mystery."

"You seem to be doing better," said Graham. "I'm glad to see it."

LARA WOULD NEVER REALLY BE BETTER. SHE WOULD grieve, in a way totally apart from grief about lost faith or lost innocence, because, for a very short time, she had been totally alive, totally in love, and totally part of another human being. All the lessons she had rehearsed for her lifetime were in preparation for some event other than this one, and yet, while her life might never again be as intense as in her moments with Michael, The Mother of God had taught her about total dedication, about constancy, about renewal and rebirth, and yes, about love.

Michael would always be with her.